A GIFT OF TIME

SARAH WYNDE

Published by Rozelle Press
independent publisher of unexpected fiction
rozellepress.com

Cover design by Karri Klawiter, artbykarri.com
Copyright © 2013 Wendy Sharp

ISBN: 1494492806
ISBN-13: 978-1494492809

❧ DEDICATION ❧

To my imaginary friend, ZeroGain, who has become my real friend, Tim. This book would not have come into being without your steady support at the other end of the instant message window. Thank you!

❧ ACKNOWLEDGEMENTS ❧

A Gift of Time went through innumerable revisions over a period of eighteen months. Along the way, I posted multiple drafts of early chapters on Critique Circle, Fictionpress, and Project Team Beta. I'd like to thank everyone who provided feedback in those forums, as well as the people who maintain those online communities. AllyrienDM, Aehvtine, World of Ink, and the anonymous reviewer who thanked me for making my characters "mature, reasonable people with good sense," get my special appreciation for continuing to read, despite the ever-changing first chapters.

I am also extremely grateful to this book's team of beta readers: Carol Bird, Barbara Gavin, Melony Grace, Lynda Haviland, Kris Hiehle, Mike Kent, Sarah Kessler, Judy Long, Amy Mendoza, Christina Pearson, Tim Nutting, and Teresa Young. Without your support, this book would have been living on a USB drive in my desk drawer indefinitely.

❧ PROLOGUE ❦

"He'll kill her. Please, can't you help me?" The woman tried to tug on the doctor's white-coated arm, but her hands passed through him as if he were as insubstantial as air. She stared at him and then backed away, turning to the nurse.

"Why won't you listen to me?" she begged. "You have to find her."

Rose wrinkled her nose. She shouldn't have stopped in the emergency room. The noise and chaos had drawn her in, but she liked visiting the hospital to see the babies, not the people in pain.

And this poor woman seemed to be in agony. She hadn't even realized she was dead yet.

Sirens in the distance grew louder. Another ambulance was arriving. Nearby voices sounded increasingly urgent, but the noise didn't drown out the words of the begging woman. "I told her to run. I told her not to say a word. You have to look for her. Please, please, please listen to me."

Rose stepped forward, her feet moving as if disconnected from her brain. Her brain was telling her to leave, to go upstairs where she could coo over the little ones in peace.

"They can't hear you," she said instead.

The woman spun, staring at Rose. She wasn't old, but her eyes held the weary look of one of life's punching bags and tired lines dragged down her mouth.

"He calls her the spawn of Satan," the woman said, her hands clenched into fists. "Thou shalt not suffer a witch to live."

"He sounds like a jerk," Rose answered matter-of-factly. A man in green scrubs rushed through her and she stepped closer to the woman, moving out of the doorway and into the room where the medical staff labored over the woman's body.

The woman choked out a surprised laugh. "Can you save her?" she asked, her frantic voice calming.

Rose opened her mouth to answer honestly. She was a ghost herself. As the woman would soon discover, ghosts were practically

1

helpless in the world of matter. Nothing either of them could do would make a difference to anyone still living. "Yes," she heard herself saying. "Yes, I can."

"Oh, bless you." The woman's shoulders sagged in relief. "Thank you so much, thank you—I can't tell you—it means so much—I'm so grateful." Tears shone in her eyes, but didn't spill over.

Oh, dear, Rose thought, feeling a tug in the center of her chest. What had she done?

❧

Much later, tromping her way through Ocala National Forest, Rose tried to be philosophical about the whole thing. The tug felt sort of like needing to pee. Not that she'd had to use a bathroom any time in the past several decades, but she remembered the sensation. First, a subtle message, a gentle push that said perhaps it was time to get up and go somewhere. Then a more insistent awareness. Now a sense of pressure, impossible to ignore.

She would have stayed far away from that emergency room if she'd had any idea what she was getting into. It was the holiday season and for the first time since her death, she wasn't trapped in the house where she'd died. She'd had plans. She wanted to visit her childhood church and listen to carols, wander around town and admire the decorations, drop in on friends, ghostly and otherwise— not trudge through the woods.

If only that ghost had stuck around long enough to answer Rose's questions. But she'd faded away in the midst of showering Rose in profuse thanks, leaving Rose with nothing but an increasing sense of urgency, a tug pulling her farther and farther into the middle of nowhere.

And then it stopped.

Rose stopped, too. She looked around her. Dappled light drifted down through trees draped in grey, wispy Spanish moss. The dense forest might have felt primeval to a stranger, but Rose had grown up in the days when visiting the cool springs made summer bearable. It felt as much like home to her as her own backyard. But what was she doing here?

The brush next to her stirred and Rose stepped quickly away. Black bear? Coyote? The moment of panic faded as she remembered she had nothing to fear from wildlife. Besides, the brown shape crawling out from the undergrowth didn't look like any wildlife she'd ever seen.

"Oh, my," Rose murmured. She took another step back and then a step closer. "Oh, dear."

The girl lifted a dirty, tear-streaked face. Her pinched look and the shadows under her eyes made Rose think she hadn't eaten in far too long, but the determined set of her chin said she wasn't giving up. She wobbled as she pulled herself to her feet, staring directly at Rose, her eyes wide.

"Good morning," Rose said brightly. "I'm here to rescue you."

The little girl didn't answer. She blinked a couple of times, but her expression didn't change.

"Sadly, I don't know how," Rose admitted, opening her hands. Even as she said the words, though, the tug started again, pointing Rose deeper into the forest.

Rose touched her chest, feeling the softness of her pink sweater under her fingers. She wouldn't have thought that was the right direction to go at all. But the pull didn't feel like a sensation she wanted to ignore.

"All right," Rose said. "Off we go then."

She smiled at the girl and the girl stepped in her direction, her face awed, lips parted, eyes alight with wonder.

They were off to a good start, Rose thought with satisfaction.

☙ CHAPTER ONE ☙

Natalya Latimer hummed as she drove down the dark and winding road leading to her cottage. *Good King Wenceslas looked out, on the feast of something. When the snow lay something-something.*

She wasn't sure why that song was stuck in her head. She hated Christmas. Worst holiday of the year. Except maybe for Valentine's Day, but at least that was a one-day excuse to eat chocolate. Christmas was just a reminder of all she'd lost, all she'd never had, all she never would have.

Sometimes knowing the future sucked.

She could remember how magical the holiday used to be: the lights, the music, the anticipation, the excitement, the love that surrounded her, flowing like warm honey. She shouldn't complain, she knew. She was lucky to have the family she did. But the magic didn't exist without children to believe in it, and Natalya would never have children of her own.

Still, this year hadn't been so bad. Her brother Zane was delighting in his role as father-to-be. Her brother Lucas seemed to be adapting to his unique family structure. Her father Max had glowed with the joy of having all his children home, and a grandchild on the way. And her sister Grace had planned the day to the dotted i's and crossed t's. The holiday hadn't been special, not the way it ought to be, but it was pleasant enough.

Her eyes narrowed, and she put a hand up to shield them. Lights—and not the Christmas decoration kind—glared ahead of her on the road.

That was odd. This road, her road, wound along the edge of the Ocala National Forest and led to a dead end. Eight houses were tucked into the trees, bordering a small lake, one of the many that dotted the region. But she wouldn't have expected any of her neighbors to be out this late on the evening of Christmas Day. The only light she should see ought to be her own car's headlights separating the blackness.

And then her breath caught in her throat and her heart froze.

A sheriff's car, door open, lights on, stood at the side of the narrow road. It was parked carelessly, half blocking her lane, half slanted into the grass.

Oh, hell.

Ten years ago, she'd foreseen this night.

She'd been waiting for it to arrive ever since.

She took her foot off the gas pedal and let her car glide to a halt behind the other. Dread flowed through her like acid, turning her muscles to jelly. For a moment, she dropped her head and let it rest against the steering wheel, fighting the urge to cry or scream.

Christmas Day? Seriously? The universe must really hate her.

Her fingers shook as she turned the key in the ignition and fumbled her seatbelt open, but her eyes were dry as she opened the car door and stepped out.

She knew exactly what would happen next.

She'd walk around to the side of the sheriff's car. In the darkness, the overhead light bar's swirling blue-and-white would cast a surreal aura over the road, the trees and grass no more than a blur of green and brown as she saw the dark-soled shoes and the long legs of Colin Rafferty, her ex-boyfriend, lying face-down in the dirt and grass.

She'd rush to him. His tawny hair would be curling at the nape of his neck, longer than usual, and she'd feel the soft tickle of it against her fingers as she slid them along his skin, searching for his heartbeat. She'd force his body over, struggling to shift him, already realizing it was too late.

There'd be no pulse. She'd feel the cool and waxy texture of death under her warm touch. His skin would be tinged with grey, his lips turning blue. She'd smell death in the air, waste in more senses than one.

Ten years ago, that was all she'd known.

The knowledge had destroyed her life.

Tonight, if she tried, she could probably capture more. When it came to the near future, her sight was as clear as the memories of her near past. If she let herself think about it, she would know everything that would happen next: the phone calls, the ambulance, the deputies showing up, the hushed voices, worried faces. The funeral, his grandmother's grief.

Instead, she took a deep breath and tried not to think. Slow and steady. She'd get through this miserable night as she had so many others: one heartbeat at a time.

But as she rounded the front of her car and stepped onto the grassy verge of the road, her feet stopped moving. She blinked and then blinked again, trying to make sense of what she was seeing. The lights, the surreal colors, Colin down on the ground—all that was right. But a shadow crouched over him, too small to be human.

She gasped in uncertain horror and the shape turned toward her, revealing a face, pale and dirty, topped with disheveled dishwater blonde hair.

Human, definitely human, Natalya realized with relief. But young. What was a child doing here? As she paused, the child's hands dropped off Colin's chest and she—he? it?—scrambled away and into the darkness.

"Wait!" Natalya called, hurrying forward along the length of the car. "Come back."

She should go after the child. It was too late to help Colin. But as she reached him, she dropped to her knees anyway, ignoring the sharp gravel pressing into her flesh as she felt for his throat. Under her fingers, the outer edge of the trachea was solid, resilient, and it took barely a moment for her to find the throbbing carotid artery next to it.

Throbbing.

He had a pulse.

His skin felt warm.

And he was stirring, lifting his head off the ground, his eyelids fluttering open and revealing his grey eyes.

"Nat?" He sounded dazed. But his words were clear, not slurred or faint or heavy with pain, nothing indicating a medical emergency. "You're here. What happened?"

She rocked back onto her heels as he pushed himself to a sitting position. "You tell me. What is this, Colin?" Anger simmered in her tone. Was he playing a practical joke on her?

But there was no smirk and no "gotcha" in his voice as he repeated, "You're here."

He reached for her, wrapping his hand around the back of her neck and tugging her forward, drawing her closer until his firm lips took hers. Startled, Natalya opened her mouth to protest but he smothered her words with his kiss.

For a split second, Natalya resisted, and then she melted. She kissed him back, her lips hot under his, the taste and smell of him filling her senses, so familiar and yet so long denied. His lips explored, caressed, his hand twining into her long hair. She felt the warmth of his touch tingling along her scalp, the pressure of his arm against her back, the heat of desire stirring in her veins.

In some back corner of her mind, she knew she should stop him. This wasn't who they were, not anymore, but he felt so good. So good, so warm... and so alive.

Through the thick fabric of her sweater, the touch of his hand on her back was lighting a fire, embers of passion sparking into life and flaring up with unforgotten heat. She let herself slide forward, let her hands slide up and over his shoulders, her body press against his, her soft curves touching his solid chest.

She wanted to be closer, to feel her skin against his, but he pulled away first, his lips leaving hers with what felt like reluctance. He let his hand drop from her neck and smooth its way down her back, resting his cheek against hers for a long silent moment.

Natalya took in a deep, shuddering breath, her lips burning, her heart racing. In a shaky whisper, she asked, "What the hell, Colin?"

"Not hell," he murmured. "Definitely not hell."

"And not heaven, either." She pulled away, a flush of annoyance beginning to replace desire. What did he think he was doing? He was supposed to be dead, not kissing her.

"You sure?" His voice held a trace of humor.

"Positive." She scrambled to her feet and looked down at him.

He looked—like himself. Brown hair, the color of the sandy dirt in the nearby pine scrub forest. Grey eyes, the shade of the 4PM sky on a Florida summer day. Even features, a straight nose, a touch of evening stubble scraping his cheeks, the mouth that fell into a natural smile. Only the faint laugh lines creasing the tops of his cheeks marked his face as any different from the last time she'd stared at it, years ago. He hadn't changed. And he looked perfectly healthy.

"What was that about?" she snapped at him, anger covering up her hurt. If this was a practical joke, it was the cruelest trick he'd ever played.

He rubbed his chest, glancing around at the night. "I'm not sure."

Her eyebrows arched. Her fury faded. He sounded authentically confused and the motion of his hand against his chest set off warning bells in the back of her head. "Are you in any pain?"

"No." He shook his head, but then added, his tone doubtful,

"Not now, anyway."

"Was it your chest?" Natalya asked. "Did it feel like squeezing? Or fullness? Any difficulty breathing?"

"Hmm." He didn't answer her, his eyes on the trees and scrub lining the road.

"Were you lightheaded? Did you pass out?" Impatience was making her skin crawl. Maybe he'd had a heart attack. She needed to get him to a hospital.

"Quit being a doctor, Nat."

She bit back the anger that wanted to spill out. Voice carefully controlled, she said, "I am a doctor, Colin. And as a doctor, I think you need medical attention. Immediate medical attention. We should call an ambulance."

"I don't need one," he answered. "I'm fine."

"You were lying by the side of the road, Colin. That's not fine! Not to mention—" She let the sentence break off.

"Not to mention I ought to be dead?"

"Not to mention that," she agreed, gritting the phrase out through clenched teeth.

"I'm not, though. I'm not." He sounded thoughtful, more surprised than doubting.

Natalya reached for his hand. His warm fingers clasped hers and she helped him to his feet. He stood too close to her, looking down, their eyes and hands locked together until Natalya turned her head away and stepped back, breaking his grasp.

The overhead lights from his car were still flashing, lending the night the surreal glow she knew from her memories. The air felt right, the temperature cool and slightly humid, but not cold. She could smell the forest, pine trees and earthy decay. Everything fit her long-ago precognition—except that Colin was alive.

"What happened?" she asked him, not letting her voice wobble. "What are you doing here?"

He frowned. "It's like a dream."

Confusion, disorientation—those were symptoms. But of what? Drugs and alcohol were obvious, but she ruled them out immediately. She might have barely spoken to him in the past ten years, but he wouldn't have changed that much. Head injury?

She scanned his head, searching for any sign of damage. No blood, no bruising, but not all dangerous head injuries were visible.

She craned her neck trying to see the back of his head, and then brought her gaze back to his face, staring directly into his eyes. His lips parted and he began to step toward her. She put a hand up to stop him and said briskly, "Your pupils are evenly dilated. No sign of concussion."

"I didn't hit my head," he said, pausing in his movement. "At least I don't think I did."

Infection? Dehydration? Shock? Stroke? But despite his confusion, he sounded much too coherent and clear-spoken for any of those conditions. She needed to know more.

"What's the last thing you remember?" she asked.

He rubbed his chest again, and started slowly. "I was driving and—"

"Why here?" Natalya let frustration win and interrupted him. Ten years ago, she'd left Tassamara for medical school and residency. When she moved back, she thought she and Colin had had a tacit agreement to stay out of one another's spaces. She spent as little time in town as she could get away with. What had he been doing on the road that dead-ended at her house?

He didn't look at her. "I wasn't paying attention. I was just driving around. Thinking."

Natalya pressed her lips together. She wanted to yell at him for being an idiot. They both knew she was destined to find his dead body. Surely he could have at least tried to stay off the roads he knew she'd be driving on? But there was no point in saying anything—they'd argued about the inevitability of her precognition for months a decade ago, back when he refused to quit his job as a sheriff's deputy.

"But I saw something," he continued. "I stopped to take a look. I got out of the car and came around to the side... "

He stopped again.

Natalya waited, trying to control her impatience.

"It's like a dream. There was a girl."

Natalya's eyes widened. She'd forgotten. How could she have forgotten? She whirled around, her gaze searching the darkness, but the child was nowhere to be seen. "That wasn't a dream. There was a girl. What could she be doing out here?"

"There was another girl, too. Older. But that was... " He let the words trail off. "No."

"What are you talking about?" Natalya glanced back at Colin. She

10

should call an ambulance. He should get a complete medical evaluation as soon as possible. He could have had a heart attack, a blocked artery, a mild stroke, an aneurysm—but he was supposed to be dead anyway. If a child was lost, they needed to find her.

"A dream. A weird dream." He stepped away from her, toward the forest, eyes scanning their surroundings and called out, "Hello? Are you out there? Can you hear me?"

He paused and listened. Natalya listened with him. She could hear the sound of her own breathing, the stirring of wind overhead, a faint distant cry that might have been coyote. But nothing that sounded like a nearby child.

"What could a child be doing here?" she asked.

Colin shook his head, walking away from her toward the trees. "Let's find her. She couldn't have gone far."

"She must have," Natalya said, pointing out the obvious. Colin glanced her way, his hands working at his belt. "It's two miles to the nearest house and we're on the edge of six hundred miles of forest. She had to have come pretty far to wind up here."

"There is that," he agreed. He turned on the flashlight he'd been retrieving from his belt, and let its illumination play over the forest outside the light spilling from his car.

Natalya could see the trees within the glare of the overhead light bar, but nothing beyond them. She'd been in the forest at night before. Without a flashlight or a full moon or a campfire, the darkness was impenetrable. Why would a child choose the blackness over the comfort offered by the warmth of the light? It wasn't a good sign.

She tried to recall what she'd seen of the girl but the sight had been too quick, too unexpected. Still, the girl had been dressed and not in rags. And she'd been thin, but not emaciated, pale and dirty, but not filthy, not with the kind of ground-in dirt that would have turned her light hair dark and her skin grey. Whoever she was, she hadn't been in the woods for months.

That probably meant she was hungry.

"Grace gave me some leftovers from dinner," she called to Colin's back as he headed toward the edge of the pool of light.

"Grace cooked?" Surprise colored his voice but he stayed focused on the forest.

"She did," Natalya confirmed, a hint of the amusement she felt leaking into her own voice. Grace was many things but a cook was not one of them.

"How was it?" he asked, the skepticism clear.

"Incredibly good. Roast beef, mashed potatoes with lots of butter," Natalya said with more enthusiasm than honesty. The beef was on the dry side and the rolls were cold. But Colin wasn't her target audience. She'd skip the mention of the over-done vegetables—she wasn't likely to entice a child out of the darkness by raving about carrots, even if they were perfect instead of mushy.

"Dessert was fantastic," she added truthfully, raising her voice so the sound would carry. "She made this strawberry trifle with sponge cake. I think she thought she was feeding an army, though—we'll be eating it all week. Unless someone else wants some, that is. I've got a bowl full of it in my car."

She paused by the passenger door of her car and waited, listening. Colin had figured out what she was doing. He turned toward her, watching. "Oh, and Christmas cookies." She raised her voice again, speaking a bit louder. "You remember the kind my mom used to make?"

"The sugar cookies?" Colin asked. "With the colored sugar?"

"Those, and also the ones with the chocolate thumbprint on top. And remember the butter frosting kind? The really sweet ones? Grace made those, too. I've got a whole tin of them here."

Natalya waited.

"I'd be happy to share," she prompted. "With anyone who was maybe a little hungry and wanted a cookie."

The rustle in the brush came from behind them, closer to Colin's car. He swung the light that way, still aiming it low, in time to see the girl crawl out from under a bush.

She stood and Colin let the flashlight follow her up. Natalya took several steps toward her, cataloging injuries. A long scratch down one cheek, visible bruises on one arm, but the dark circles under her eyes were exhaustion, not damage.

As Natalya got closer, the girl flinched, taking a single step backward and glancing over her shoulder as if checking for an escape route.

Natalya froze. In a voice as gentle as she'd use with a wild creature, Natalya said, "What's your name?"

The girl's chin rose, but she didn't answer. Her blue eyes, as they looked from Natalya to Colin and back again, were wary.

Natalya crouched, putting herself closer to eye level with the girl. "I'm Natalya." She tilted her head toward Colin. "That's Colin. We'd like to help you."

The girl didn't answer. A dozen questions burned in Natalya's brain, but she settled for asking only the most important. "Are you hurt?"

The girl's throat moved as she swallowed, but she didn't speak.

"I'm a doctor," Natalya continued, voice still gentle. Behind her, she could sense Colin shifting to the side. He stayed a comfortable distance away, but he was working his way, as if casually, between the girl and her path back to the trees. "I can see the scratch on your face and some bruises on your arm. Does anywhere else hurt?"

The girl's hand rose to touch her face before dropping again. With a hint of defiance, she lifted the edge of the ugly brown dress she wore. Her knees were scraped, her legs scratched and dirty. Blood oozed out along the strap of her cheap plastic sandals.

"Your feet?" Natalya made no move to touch the girl.

The girl nodded.

"I can help with that. Let's get you some food first and then we'll get you cleaned up. Okay?" Natalya waited, not standing until the girl tilted her head in a barely perceptible nod.

"If you want to grab the cookies, I can take her to the station." Colin spoke quietly. He'd managed to move around the girl to the side of his car.

"No way." Without taking her eyes off the child, Natalya gestured with an open hand toward her own car. The girl began to limp toward her.

"What's that supposed to mean?" Colin asked.

"I found you unconscious by the side of the road not ten minutes ago." Natalya kept her voice soft. "And you think I'm going to let a kid ride in a car you're driving? Not a chance."

The girl looked at her sideways as she limped past, her lip curling in what looked like satisfaction. She went straight to the back passenger-side door and tried to open it, then glanced at Natalya. Natalya fumbled in her pocket, then pulled out her keys and pushed the button to unlock the door. The girl opened it and climbed inside.

"Fair point," Colin said, moving to join Natalya where she stood. "Do you want to take her to the station?"

"We should probably take her to a hospital, get her checked out first," Natalya said with a frown. The nearest emergency clinic was forty-five minutes away, the hospital even farther.

"She seem that badly hurt?" Colin asked, turning off his flashlight and reattaching it to his belt.

Natalya made an equivocal gesture with her hand. "Did you look at her?"

"Yeah. Scratches, some bruises, nasty blisters."

"Those bruises aren't fresh. From the dirt, the scratches, the tangled hair, the dried blood—she didn't wander away from home two hours ago. She's been lost for a while."

"Not feral, though," Colin said. "She's no stranger to automatic door locks."

Natalya nodded in agreement. "She's thin, but not emaciated. But she could be dehydrated. If not, she's been drinking untreated water, which in Florida means parasites. Giardia lamblia. Cryptosporidium."

"Brain-eating amoebas?" Colin asked, an edge of humor in his voice.

"Wrong time of year," Nat replied. "Those need warm temperatures."

"Well, that's a relief."

"Not much to do about any of it unless she gets sick, though," Natalya said. "It might be better to try to find her parents first. You should get to the hospital, though."

"I'm fine," Colin answered.

"You don't know that."

Colin thumped himself in the chest. "Heart's beating like a champ. No pain."

"You were rubbing your chest before. It hurt then, didn't it?"

"It was indigestion," he told her. "Hurt like a mo—hurt a lot. But it was just gas."

"That's not how it works. Time equals muscle when it comes to heart attacks." Colin didn't look convinced, so Natalya continued, her worry lending persuasion to her tone. "A heart attack happens when the blood supply to part of your heart is blocked, damaging heart muscle. If the rest of the heart works, the pain can stop. People have heart attacks and walk around afterward as if nothing happened, but that doesn't mean the damage isn't there. And if an artery is blocked, you could have another heart attack any time."

Colin frowned. "I need to start an investigation. I've got to call around, see if anyone's reported a missing child. Check missing person reports, get some dogs out here to retrace her trail, get in touch with DCF—I've got a lot to do."

"One of your deputies could do all that," Natalya suggested.

"What about—" He paused and tugged his earlobe thoughtfully.

"What are you thinking?" Natalya recognized that look. He was going to try to talk her into something.

"Your lab is what, five minutes away?"

"Yeah," Natalya answered warily.

"You could check us both out there. You've got some fancy-pants scanner, right?"

Natalya stopped herself from rolling her eyes with an effort. Fancy-pants was not the word she'd use to describe the multi-million dollar imaging system she used for her research. "I have a high-end imaging system, yes."

"Could you use that to see if anything's wrong?"

"I'm not a cardiologist or trauma specialist," Natalya started, before pausing. Her imaging system was probably the best system in the state of Florida, certainly better than anything at a local 24-hour clinic. And although General Directions wasn't a medical facility, it was well-stocked with medical supplies. She could run the same tests a hospital would run.

She should send Colin to a hospital.

She shouldn't get involved.

But it would save a lot of time.

"I can't treat you at GD. I don't have the right drugs and I'm not about to do an angioplasty. But if you do have a blocked artery, we could get Dave to fly you to Orlando or Jacksonville. You'd get better cardiac care there, anyway."

"That's the ticket." He grinned at her. "And I can get a missing person investigation started."

"Found person, surely," Natalya murmured, wondering if she was making a mistake.

"Same difference, happier ending." He looked away, back toward her car and the hidden child. She could see his frown, but the word was barely audible as he added, "Maybe."

⤫ CHAPTER TWO ⤬

Colin slid into the passenger seat of Natalya's car with a wince. He hated being a passenger. Nat's pointed question about whether it was safe to drive when he didn't know why he'd passed out was valid, though.

Why had he passed out?

And what had happened while he'd been unconscious?

He reached up and flipped open the mirror on the sun visor, angling it so he'd be able to see the girl in the backseat. In the darkness, her face was shadowed, so he pushed on the overhead light. While he'd been radioing in and parking properly, Nat had given the girl food. She sat now with the open tin of cookies by her side, a Santa Claus sugar cookie clutched in her hand, but her eyes were glazing over, the lids fluttering down. Her head tipped to one side and she jerked it back upright, eyes flying open. She saw him looking at her and scowled, eyes narrowing and lips setting stubbornly, before her scowl disappeared in a yawn.

Colin smiled as he turned off the overhead light and settled back into his seat. He didn't mind her glare. It was a good sign, he thought, that her fear didn't have her cowering in the corners.

"Is she asleep?" Nat asked, her voice barely above a whisper.

"Getting that way. Did she say anything?"

"Not a word." Nat shot a quick glance at him. "So tell me what happened."

He rubbed his chin. "It's going to sound crazy."

She raised a skeptical eyebrow. "I have very high standards for crazy."

His answering chuckle was wry. Living in Tassamara was like that. On the surface, Tassamara was a sleepy rural town, supported by the occasional tourists passing through and business from the local farms, orchards, and ranches. Underneath that façade, though, lay a vibrant community composed of open-minded scientists, psychics, and people who didn't quite fit in the outside world.

Long-time residents claimed the town was built on a convergence of ley lines or a vortex point. They said it had been a place of

17

dimensional energy that nourished spiritual gifts for thousands of years, always attracting people with unusual abilities. Maybe it was true. As sheriff, he'd certainly had to deal with his share of strange events and odd occurrences. Still, this night was one of the weirdest of his life.

"It was like a dream," he said.

Nat shook her head. "Don't start there. Start at the beginning. You were in your car and—?"

He'd been driving aimlessly, after a long day capped a long week. Earlier in the month, an apparent double murder turned into a massive drug case involving Feds from all sorts of three-letter agencies. Two days ago, it culminated in a debacle of a raid, leaving three people dead, one in the hospital. The agencies would be pointing fingers and fighting about responsibility for weeks. Despite the holiday, he'd spent hours working on his share of the paperwork.

He didn't blame himself. It might be his town, but neither the drug trafficking nor the botched federal raid were under his control. But the combination of death brushing its wingtips too close and the holiday had him pensive. And nothing could soothe him like the stillness of a dark night and the feel of an automobile engine humming. He loved the solitude of the quiet roads, the control and power of having his hands on a steering wheel.

He'd been waiting to die for a decade. He could still remember the exact moment Nat had told him what she'd seen, as vividly as if it were happening in real time. When she'd started talking, most of his attention had been on the overflowing recycling bin, wondering if they'd missed the right day to take it out, until her words dragged his gaze to her luminous blue eyes.

As the years passed, he tried not to dwell on it. Nothing he could do, no way to change it. Nat's foresight was inevitable, immutable, destined to happen as forecast. Still, knowing death was impending changed a man's perspective.

"I saw a lump by the side of the road," he said. "I thought trash at first. Figured someone dumped something. And then it moved, so I thought animal—maybe a raccoon? But it didn't fit. Wrong size, wrong shape. Too small for a bear and dog didn't make much sense. I was already past it, so I stopped and started to back up, just to check on it."

He fell silent. He'd already been feeling bad, but not bad-bad, just

18

kind of off. Indigestion, he'd thought. Too much of his gramma's turkey and stuffing, although they'd eaten dinner at noon, hours earlier. But as he'd turned to look over his shoulder, raising his right arm to rest it on the back of his seat, a sharp stab of pain had broken into his concentration. Gasping, he'd dropped his arm, turning his hand to push on his chest as if pressure would relieve the tension, hunching his shoulders into the hurt.

He'd known then.

It was time.

It was over.

He'd tried to take a deep breath, but could only suck in shallow gasps of air.

"I felt this—pain." The word seemed entirely inadequate. Pain was a sprained ankle, a broken toe, a bad bruise from a game of touch football that got rough. This was something more like agony. "But then it eased off. It hurt but not so much."

He'd figured he'd made a weird move. Pulled a muscle, maybe. Or pinched a nerve. The sweat on the back of his neck had cooled rapidly and while he still hadn't felt well, sort of fuzzy and shaky, the stabbing misery had disappeared as if it had never happened, leaving only the dull grinding pain of his previous indigestion.

"I stopped, got out of the car and then..." He fell silent again. The lump he'd seen had moved, had raised a head. He'd seen the blonde hair, the eyes, and realized he was looking at a child. It made no sense. What was a child doing by the side of the road, this road, after dark on Christmas Day?

But he couldn't think it through, because the pain had returned, intense and churning. He'd put a hand on the car, bracing himself, hoping the cold metal would break through the fog of agony clouding his vision.

It didn't.

He could barely feel it. His hands had felt far away, disconnected, almost like they weren't part of his body any more.

"The pain was back?" Nat asked.

He nodded. He turned again and looked at the child in the backseat. Her eyes were closed, her head tilted to the side. She'd dropped the cookie.

"And then what?"

"I stepped out." His voice was quiet.

"Out of what? The car?"

"No. No, I was already out of the car."

"Out of what then?"

He glanced at Nat. She was focused on the dark road, not looking at him. "Out of my body," he answered.

"You—what?" She turned her eyes to him for a brief moment, before returning her gaze to the road.

"I know," he said. It sounded ridiculous. But it was what had happened. He suspected he wasn't going to be sharing this story with too many people.

There was a moment of silence before Nat said, "Okay. Keep going."

He felt his lips curling up, amusement stirring. If Nat was having trouble with this first part, she was never going to believe what came next. "This is when it started to feel like a dream. There was a girl there."

"Not her?" Nat tilted her head in the direction of the backseat.

Colin shook his head. "No, another one. Older. A teenager. Wearing a costume of some kind. And she was not real happy with me."

"A costume?" Nat sounded disbelieving.

"Not like Halloween or MegaCon. She wasn't a superhero. God, that would have been strange."

Nat coughed slightly and he could see her trying to hide a smile.

"Well, yeah, it was strange anyway. Stranger, I guess," he admitted. "No, she was dressed old-fashioned, that's all." He ran a hand through his hair, then over his face, trying to remember. "It gets blurry. I think I asked her if she was a shinigami."

"A what?"

"You know, like in—never mind." No way would Nat know. She'd never gotten into manga. "She didn't know what a shinigami was either. Or a reaper."

"A what?" Nat asked again.

He sounded crazy. He knew it. He'd warned her. "You know, like a spirit guide, someone to take me on to the next plane of existence, the afterworld. But she laughed and said if she was a spirit guide, she'd be the kind stopping and asking for directions every five minutes, because she was as lost as a goose in a snowstorm."

"Okay, let me get this straight. You've left your body. You think you're dead. And you're talking to a girl in costume who's making jokes about geese?"

Put like that, it didn't sound crazy. It sounded ridiculous. "I told you, it was a dream."

Nat shrugged. "Maybe. Then what?"

It was a dream that had felt very real, though, in its own way. He hadn't been in a strange place or a surreal world. He'd been exactly where he was, standing above his body, talking to the teenager. The little girl had darted into the underbrush at the side of the road when he got out of the car, but she'd crept closer, wide-eyed and uncertain. She'd reached a tentative hand out to him and patted his back gently. His body hadn't moved, but he had, crouching down next to her as he asked the teenager about her.

"The little girl moved me," he said, remembering. She'd tugged at his body, pulling on his arm, working hard to turn him over. And the bigger girl, she'd said something. But it was gone, whatever it had been. The memories were slipping away, the rich, vivid images fading like a dream after being awake for too long.

"Rolled you over?" Nat asked sharply.

"Yeah, I think so."

Nat looked over her own shoulder at the girl. "Not easy. She's what, maybe fifty pounds? You would have been a dead weight. No pun intended."

"No," Colin agreed. "The other girl helped, I think." Had she? She'd crouched down, too, almost on top of them both, her hands and arms passing straight through the smaller one. They'd touched his face, both of them, soft touches, but then the bigger girl shifted, directing the little girl down to his chest.

And then... he didn't know what had happened then. There'd been light and heat and pain again, the burning in his chest back for a moment that lasted forever, and then Nat over him.

That had seemed as much a dream as anything. Ten years had passed since she'd touched him, a decade without her blue eyes the first sight he saw as he woke. Yet opening his own to meet hers had felt like falling back into the world as it should be, as it was meant to be.

"You know everything else," he said. "I woke up. You were there." The words sounded so simple. So easy.

Nat was silent.

21

"What do you think?" he asked her.

"We don't dream when we're unconscious," she said.

"What does that mean?"

"No idea."

They'd reached the gate barring the way into GD. The security booth was dark, no guard on duty, but Nat pulled to a stop and rolled down her window. She punched a code into the computer pad next to the gate.

"She's asleep, right?" Nat asked without looking back.

"Yeah."

"So we'll run some tests on you first. See what we find. Did you call DCF?"

"Not yet. I've got dispatch checking missing persons and making some calls."

She frowned at him. "Child Protective Services will need to send a caseworker. They'll probably want a psychologist present when you interview her."

"Yeah, yeah," Colin agreed. "But it might not be that complicated. How does a kid wind up lost in the forest?"

Nat's brows drew down as she pulled the car forward. "Camping?" she offered. "Hiking?"

"That'd be my guess. So maybe the rangers and some frantic parents are searching for her already."

"You're thinking she just wandered off?" Nat asked.

"Maybe, yeah."

Nat looked skeptical. "On Christmas Day?"

Colin shrugged. "Big meal, maybe the parents took a nap afterwards. Kid gets bored, next thing you know..."

"It's a long walk from the nearest campground. I don't think a child could cover that much distance in an afternoon." Nat pulled into the parking space closest to the cobblestoned walkway leading to the front door. A lamppost shed a warm glow of golden light, while the bushes and shrubs that lined the path and bordered the building were sprinkled with the delicate white glimmers of hundreds of tiny holiday lights.

"Next possibility then." Colin glanced over his shoulder at the sleeping child, then gestured to indicate they should talk about it outside. Stepping out of the car, he turned, leaning on the roof. In a quiet voice, he suggested, "The parents could have been in a car accident on one of the back roads."

Nat winced. "Okay, that sounds more plausible. But still, to get to where we found her? It's more likely she was on a trail. Maybe an ATV accident?"

"Yeah." Colin nodded in agreement, his face grim. "No helmet, though."

"And wearing a dress and sandals." Nat shook her head, but not as if she were ruling out the possibility, more as if she were regretting the chances parents were willing to take. "It makes sense."

"With any luck a couple of phone calls will clear it up. We'll get her home before morning."

Nat didn't say anything, but then she frowned, blinking a few times as if perplexed.

"What is it?" Colin asked immediately.

She licked her lips. He felt an immediate and unsurprising surge of lust. Haloed by the light from the lamppost, Nat's dark hair glinted with color, while the shadows made her blue eyes mysterious and smoky. She was beautiful. And he was alive.

Alive.

The smile felt like it started in his chest and built its way up until it reached his face. He knew he was grinning at her like an idiot, but he couldn't stop himself.

Alive.

And with Nat.

Sometimes it felt as if he'd loved Nat forever.

He hadn't, though.

It had only been thirty years.

He'd been a stubborn five-year-old, desperately trying to convince his mother—who already had seven children—that he needed a baby sister, one who would be all his. He would get to boss her around like his older brothers and sisters bossed him around, but he would never, ever hit her and he would play with her whenever she wanted. She could be Princess Leia when they played *Star Wars*. He needed someone to be Princess Leia. Unfortunately, his mother had remained resolutely unconvinced of the importance of his need.

Then, on the first day of kindergarten, he'd met Lucas. Lucas didn't just have a baby sister; he had a baby brother, too. He didn't seem to be as convinced as Colin was of his incredible luck, though, and he'd generously offered to share. Colin distinctly remembered his first visit to the Latimer house. He hadn't even seen baby Zane. One look at the wide blue eyes and round cheeks of Natalya's three-year-old self and he'd decided. Mine.

The arrangement had worked well for a long time. Through high school, through college, past graduation, up until the moment he got his first job as deputy and she had her premonition of his death—and then they'd hit a dead end. He'd let her go. Made her go, really, and not without hurting her.

She'd gone to medical school and they didn't speak for years. After the bitter words of their last fight, the first time he'd spoken to her had been at her mother's funeral. He couldn't remember what he'd said, but she'd said, "Thank you," her voice calm, collected, but her eyes showing the depth of her pain. After completing her residency, she'd returned to Tassamara.

He'd managed to draw her into a precarious almost-friendship— he could say hello to her on the street without her glaring at him— but it survived through a careful dance of manners and caution and patience on his part. He knew—or suspected—that if she had her choice, she'd never speak to him again. But Tassamara was a small town. That hadn't been an option.

And now—well, he was alive. Now everything changed.

"I can't—nothing," she said abruptly, ignoring his grin. "Let me get the security guard to carry her in."

She turned away. Before she'd gone two steps, Colin called out. "I'll get her."

She turned back. "Unconscious, remember?"

"Not without warning." He dismissed her concern as he reached for the car door. "If it happens again, I'll have plenty of time to set her down."

The girl had fallen asleep slumped against the door. Her hand had crept up to her mouth, the thumb not quite inside but tucked next to her lips as if she would have been sucking it if she'd been a little younger. Carefully, Colin opened the door, slipping one hand in to catch her before she started to slide out. She stirred but didn't open her eyes.

As he unbuckled her seatbelt, he considered his approach before taking the most straightforward route. Sliding his hands under her arms, he tugged her out and up, lifting her high and drawing her close, before tucking one arm underneath her legs. She wasn't light, but something about her weight balanced in a way that made carrying her totally unlike picking up a fifty-pound sack of mulch for the yard. As if automatically, she wrapped her legs and arms around him before dropping her head into the curve of his neck.

"Da," she muttered.

Colin froze. The tiny voice, the weight of her head, the soft tickle of her hair against his skin, the smell of light soap and sandy dirt, no hint of the tang of sweat—it was a visceral punch to the gut. Somewhere out there, in the forest or not, a man, a father, had lost this child. He'd get her home to him, he swore silently. He'd find her da for her.

"Colin?"

He could hear the worry in Nat's voice. He turned and started toward the door, before saying, his own voice hushed so as not to wake the girl, "She spoke."

"Oh, good," Nat answered, hurrying to catch up with him. "Selective mutism from trauma isn't uncommon, but maybe when she wakes up she'll be willing to tell us what happened."

At the door, she pressed a keycard against an unobtrusive black pad, reaching for the handle at the sound of a loud click. As she opened the door, she looked back at Colin. "What did she say?"

Colin's gaze met Nat's. Her face was open, her eyes clear. He could feel the warmth of the girl's arm against his neck, her heartbeat against his arm. He opened his mouth to answer and then stopped, staggered by the moment.

This.

This should have been his.

Theirs.

If their lives had been what he wanted, what they wanted, how many times would he have already carried a sleeping child from a car while Nat held the door for him? Dozens? Hundreds?

This should have been theirs.

"Da," he answered, his tongue feeling thick in his mouth, not able to hide the sorrow he felt.

A flicker of a frown passed across Nat's face as if she were confused by his reaction, but he could see the exact instant she recognized what he was thinking as her face stilled and her chin angled up. They stood there, motionless, staring at one another.

He wanted to say so much to her. He shifted the sleeping child, but before he could summon the words, a security guard was pushing open the door.

"Dr. Latimer. Everything okay?" The guard's eyes were wary, his hand close to his weapon, but he nodded at Colin in acknowledgement of the uniform. Colin nodded back, not sure whether to be annoyed or grateful for the interruption.

"Everything's fine," Nat said smoothly. If her smile looked forced, Colin didn't think the guard noticed. "We're just here to run some tests." She stepped inside the building, moving briskly.

Colin followed more slowly. Maybe it was a reaction to almost being dead, but he felt close to battered by the intensity of the emotions flowing through him. Joy, relief, grief, regret on high-speed cycle.

Feeling so emotional was damn exhausting, he thought. He hoped he'd get over it soon.

❧ CHAPTER THREE ❧

Natalya rubbed her forehead, then pinched the bridge of her nose. It was late, she was tired, could she be misreading? Could she have done something wrong?

"Aren't you done yet?" Colin's call from inside her scanner was louder than it needed to be. She'd told him she could hear him if he whispered. His volume probably indicated his mood: she'd had him in the machine for almost forty-five minutes, longer than any typical scan.

But then this wasn't typical. She pressed her speaker button and said flatly, "No."

She picked up the test stick again. It was idiot-proof. She couldn't have done anything wrong there. Drip some blood on the piece of plastic, wait fifteen minutes, look for a line. The line said, clear as day, that Colin had suffered a heart attack.

She looked back at her screen and began rapid cycling through images. Doctors, typically, neither gave the blood tests nor ran the scanner. Technicians did both those jobs, leaving doctors more time to treat patients. But when Natalya had returned to Tassamara, she'd retreated to a lab and research with relief. It wasn't that she didn't like working with people. She did. But medicine and foresight made for an uneasy combination.

She closed her fingers around the test stick, closing her eyes for good measure. She didn't often try to induce her foresight; it came on its own, unwanted, ill-timed. But now, when she did want to know what the future would bring, she saw exactly nothing.

Nothing.

She opened both fingers and eyes, letting the plastic stick drop to her desk with a slight clatter. Reflexively she glanced over her shoulder at the tiny figure curled up on a nest of cushions on the floor behind her, but the girl hadn't stirred at the noise, any more than the sound of Natalya's voice had moved her. She'd been out cold since she'd fallen asleep in the car, her exhaustion overruling her hunger. Natalya hadn't wanted to leave her alone in a more comfortable room, so she'd grabbed some over-sized pillows from the couch in an upstairs reception room on their way down to the scanner.

Natalya turned her gaze back to her computer screen. Colin's heart was perfect. Her hands flew over her keyboard, increasing the magnification of the images by two hundred percent, then three, then four. She stared at the screen, searching for evidence of microinfarcts, subtle tissue damage, but there was none. His arteries were lovely. His entire cardiovascular system looked stellar. If she'd been reviewing these images for a physical, she would have happily signed off on any activity.

"Come on, Nat. You've gotta be done by now." Colin's tone this time was closer to a mumble, a protest he didn't expect her to hear.

Natalya rested her forehead on her hand for a second or two, trying to think. With a long exhale, she stood. She'd run the troponin test again.

She pushed the button to slide the table out of the scanner. Standing, she crossed to the door between the two rooms, and as Colin sat up, told him, "I need to take more blood."

His sigh of relief at being out of the machine turned into a sigh of exasperation. "Seriously?"

"If you were in Gainesville or any reputable hospital, they'd be checking the enzyme counts in your blood every hour. Don't be giving me a hard time about this." With one last glance at the sleeping child—still motionless—she gestured for Colin to follow her and headed to the small exam room down the hallway. GD was a research facility, not a clinic, but she routinely checked her subjects' basic vital signs, including blood pressure, heart rate, and temperature, before proceeding with their imaging.

Colin didn't complain, but as she slid the hypodermic needle under his skin, he grimaced. "I think you're turning into a vampire."

"Overgrown mosquitoes. Not a chance," she responded automatically, as she watched the syringe fill with red. Pulling it out, she pressed the cotton ball she had ready onto his skin and slid her hand up his forearm, gently forcing him to close his arm around the insertion point. And then her eyes met his.

His were hot, almost smoky. She could see the thought, the memory, as clearly as if her gift were telepathy. His old apartment. The television on. Him trying to convince her to watch. Her huffing in disgust. Vampire shows. Pfft. And then... how many times had five minutes of television turned into heated kissing on the couch, his hand sliding up her shirt, her hand sliding down his?

Too many.

Her lips parted, the heat rushing into her cheeks, flooding the rest of her. She dropped his arm as if it burned, turning away and fumbling with the vial of blood.

Without a word, she marched off into the adjacent storeroom.

He followed her. He was bare-chested, only half-dressed so she could scan his heart without interference from his shirt. She'd look like an idiot if she told him to put some clothes on, but she was much too aware of his presence behind her as she set the vial of blood down on the counter.

She opened the industrial-size refrigerator. Her eyes skimmed down the full boxes to the one she'd located earlier and she grabbed it and slid another test pouch out.

"Why do you guys have all this stuff?" The question was casual, but she could hear the tension underneath it.

How many years had it been since the two of them were alone together?

Too many.

Not enough.

Natalya frowned down at the test instructions, trying to focus on the present, not the past. What had he asked? Oh, right. The over-stocked refrigerator.

"Zane. And Grace," she added, to be scrupulously fair. Really, Grace should have known what she was doing. She scanned the instructions, looking for any place where she might have gone wrong before. She was no expert but they seemed perfectly straightforward. Drip whole blood on the test unit, wait fifteen minutes, check the line.

"Not really an answer," Colin murmured.

She glanced at him, surprised, and then chuckled. It felt like a complete answer to her, but then she'd been working with her siblings for the past few years. "Grace didn't have time to do her usual emergency preparedness planning this year. So she told Zane to take care of it."

Natalya ripped open the pouch, taking out the test stick. "She didn't give him a budget. Instead of working his way down her checklist and updating our water and canned food supplies, which

I'm sure is what Grace intended, Zane sent out an email to everyone in the company, asking what they thought we'd need in the event of the zombie apocalypse and promising a prize to the person who sent the most complete answer, quality of the prize to be determined by the quality of the answers." Bending over the test, she carefully dripped blood into the test well, before looking at the clock on the wall to check the time. Almost one.

"And?" Colin prompted.

She yawned, covering her mouth with her hand. "You know how people work here. The answers were in-depth. Thorough. A little crazy. We probably lost a solid couple of day's work from every researcher on staff."

"You're kidding. How much detail is possible?"

"One person wrote a novel," she told him. "I read it. It wasn't half-bad." She'd actually enjoyed the story of how Tassamara survived and thrived during the zombie apocalypse, although she had serious reservations about whether Max's actions were at all plausible.

"What?" Colin's laugh held disbelief.

"No, I'm not kidding. People got—well, they know Zane. Anyway, after he received all the answers, he had an admin compile the results, and order anything at least three people mentioned. We've got more than three doctors on staff, so—" She waved at the refrigerator. "In the event of an emergency, we're stocked."

"Don't you mean in the event of the zombie apocalypse?"

"Not gonna happen," she told him wryly. "Our next hurricane, however, is inevitable." The words didn't inspire foreknowledge and she frowned. But she'd seen it before: the tree branches, Millard Street, the window of the bistro shattering. With a shake of her head, she added, "As are our next tornadoes."

"What did you see?"

Natalya turned away and picked up the plastic stick. "Nothing."

"Nat."

She glanced at him. "Nothing."

"I'm the sheriff. My job is to keep the town safe. If you know something that could help me do that, I want to know what it is."

Natalya stared down at the test stick in her hands, barely seeing it. "I don't tell people what I know about the future anymore. It serves no purpose."

Silence.

It dragged on, became pronounced. Natalya could hear the sound of the clock ticking on the wall, her own breath, even the tiny hum of the overhead light.

And then they both spoke at once.

"It isn't because of you, because of what happened with us."

"You're not responsible for what you see."

Natalya's hand shook and she steadied it, consciously inhaling. Straight to the heart. Damn it. And then they both spoke, again talking over one another.

"I know that," Natalya said.

"I'd be sorry if it was."

Colin half-laughed and Natalya started to set the test back down on the counter, then blinked at it and paused. "Damn."

"You go first," Colin offered.

Natalya shook her head. "Not that." She offered him the plastic stick. "Pink line. You have excess troponin in your blood. It's an indicator of heart damage."

"Ah." Colin took the stick and looked at the line, his mouth twisting. "How bad is it?"

"It's not." She crumpled up the waste from the test kit and dropped it into the nearby trash can, then took the vial with his remaining blood and walked back toward the scanner monitoring room.

"What does that mean?" He followed her, of course.

"It means I'm a radiologist, not a cardiologist, and I don't know what I'm doing." She set the vial of blood down on her desk next to the first one and stared at her computer screen for a moment, not really seeing it. She tried to think, tried to remember any facts that could make sense of the contradictory data, but her brain kept returning to the moment when she rounded the back of his car and reality began deviating from her foreknowledge. Why was he alive? Why wasn't he dead?

"Come on, Nat, that scan took forever. You must have lots of pretty pictures of my heart by now."

"And a very pretty heart it is," Nat answered, half-sarcastic, half-serious, before grabbing a pen and reaching for the sheet of labels she'd gotten out earlier. As she filled out the sticker with his name, the date, and the time she'd drawn the blood, she added, "But there's nothing wrong with it."

"So did I have a heart attack or didn't I?"

"Your troponin levels say yes. But your heart shows no evidence of damage, which means no." She set the pen down, and then placed the label neatly on the vial.

"I'm confused."

"Join the crowd," she muttered. She looked in his direction, trying not to notice his physicality. She'd gained at least fifteen pounds, probably closer to twenty, in the past decade, but he'd added muscle. The definition in his upper arms and chest was noticeable. And regrettably hot. "You weren't exercising strenuously a couple of hours ago, were you?"

Colin grinned at her. "Not unless eating an extra slice of cake counts. All that chewing, you know."

She didn't smile back. "Elevated troponin levels indicate damage to muscle, usually cardiac. But your heart is fine."

"That sounds like good news."

"I suppose." She pressed her lips together. "If you went to a hospital, they probably wouldn't even keep you overnight for observation. Troponin tests can be wrong, but the scan should be conclusive."

"So I'm going to live?" All humor had disappeared from Colin's face. His grey eyes were intent on hers, his strong mouth set in an even line.

Natalya spread her hands. "Your guess is as good as mine."

"Come on, Nat, you can do better than that. Tell me my future." She could see he was making an effort to sound casual, but his eyes were anything but.

"I don't do that anymore, remember?"

"Exigent circumstances," he responded. "When am I going to die?"

She licked her lips, waiting. But his question didn't spur anything in her mind, no flood of images, no quick fleeting glimpse of an unknown place that still seemed familiar. She shook her head in his direction.

"Will I die tomorrow?" he persisted. "This week? Next week?" He stepped closer to her until he was so close she could almost feel the warmth radiating from his skin and she had to tilt her head up to look into his face.

She shrugged. "No idea. I don't see it." He was in her space. She should step away from him or at least order him to back off, but she didn't, torn by her own mind's mixed messages. She didn't want him to affect her. She didn't want to show him he affected her. But part of her—maybe it was the girl who had taken his presence in her life for granted, believed they were for always—simply wanted to lean into him and exult for a moment that he was still living, still breathing.

A smile broke over his face, curving his lips, lifting his cheeks, crinkling his eyes. And then his hands were on her, tugging her close. Her mouth opened to protest, but he was kissing her before she could form the words.

His kiss earlier had been questioning, searching, but this kiss demanded and took. She kissed him back. It was impossible not to. Her eyes closed and she lost herself in the moment; familiar, yet different, the long-suppressed craving bursting into life, heat rushing through her and pooling in her core. Their lips parted and returned, tongues tangling, little gasping breaths escaping, until Colin began stroking his way along the line of Natalya's cheek, lips teasing and nibbling.

She let her head fall back, giving him better access to her sensitive neck and ears. He knew just how to kiss her, just what she liked. That hadn't changed.

He caught the lobe of her ear with gentle teeth. "Boy or girl?" he whispered.

She froze. The words ricocheted in her mind like bullets hitting the memories of the times he'd asked the same question, teasing, silly, a joke. Lying by the lake at sixteen, in their first shared bed at twenty, and then the last time, the very last time, the day before he told her good-bye.

She pushed herself off him, shoving with enough force that he took a couple of steps backward, and she reeled away and into the edge of her desk, almost onto her computer. The heat of passion was gone, lost in a wave of such searing anger that her tensed muscles quivered with it.

Fists clenched against the urge to hit him, to hurt him like he'd hurt her, she grated out the answer. "We are never having children. Because we are not a couple and never will be again."

He put a hand on his chest. Maybe he was touching where she'd shoved him, maybe he was covering his heart. She didn't know and she didn't care. "Nat."

She glared at him.

"I'm not going to die."

"Apparently not. Congratulations." She turned away, feeling tears well up in her eyes and not wanting him to see them. She'd told herself years ago that it was stupid to keep hating him. That she needed to let go. Maybe not forgive, maybe not forget, but move on with her life. But she'd always known this night was coming. She'd been waiting for it, even if it hadn't ended the way she'd expected.

She took a deep breath and exhaled slowly, making a conscious effort to relax her muscles and clear her mind.

"I'm not dying," Colin repeated.

She turned back to him, in control again. "No, you're not." She managed a tight smile. "But that doesn't change the past. It doesn't change the fact that when you thought you would, when you thought you only had a little while to live, you chose not to spend that time with me."

He opened his mouth as if to protest, but she raised a hand and snapped, her tone fast and furious. "Don't. Don't even start. I don't want to hear what you have to say. I don't care what you have to say. I'm glad you're alive but that doesn't mean anything between us changes."

He ran a hand through his hair, "Everything changes, Nat."

"Not us. We don't change. You dumped me. And I don't forgive you."

In the other room, a phone rang. His. It rested with the other items from his pockets on a small table next to the scanner. He glanced in that direction automatically, then looked back at her and started. "Nat—"

"You should get that," she interrupted him, voice cold, expression colder. "It's probably about the girl. Maybe they've found her parents or know who she is."

He didn't move.

A rustle behind her told Natalya the girl was sitting up. She tried to school her expression, to not let the anger seething under her surface show, but her hands were trembling as she turned toward the child, taking the two steps that put her next to the pile of cushions. She crouched down. "Hey, sleepyhead."

The girl looked fearful, eyes wide.

"Don't worry." Natalya reached out and put a gentle hand on the girl's shoulder. "You fell asleep in the car and we carried you down to my office. But you don't need to be afraid. We'll get you home."

The phone was still ringing. With a muffled sound falling somewhere between a sigh of resignation and a growl of frustration, Colin went to answer it.

The child still looked scared and Natalya let her hand drop to her side. Poor kid. Natalya's anger faded, lost in guilt and sympathy. Bad enough to be lost and alone without waking up to strange adults screaming. "Did I wake you up by yelling at him? I'm sorry."

The girl blinked, but the stiffness in her body didn't ease.

"I've known him for a long time, since I was a little girl. Littler than you."

The girl's eyes narrowed slightly, a tiny movement, but her skepticism was plain.

Natalya had to smile. "Really. He was a little boy then, of course."

The girl's head tipped back, away from Natalya. She looked toward the door where Colin had disappeared and then back at Natalya.

"I might get mad at him sometimes, but he's a good guy. You don't need to be afraid of him. Or of me," Natalya said, still trying to reassure her.

The wariness remained, but the look of fear was gone. For a moment, Natalya debated questioning her—asking again for her name and the story of how she'd come to be lost in the forest—but she suspected from the girl's silence, the tension in her shoulders and the closed-off way she was holding her arms tight to her sides that she'd be no more helpful than she'd been earlier.

From the other room, she could hear the rumble of Colin's voice, but not what he was saying until he appeared in the doorway, phone in hand. "No luck, I'm afraid."

"Nothing?"

"No reports of a missing child. There's a ranger out looking for accident sites, but even knowing where she wound up, there's a lot of ground to cover. We'll get a real search started at first light." Colin glanced at his watch.

"What now?" Natalya asked.

"The DCF call." He grimaced. "I'll start with the hotline. It's probably going to take a while, though. Working my way through a state bureaucracy on Christmas Day won't be easy."

"You might be surprised," Natalya answered. "Our local agency is very well-run."

She didn't say any more, but her mother had supported Florida's shift to private, community-based foster care. When Natalya moved back to Tassamara, she'd taken over her mother's former seat on the board of directors at the local agency, so she knew—and admired—the people who ran the non-profit. They had hard jobs, but they did them well.

"I'll find out." Colin turned away, punching the number into his phone without hesitation.

Natalya looked back at the girl. "Let's get you cleaned up and put some band-aids on those blisters," she suggested.

The girl didn't argue, so Natalya stood. She held out a hand but the girl ignored it as she scrambled to her feet. Without comment, Natalya led the way to the exam room.

The blisters were bad and must have hurt, but Natalya saw no signs of infection. Natalya sprayed them with a topical numbing agent before cleaning them but even so, the girl was wincing, feet twitching away from Natalya's fingers, before she was done. She still didn't make a sound.

"Sorry about that." Natalya dropped the used antiseptic wipes into the trash can. She pulled open the cupboard door and looked at the bandage options. A basic adhesive would be fine, but she wished she had a fun choice, instead of the plain brown. Zane's zombie planning apparently hadn't taken into account the need to cheer people up. "All of our band-aids are the boring kind, I'm afraid. I wish we had fun ones for you."

She turned back to the girl and paused. Something had drawn a smile from her, a faint one, curling around her lips like a wisp of sunshine on a grey day. Natalya smiled back at her as she sat down and began applying the bandages.

"No. That's not acceptable." Colin stepped into the exam room and dropped his phone to his side. "How old do you think she is?"

Natalya raised a questioning eyebrow, before looking back at the girl. If she ran a scan, she could probably pinpoint her age within a year from the growth plates on her bones, but without more information, she'd be guessing. Still, children were sometimes predictable with how they behaved when their ages were mentioned.

Deliberately, she guessed low. "Five, I'd say."

The girl's eyes widened and her lower lip slid out.

"No?" Natalya asked. "Six? Seven?"

At the last number, the girl's chin jerked down in a tiny nod.

"She's seven years old," Colin said into the phone. "An emergency shelter with teenagers is not appropriate."

Natalya frowned and pushed her sliding chair away from the girl, turning so she could see Colin more easily.

"I understand it's a holiday. And the middle of the night. What else have you got?" Colin listened for a moment. "That's almost worse. Refusing to speak doesn't mean she's emotionally disturbed. She's been through a traumatic experience. She'll talk when she's ready." He fell silent again, but as the person on the other end of the line continued to speak, he began shaking his head as if rejecting her words.

"Who is it?" Natalya mouthed.

He covered the mouthpiece with one hand and whispered, "Carla something. Didn't catch it. Community Family Services."

Standing, Natalya gestured for Colin to hand her the phone. She'd take care of this. He scowled but she wiggled her fingers at him, demand clear, and he passed the phone to her.

"Carla? Natalya Latimer here."

"Dr. Latimer! The sheriff didn't mention you." The woman sounded surprised, her tone tense.

"We must have woken you up," Natalya said, making her tone sympathetic. "And on Christmas. How did you get stuck with this shift? You've been with the agency what, four, five years, now? Shouldn't one of the new girls be working the holiday?"

"It'll be six in March," Carla answered, sounding more relaxed. "And I'll tell ya, if I'd known what today was gonna be like, I sure wouldn't have signed up for this shift."

"Bad day?"

"A home visit that didn't go well and two emergency placements. Plus all the usual juggling around the holidays. The Ruiz's needed to visit out-of-state family—Marco's mother is ill—and the Thompsons have visitors."

"What about Mrs. Watson? Is she available?"

"She's got a toddler and a baby, so she's at capacity."

"Who else do you have?" Natalya asked.

37

As Carla rattled down a list of names and reasons why each one wouldn't work, Natalya turned some of her attention back to the exam room. Colin had picked up his shirt and was shrugging into it, but his eyes were on her.

"It sounds as if we need a new recruitment drive," Natalya said, interrupting Carla."

"This isn't typical, it's just—" the woman started.

"I'll make sure it gets on the agenda for the next board meeting." Natalya spoke over her. "Meanwhile, though, what do we do for the moment? I've got a little girl here who needs a bed to sleep in."

"I've got space free at the juvenile facility and Hart House, but as I was telling the sheriff, that's it. That's all I've got. I can start calling out of county, but I can't tell you how long it'll take."

"Hmm." Natalya considered the options. Her role on the board was mostly symbolic, based on General Directions and the Latimer family being the largest financial contributors to the agency. She had no experience navigating the system.

"What are you doing there, anyway?" Carla asked. "Why did the sheriff call you?"

"Oh, just a little emergency first aid," Natalya answered.

"Is she hurt?"

"Not seriously, no."

"A hospital might be an option, though. I realize they won't want to keep her, but if there was a bed on the pediatrics floor, maybe we could justify an overnight observation."

"What about an emergency placement?" Natalya asked slowly. "For the same reason?"

"What do you mean?"

"I'm not licensed, but I took the training class last year as part of the development planning. And I've got a guest bed."

"You'd let her stay with you?"

"For the night," Natalya clarified hastily. "To keep her under medical supervision. Just in case."

"That would work," Carla said, sounding eager. "Up to twenty-four hours. And beyond that, thirty days if a judge signs off."

It couldn't take a month to find the girl's parents. Surely they'd find them tomorrow. Maybe even by morning if the rangers got lucky.

Without even thinking about it, Natalya concentrated, expecting to see what would happen. Would it be a phone call, reporting the news? Or would someone show up at her door? Would they be at the sheriff's office? But nothing came to her.

She tried to summon a recent memory and it was easy: standing on the porch of her childhood home, the lights sparkling, the poinsettias red against the white porch, her father's deep voice telling her to drive safely, Grace shoving food into her hands. But when she thought of the future, her mind was blank. Empty.

A paranoid person might think the emptiness meant she had no future.

Good thing she wasn't paranoid.

❧ CHAPTER FOUR ❦

"Hannah." Natalya's eyes flickered open.

"Emily." She lay still, motionless for the second or two it took to identify her location.

"Jane." Her own bed, with its soft cotton sheets and thin, lightweight quilt.

"Anne?" Her own room, cream walls, moss-green trim, a careful selection of her own colorful artwork hanging within easy eyesight. But something wasn't right.

"Am I totally off-track here?"

The voice was part of it. She recognized it, of course. Grace, her tone one of mild complaint. But what was she doing here? As Natalya sat up, she waited for her foresight to kick into action, for her brain to preview the next few minutes for her and answer her question, but her mind refused to cooperate, staying stubbornly blank.

"Should I be trying names like Sunshine? Harmony? Dharma? Cosmic Bliss?"

The light. That was what else was wrong. She'd overslept. Morning sun scattered its rays along the hardwood floor as she threw off the quilt, fumbling for a robe, and hurried into the short hallway leading to the adjacent kitchen.

Grace was sitting at her table, watching the little girl across from her eat. "More?" Grace offered, reaching for the cereal box.

Natalya tried in vain to recall what would happen next. Nothing. "What are you doing here, Grace?"

"I was going to make you come shopping with me," Grace answered, pouring more granola into the girl's bowl. "But I got distracted by the burglar in your kitchen."

"She's not a burglar." Nat crossed to the sink and pressed the On button on her coffee maker. The low water light blinked at her, so she grabbed the sprayer from the kitchen sink to refill the reservoir.

"Depends if you want cereal for breakfast, I guess. That's the end of your granola." The girl's spoon clattered against her bowl as she dropped it.

41

"No, no," Grace said hastily. "I was just kidding. I'm the one who fed you, so that makes me the burglar." She nodded toward the bowl. "Go ahead, eat. Nat'll find something else."

"There's plenty of food." Natalya turned to reassure the girl, noticing too late that she was letting water splash out of the coffeemaker. Oops. With the coffee started, she grabbed for a dishtowel and wiped up the water on the counter.

"Neighbor have a childcare emergency?" Grace asked as the girl started spooning cereal into her mouth, neatly but too quickly, her eyes down.

Cleaned up and wearing a brightly-colored t-shirt Natalya had given her to sleep in, she could maybe pass for a neighbor kid—if, that is, Natalya had any really crappy neighbors whose kids were half-starved, bruised and scraped, wary and silent, which she did not.

"Not exactly, no." Natalya leaned against the sink, waiting for the machine to finish brewing.

"So where'd you get her?"

"I, um, found her." Natalya ran her hands through her hair and yawned. She was going to have to tell Grace the whole story, she realized. Beginning to end. Finding Colin on the road. Colin not dying. The premonition. The past. Her foresight going wrong. Her foresight being gone.

"You found her? Like how? Like you'd find a stray kitten?" Laughter underlay the surprise in Grace's tone.

"Something like that, yeah."

"Have you called the police?"

"No." Hell. Natalya wasn't ready to cope with Grace being efficient. She needed caffeine. She reached for the coffeepot.

"Why not?" Grace demanded.

"I didn't need to. I mean I—" Coffee pot in one hand, Natalya turned, stepped, and slipped in a puddle of water on the floor. The coffee pot went flying.

Grace almost caught it.

Almost.

A yelp from Grace as the glass burned her hands and she tried to juggle the coffee pot, a crash-smash as it hit the floor, a squeak of dismay from the child, a scrape as she pushed her chair away from the table and fled, and instant, profuse, apologies from Natalya.

"I'm so sorry, I'm so—sink!" Natalya finished with the order, grabbing her sister and tugging her over to the kitchen faucet.

Grace stared at the coffee staining the shirt, the brown liquid rapidly soaking into the sleeves. "Ouch?"

"Take it off," Natalya ordered, turning the handle and shoving Grace's arms under the cool water.

"I can't take my shirt off when you're pushing me around." Grace protested automatically, before shoving both arms together and lifting them up so the water trailed down and dripped off her elbows. "What the hell, Nat? How did you not know that was coming?"

Natalya closed her eyes, feeling sickness wash through her. She'd burned her sister. But she never had accidents. Never. Her foresight should have kicked in the moment she heard Grace's voice. She should have known what was coming before she even got out of bed.

"Don't worry about the shirt," she corrected herself. Lavender oil. Where was it? Her bathroom, probably, from the last time she'd used it in the tub as a relaxing aromatherapy. "Wait here. Keep your arms under the water."

She hurried away. Breathe. Breathe. Breathe. Her friend Tim's medical school litany swam through her head, 'Fear is the mind killer. Let it go. Focus on the now.' But it didn't work.

Grace was burned. It was Natalya's fault. And her foresight, her vision, the gift that had so often felt more like a curse, was gone. Nausea churned in her stomach and her pulse thudded in her ears.

With the lavender oil clutched in her palm so tightly her nails dug into her skin, she returned to the kitchen. "Okay, I've got it."

But she wasn't the first one back. The little girl stood next to Grace, on tiptoe, peering over the edge of the sink, her hands holding Grace's arm while the water sluiced down. The girl met Natalya's eyes, then soundlessly, she dropped Grace's arm and darted toward the archway leading to the front room.

"Wait," Grace said. "What was that? How did you, what did you, come back!"

The moment felt familiar. The little girl had run again, just like last night. But why? Natalya listened but there was no sound of the front door being pulled open, so with a worried frown, she turned her attention to her sister. "Take off your shirt."

Grace shook her head, but not in refusal. Her hands started working the buttons as she said, "I think I'm fine. Really. It doesn't hurt."

Natalya's mouth twisted. Burns could be deceptive and a lack of pain wasn't always a good sign. But as Grace dropped her soaking shirt into the sink and held out her arms, Natalya's frown deepened.

Grace's arms were pink. Pink like skin run under cold water.

"Uh..." Natalya started, holding the lavender oil up. "Where does it hurt?"

Grace shrugged. "I told you. It doesn't."

Natalya set the oil down on the counter and took Grace's left forearm into her hands. She turned it this way and that, holding it up to the light from the kitchen window. No red, no blisters, definitely no dead white skin. She dropped it and reached for Grace's other arm. Same thing. With no vestige of embarrassment, she scrutinized Grace's chest and stomach. Pink healthy skin, no evidence of a burn. Not even a mild first degree burn.

"Nice bra," she said absently, trying to visualize the accident in her head. She'd spilled the coffee on Grace. The shirt proved it. The pot was straight from the burner so as hot as coffee ever got, certainly hot enough to burn skin. And yet—Grace was fine.

"Freya Deco," responded Grace promptly. "Expensive, but worth every penny."

Natalya nodded. She'd have to give them a try. And then she waved a hand back toward her bedroom. "Go grab a clean shirt," she ordered. "You're not burned."

Grace reached for the dishtowel hanging off the oven and carefully patted her arms dry. "Isn't that..."

"Unexpected?" Natalya provided the word for her. "Yeah."

"Weird was what I was going for," Grace said. She held the dishtowel out to Natalya and then headed back to Natalya's bedroom to rummage through her sister's closet.

The kitchen smelled of burnt coffee from the drops splashing onto the warming plate and overflowing along the counter. The tiled floor was a mess of brown liquid and broken glass. The little girl had run off somewhere, hopefully not outside. And Natalya still didn't have any caffeine in her system.

With a sigh, she grabbed a mug and slid it under the dripping coffee, and then started to clean up. As she crouched, carefully picking up pieces of glass from the floor, she noticed a slight stinging on her bare leg, above her knee. She brushed at the red spot. It was a very minor, very small burn. First degree, no worse than a drop of sunburn. She must have been hit by a backsplash of coffee.

But if the heat was enough to burn her, then how had Grace escaped?

"All right, that was really weird." Grace came back into the kitchen, flipping her blonde hair out from under the collar of a turquoise shirt.

"I don't understand why you're not burned," Natalya admitted, rocking back on her heels.

"I don't understand why you spilled coffee on me," Grace said, accusation in her voice. "What's up with that?"

"That, too." Natalya let her hair fall across her face, ignoring the way the dark straight strands dropped into the coffee puddle on the floor.

"Nat?" Grace sounded worried. "Are you okay?"

"It's a long story." Natalya stood, pieces of glass cradled in her hand and then paused. She was standing barefoot among broken glass. And she didn't know whether she would cut herself. Damn it. She didn't like this. "I'll tell you the whole thing after I get some shoes on, finish cleaning up this mess, and, please God, have a cup of coffee."

Grace chuckled. "All right, I'll give you a hand."

Natalya dumped the glass into the trash can and navigated the floor, avoiding coffee and glass, as Grace grabbed a mass of paper towels. Heading for the front door, where she typically left her shoes, she added a task to her list: check on the little girl.

Her cottage wasn't very big. There weren't too many places a child could hide. But Natalya didn't see her in the living room as she crossed to the front door and grabbed her sandals. Slipping her feet into the flat-soled slides, she let her eyes skim over the comfortable, overstuffed furniture and under the tables, before stepping back to the door by the front bedroom where the child had slept.

Most of the room was her studio, a paint-splattered tarp spread across the floor, canvases piled against the walls. A seldom-used bed was shoved against one wall, sheets neatly pulled up, comforter folded at the foot of the bed. And there the girl was, crouched in the corner next to a wooden table holding paints and brushes, linseed oil and sketchbooks. Her eyes were closed, her thin arms wrapped around her knees, her head bent.

"It's okay." Natalya kept her voice gentle and didn't move from

45

her spot in the doorway. "Grace is fine and we're cleaning up the mess. You didn't step on any glass, did you?"

The girl lifted her head. On her pale face, the shadows under her blue eyes looked almost like bruises. Her fear was palpable.

There is more troubling this child than a day or two lost in the woods, Natalya realized with a jolt. "Can you tell me why you're afraid?" she asked.

The girl didn't answer. Her stare was so blank she might not even have understood the question.

Natalya sat down where she stood, crossing her legs and propping her elbow on her thigh, her face on her fist, as if she planned to stay there awhile.

She wasn't a trained therapist. The child needed to talk to a forensic psychologist, someone with experience in asking the right questions, providing the right reassurances. But Natalya couldn't leave her hiding in a corner.

She thought back to the foster parent training she'd taken, but she'd had no intention of becoming a foster parent and much of it had to do with the rules and regulations and procedures. Still, help the child feel safe—that was pretty basic.

"Grace was trying to guess your name, and you weren't answering," she said slowly. "But I need something to call you. Is it okay if I give you a name? Just for now?"

No response. Natalya hadn't really expected one.

"Kenzi," Natalya said. Now where the hell had that come from? Oh, right. Television. "Can I call you Kenzi?"

The girl's eyes opened wide and then she blinked twice in rapid succession.

Natalya decided to take that as a yes. Carefully, picking her words with caution, she continued, "Okay, Kenzi, here's the deal. I'm a doctor. That means sometimes I have to hurt people, like when I cleaned up your feet last night and it stung a little."

She waited but got no response, so she went on. "But doctors swear an oath." She paused, suddenly doubtful, as she asked, "Do you know what that is?"

Kenzi didn't move but something about her air of tension looked uncertain to Natalya, so she explained. "It's a promise. A really serious, really important promise. The most important promise a doctor makes is to do no harm. Do you understand what that means?"

Natalya hoped for a nod, at least one of the tiny inclinations the girl had managed the previous evening, but Kenzi just looked at her, unblinking.

Natalya sat up straighter, resting her hands on her knees, and wished she knew what she was doing. "It means I will do my best never to hurt you on purpose. If you do something wrong, I won't hurt you. If you do something bad, I won't hurt you. If you make me really, really mad—which is pretty hard to do, I don't get angry easily—but if you do, I might yell a little, but I won't hurt you. You're safe here. I don't know why you're scared or what you're scared of, but I promise, you you're safe with me and safe here in my house."

She waited. Two seconds, five seconds, ten seconds, and then Kenzi took a deep breath and let it out on a shaky exhale, the kind that said tears might be close to the surface.

Good enough. Natalya didn't know whether she should follow up and try to get the girl to talk or leave her in peace. Best bet, though, would be to leave the talking to the professionals.

Gently, Natalya said, "You can stay where you are if you want or you can come back and finish your granola." She pushed herself up, off the floor, tugging her robe back around her. "Or maybe have something else to eat, some fruit? Or eggs if you like eggs?"

Kenzi stayed motionless in the corner, so Natalya added, "All right, I'm going to get my breakfast. You come whenever you're ready."

As she headed back to the kitchen, she frowned with worry. She didn't feel qualified to analyze a troubled child. But why was Kenzi so frightened? Grace hadn't scared her. She'd been eating breakfast quite peacefully. Could it have been the crash of the glass? But why had she come back and then run away again?

Grace was almost finished cleaning the floor, wiping a damp paper towel across it in wide swathes. "Everything okay?"

Natalya grabbed her mug of coffee and took a cautious sip, then a larger swallow. "I wish I knew."

Grace tossed the towel into the trash and sat down at the table. "Talk," she ordered. "What's going on?"

Kenzi's bowl was in front of the chair Natalya usually sat in, so with a sigh, Natalya slipped into the corner seat, back to the window. "Last night was the night I found Colin."

Grace looked blank for a moment and then understanding and immediate sympathy darkened her eyes. She started to rise, reaching out to her sister, saying, "Oh, honey, I'm so sorry—"

Natalya waved her off before Grace could finish. "No, no, it didn't—he didn't—it went wrong. Or right. Or—I don't know. I'm so confused."

Grace sank back down in her seat. "You saved him?"

"No." Natalya shook her head. She stared down at the black surface of her coffee. "No," she repeated more quietly.

"Well, Nat, damn it, you should have called. You shouldn't have had to go through that alone." Grace was on her feet again. She reached across the table to put a hand on Natalya's shoulder. "We would all have come, you know that. Did you let Lucas know? He'll want to fly back from North Carolina today."

"No, no," Natalya protested again, putting her hand up and over her sister's. "I'm sorry. I'm not explaining this right. Colin's fine. He's alive and well and based on the scan I did, in perfect health. Likely to live for years."

Grace put her hands on her hips. "Okay, you're not making any sense at all," she said bluntly. "Was last night the night Colin died or wasn't it?"

"Sit." Natalya waved at Grace's chair. "Let me tell it my way."

Obediently, Grace took her seat as Natalya gathered her thoughts. Grace knew about her premonition, of course. The whole family did and probably half the town. Natalya and Colin's break-up had been the hot topic of gossip in Tassamara for a solid six months, only diminishing with Natalya's unexpected departure for medical school. So she started with the drive. "It was exactly like I'd seen it."

She told Grace almost the whole story, skipping only a few details. Like that heated kiss by the side of the road. The rush of desire that filled her in the exam room. The question he'd asked and her angry response. The unimportant stuff.

"Why do I have the feeling you're not telling me everything?" Grace mused when she'd almost finished.

Natalya could feel a prickle of heat along her cheekbones but she ignored the question. "And my vision is gone."

"The vision of Colin?" Grace asked, puzzled.

"No, I mean my foresight. It's gone."

"Gone, how? Gone like you can't see anything about Colin any more or gone like—"

"Like I'm blind," Natalya interrupted her.

"Future blind." Grace seemed to be turning the idea over in her head and not liking it.

"Actually, it feels more like I'd imagine amnesia feels. There are things I should know, things I used to know, that are just... gone. And I keep reaching for them. Trying to remember. But there's nothing there."

"That sounds unpleasant." Grace's eyes were worried, her brows drawn down.

"It's different, anyway." Natalya forced a chuckle. How many times in her life had she asked for just this? Knowing the future had never felt like a gift to her. She'd become practiced at not thinking about it, at living in the present moment and appreciating where she was while accepting that the future was not hers to control. She hadn't realized how much she took her foreknowledge for granted. Serenity, it turned out, came easier when you knew exactly how your day would flow.

"So you don't know anything about the little girl?"

Natalya glanced at the clock on her microwave. Almost ten. "Colin said they'd start a real search at daylight. They're trying to track her path back through the forest, and the rangers are driving all the back roads, looking for an accident."

"It's a big forest."

"Yeah, but she's a little girl. She couldn't have gone too far."

"And she won't talk." Grace's voice was thoughtful. "Did you see if she could write? What does she do with a pen and paper?"

Natalya felt stupid.

"It was late," she said. The excuse sounded weak. But the girl had been sleepy and hungry, had needed her scrapes bandaged, a hot shower, clean clothes—Natalya had been so focused on the priorities of the moment that she hadn't even thought about other methods of communication. Still, given that they knew the girl could talk and wouldn't, how likely was it she'd be willing to write?

She gulped down the rest of her coffee and stood. Grace had shoved another mug under the dripping filter. It was half-full, so she switched mugs, and took a sip from the fresh one. "Oh, sorry," she said, realizing she was being rude. "Do you want coffee?"

"Not the way you make it," Grace answered.

"Snob," Natalya retorted mildly. "Lighter roast has more caffeine."

"And less taste. Stop stalling. Do you want to try this or what?"

Natalya leaned against the sink. They should leave the questions to the psychologist Kenzi would surely see within a few hours. But asking if she'd write her name—how could that hurt?

"All right," she said. Automatically, without even thinking about it, she tried to look into the future, to see the outcome of this choice. Not knowing felt uncomfortable, like an itch she couldn't reach to scratch. "If she's willing."

Setting her coffee cup down on the counter, she crossed to the living room. "Kenzi? Will you come here, please?"

"Kenzi?" Grace asked from behind her.

Natalya shrugged, watching the door to her studio. "I needed something to call her."

"Isn't Bo the lost one?"

"Matter of opinion, I guess." Natalya looked over her shoulder at her sister with a smile until a shuffle of noise drew her attention back to the front rooms. Kenzi stood in the doorway of the studio, looking at her warily.

Natalya's smile didn't change. She tilted her head toward the kitchen to let Kenzi know she wanted her to join them, then turned and went back to the kitchen table. Kenzi would either come or not. The choice was up to her. But it was only a few seconds before the little girl appeared at the door.

"Cool," Grace said cheerfully. She hopped up and rummaged in the junk drawer by Natalya's phone, pulling out a pad of paper and a pen. Crossing to the little girl, she set the pad down on the countertop next to her. "Here," she said, handing her the pen. "Can you write your name for us?"

Kenzi didn't refuse to take the pen and she wasn't running, but she didn't look eager to cooperate, either. Her eyes flickered from one of them to the other as if she were trapped.

"Hmm." Grace crossed her arms, looking down on Kenzi speculatively.

"Gently, Grace," Natalya cautioned her sister softly. They had no idea what sort of trauma this child had experienced. She didn't want to push.

"How about we negotiate?" Grace said to Kenzi.

A flicker of doubt creased Kenzi's forehead.

"A deal," Grace said. "We'll make a deal."

Kenzi licked her lips. Natalya's curved up in reluctant appreciation. Grace was CEO of the family company. Trust her to think of problems in terms of business.

"Which do you like better, clothes or toys?" Grace asked.

Kenzi blinked at her, her uncertainty obvious.

"Hang on." Grace stepped past Kenzi and disappeared into the living room. Kenzi glanced at Natalya and Natalya shrugged as Grace returned, smart phone already in hand, head down. "No, not that one," Grace muttered. "No, no, ick, no. Ah… okay, that'll do." She turned the phone around and showed Kenzi the screen. "What do you think?"

Kenzi's eyes widened. She looked up at Grace.

"You write your name on this piece of paper," Grace said, pushing the pad closer to the edge of the counter. "And I'll buy you that doll. I'll even pay for overnight shipping so you get it tomorrow."

Kenzi looked torn. Her fingers tightened on the pen in her hand. But she didn't make any move to write.

"Tough bargainer, eh?" Grace said. "All right, I'll also buy you a new dress. Pink. With ruffles. And lace. And glitter." She left a pause between each new addition to the dress's description.

"What next, wings?" Natalya murmured.

Both Grace and Kenzi glanced toward her, Kenzi's eyes wide.

"And wings," Grace said promptly, before adding with what sounded like regret, "although not ones that would let you fly, that's a bit beyond me. But I'm sure I could find ones that sparkle."

Kenzi lifted the pen and set its tip on the paper, but she didn't write.

"Come on, sweetie." Grace's voice was gentle. "We need to know your name to help you get home."

The little girl's chin went up. Natalya's eyes narrowed. And then the girl pulled the pad closer to her and with short, sharp, strokes, wrote a few quick letters.

"Ha," said Grace, watching her write. "Very funny."

The little girl's mouth twitched as if she were trying not to smile. Or was it trying not to cry?

Grace's expression was unreadable, before she looked back at the girl. "That's what you want to say?"

The girl nodded.

"Nothing else?"

The girl shook her head.

"All right." Grace looked down at the paper and her shoulders lifted, part shrug, part chuckle. "I'll buy you the doll anyway."

"What did she write?" Natalya asked. She'd already guessed it wasn't a name, but was it something horrifying? Words an abusive parent might have called a stubborn child? Or something milder but resistant, like 'none of your business'? Only in fewer letters, because she couldn't have written a whole sentence.

Grace didn't answer for a moment as she tapped on her phone. Finished, she reached out and placed a gentle hand on the girl's blonde hair, before saying calmly, "Welcome to the family."

"Wait, what?" Natalya stood. "That's not—she's not—she's only here for the night, Grace. I have to bring her to the sheriff's office this morning."

Grace laughed. Picking up the pad, she turned and tossed it in Natalya's direction. As it fluttered down to the kitchen table, Grace said, "You obviously can't come shopping with me because of your little friend here, but I assume you'll be needing some girl's clothes? I'd guess a size six, maybe seven? I can take care of that for you."

"Hang on, what are you—" Natalya reached for the pad as she started to protest. What was Grace talking about? And then she saw what the girl had written on the pad.

KENZI.

❧ CHAPTER FIVE ❧

Colin dropped into his office chair, exhaling with relief. Ten minutes alone, that was all he needed. He pulled open his desk drawer and grabbed a candy bar. He should eat a real meal, not sugar, but he didn't have time. Nat and the girl would be arriving for a handover to the DCF caseworker any minute and he needed a chance to organize his thoughts.

He'd rousted two deputies and a bloodhound out of bed before dawn to trace the girl's path through the woods. The dog had quickly made it clear that Colin was an idiot. He knew exactly where the girl's trail ended: at the road where she'd been found. What Colin needed wasn't a search-and-rescue dog, but the kind of fabled Native American tracker who could follow a broken path through the woods, spotting every indentation or broken leaf. Unfortunately, he didn't have one.

He and the deputies tramped around for several hours, looking for any evidence of the girl's passage through the forest, following paths until they disappeared, and then circling around to try again. He'd thought at one point they'd managed to get lost in the pine scrub themselves and wouldn't that have been embarrassing? The thought of having to call a ranger for help made him cringe. Fortunately, they'd found their way out. But it had been a gigantic waste of time.

Or it would have been if not for the pure pleasure of being out in the forest. The air felt crisper today, colors brighter, smells more intense. Colin had thought it was a weather change, maybe a cold front moving in. But even here, sitting in his barren office, the sensation remained.

As he bit into the chocolate, he found himself admiring the green of the truly ugly office chair on the other side of his desk. How had he never noticed before how closely it matched the olive shades of swamp water? And the coffee that had been sitting on the burner since he'd gotten back here at 4AM smelled nutty and rich and deep, if a little burned.

Life was good. No, life was amazing.

53

Finishing his candy in two quick bites, he tossed the wrapper into the wastepaper basket and clicked open his pen to start making notes.

Missing person reports? Check. They'd looked at local records, the FBI's database, and the national NamUS Missing Persons system without finding any cases matching the child's description. Still, maybe he should have someone start checking neighboring states, just in case. A recent report might not have made it into the national systems yet.

Rangers? Check. He'd had an early morning phone call from Shelby, the deputy district ranger stationed at the nearby springs. She hadn't found any sign of an accident after a slow drive down the closest back roads, but she would be checking with the campgrounds to see if any campers hadn't returned to their sites. He hadn't heard back from her yet, but he was sure she'd call as soon as she knew anything.

Media? No check. But it was an obvious next step. Tassamara was much too small to have any local news outlets, but maybe they could get the word out in nearby towns. If one of the television stations in Orlando or Gainesville put her picture out, surely someone, somewhere, would recognize her. Maybe it would even get picked up nationally.

DNA? Maybe. Would there be any point in testing the girl's DNA? The lab they used for testing would be backed up over the holiday, because of vacations. If he wanted to get a sample in, he should do so as soon as possible. Did he need to, though?

State police? He hadn't contacted the highway patrol yet. Should he?

With a sigh, he set down his pen, carefully lining it up on top of his notepad. He was taking the wrong approach, he realized. He needed to look at the facts and see what they added up to, what the possibilities were, before he determined on his own course of action.

Fact number one: a seven-year-old child was found alone, at night, on a road near a national park. The obvious answer was that she'd wandered away from her parents and gotten lost. Simple enough.

But fact number two was that no one had reported her gone. That detail made the situation darker. He hadn't wanted to think about it last night. But as he watched her limping toward Nat's car and saw her clearly in the headlights—the tangled hair, the dirt, the bruises, the bloody feet, the disheveled clothes—he'd known she'd been in the forest for longer than an hour or two. She'd been lost for a while. And if anyone in the vicinity had reported a child missing, he would have heard about it. Hell, he would have been out searching.

Yes, her condition was fact number three. The surface damage was bad enough but not the whole of it. Maybe she was naturally thin, but maybe the pinched look around her face meant she'd gone hungry for more than a missed meal or two. Maybe her quiet was exhaustion and fear, but maybe it told a deeper story.

He sighed, rubbing a hand across his chin. So... a missing child not reported missing. What did that give him?

Picking up his pen, he wrote:

Parents failed to report

Parents unable to report

Parents don't know? (Not with her parents?)

As he stared at the paper, wondering what he wasn't seeing, the phone rang. Leaning forward, he picked it up. "Sheriff's office."

"We got nothing." The skipped greeting revealed Shelby's concern, though her tone was as laconic as always.

"Nothing?" He could hear his own dismay. He hadn't realized how much he'd been counting on the rangers to find the girl's family. His favorite scenario had been a dad on a trail with a sprained ankle, a frantic mom at a campsite with a dead cell phone.

"Nada. Zip. Zilch."

"How far have you looked?"

"As far as we could, but you know the problem. We've got over 200 miles of off-road trails, hundreds of lakes and ponds and springs, fourteen major campgrounds, numerous recreation sites. Even assuming the girl couldn't have walked any long distance from where you found her, it's a lot of ground to cover."

Colin snorted in agreement. He felt as if he'd covered quite a bit of it this morning, but they'd only explored a small area.

"But everyone's accounted for at the nearest campground," Shelby continued. "No missing kids have been reported. And no accidents have been found on the closest roads and trails."

Colin rubbed his chin again. He needed to shave. And he needed to sleep. But neither of those things would happen any time soon. "What about the water?" he asked. "Anyone rent a kayak and not return it?"

"I'll check," Shelby answered. "Good idea. Except, of course..."

She let the sentence trail off.

"Yeah." Colin didn't need her to explain. If the girl had somehow survived a boating accident, but the adult who'd been with her had disappeared, chances were they were looking for a drowning victim. "Her clothes were dry, though." He'd take another look at the dress she'd been wearing, see if he could detect any sign it had been in the water. He scribbled a quick note on his pad.

"It was a warm day yesterday." Shelby didn't sound optimistic. "Only takes an hour or two to dry off."

"Yeah, but let's not go there yet. Let's find a kayak first." Colin wasn't ready to give up on the picture of joyful reunions his imagination had painted.

"I'll start making calls right away," Shelby promised.

"Damn it," Colin muttered. He'd hoped this would be easy. He tilted back in his chair and stared up at the ceiling. "She didn't get dropped off by aliens."

"You thinking flying saucer aliens? ET and friends?" Shelby's tone held a smile.

"Not seriously, no."

"Hmm. It could be the other kind of aliens, you know," Shelby said, the humor gone.

"Illegals?" Colin tipped forward again. Parents afraid to report a missing child. Now that was a scenario he hadn't thought of.

"You know we get squatters out here. It's a big park. Policing almost four hundred thousand acres—well, there are corners we don't get to so often."

"I don't know," he said, doubt replacing his first enthusiasm. "She understood English. Recognized automatic door locks."

"Did she look Hispanic?" Shelby asked.

Colin picked up his pen and tapped it on the desk. "Not so much, no. Light brown hair, blue eyes."

"Central America's got plenty of blue-eyed blondes. Guatemala, Argentina. Even Mexico's got some."

His response was a noncommittal hmm. It didn't feel right to him, but he'd keep an open mind. "Will you keep looking?" he asked.

"Oh, yeah, of course," Shelby assured him. "And I'm spreading the word. It'll take hours, maybe more, to make sure every family is accounted for at the campgrounds. I'll check on the kayaks, and we'll be watching for abandoned cars, too. Maybe they were out for a day hike and something happened."

Colin grimaced. Ocala was a wilderness and people sometimes underestimated its risks. Snakes, bears, and of course, other human beings. He hoped to God the girl's family hadn't fallen prey to a human predator. A bear would be bad enough.

"We'll put the word out to the volunteers and guests, too," Shelby added.

"Great. The more eyes looking, the better." Colin thanked her and said good-bye before disconnecting.

He pulled the pad closer to him, looking down at his notes. Where to start? A soft knock on the door interrupted. He looked up absently, still focused on his list, before starting to his feet, almost knocking his chair over.

He'd been expecting them and yet somehow seeing Nat, here, in his office, was still a shock. If the sky looked bluer today and the trees greener, Nat looked more beautiful. The lightweight red sweater she wore over blue jeans wasn't tight, but caressed her curves just enough to make him want to touch, while her dark hair was twisted down her back in one of those complicated braids she liked. For a fleeting second, he entertained a fantasy of pulling off the hair tie and running his hands through the silken strands as he spread them over her shoulders—and then he swiftly brought his recalcitrant brain back under his control and said hello.

Nat returned the greeting, but the girl by her side just stared at him, her expressive face solemn. Clean, her hair brushed, dressed in pink leggings and a faded t-shirt, she should have looked less lost, more relaxed, but she held herself in a way that looked poised to run, as if wiry energy coiled its way down her legs.

"This looks like you," Nat said, glancing around his office.

Colin raised an eyebrow. "Sterile and industrial? Sorta rundown?"

His office was scrupulously neat, with all files tucked away into the racks of steel-grey cabinets lining one wall, but the building had been built in the 1970s and both the room and the furniture looked their age. Okay, so maybe the swamp green of the chairs wasn't as ugly as he'd always thought, but that was about all he could say for it.

"I think I've been insulted," he added in a stage whisper to the child. She didn't smile, so he winked at her to let her know he was kidding.

"I was thinking orderly and practical," said Nat. "No personal touches? No family pictures?"

Colin rolled his eyes. "You know how my family is. The walls would be covered if I let them get started."

Nat's lips quirked up. "How many nieces and nephews do you have now?"

"Uh…" Colin squinted and started counting. His six siblings were all married, all with kids. He could probably add them up, except that because his sisters had started having babies when he was a kid himself, some of them felt more like cousins. And some of those cousin-types were now grown, having babies of their own who called him "Uncle Colin." Did they count? He supposed technically they did. Wouldn't he be like a great-uncle or something to them? And his sister Jenna was on her second marriage, this one to a man with three kids of his own. Should he include his step-nieces and nephew? They felt more like relatives than his brother Brian's kids did, because Brian lived in California and Colin hadn't even met his youngest yet, so yeah, he should probably include Jenna's step-kids.

"You don't know the answer?" Nat interrupted his thoughts.

"I'm a great-uncle," he protested.

"I wouldn't doubt it," Nat said stiffly. "You always liked kids."

"No, no, I mean, I'm a great-uncle and a step-uncle and a regular old uncle. Cecily's got two and Minerva's pregnant and Mitch—" He waved a hand in the air. "You get the idea. There's a lot of 'em and they keep making more." He pointed at the bottom drawer of the file cabinet closest to the front wall. "Filled with drawings made by visiting munchkins. If I let them put them on the walls, they'd go floor to ceiling. Kinda tough to take your local law enforcement seriously when the office looks like a kindergarten classroom."

A real smile crossed Nat's face, humor lightening her eyes. "Well," she said, her hand gently brushing the top of the head of the girl next to her, not a stroke but a butterfly caress, "maybe Kenzi can make you one more."

"Kenzi?" Relief leaped in Colin's chest. They had a name. If it was her first name only, it wasn't much, but it was a starting place. He could work with that.

But Nat must have heard the excitement, because she was shaking her head. "No, sorry. I just needed something to call her."

"And you picked Kenzi?"

Maybe his surprise sounded critical because Nat arched her

eyebrows at him and said, frost tingeing her tone, "We like it." The little girl looked up at her and gave a smile, her first sign of emotion.

Colin spread a hand in defense. "Hey, works for me." Changing the subject, he added, "The caseworker's down the hall. If you want to go fill her in, Nat, I can set Kenzi up with some crayons and paper here while we wait for the psychologist."

Nat paused, before offering a reluctant nod. Her hand opened toward the little girl as if she wanted to touch her, but she pulled it back, turning the gesture into an encouraging wave into the room. Kenzi's smile vanished, but obediently she took two steps forward, as Nat said, "All right. I'll be back in a few minutes."

As Nat disappeared down the hallway, Colin opened his top desk drawer. He kept a box of crayons in it. But they weren't the only personal item. His fingers brushed against a leather folder. He did have family photographs, but he kept them tucked away. A half dozen or more hid behind the closed cover: his parents, his grandmother, a family photo taken in his childhood with all of his siblings, and then, of course, Nat. Their prom picture, a snapshot from their college graduation, a photo of her laughing from a summer day spent at the beach.

For so long, he'd known death waited for him. And he'd been waiting for it. Sure, he'd kept his office professionally neat, but he also kept it easy to clean out. When it happened—when the day came that he would never show up to work again—it would have taken his deputy five minutes to drop everything that mattered to him in a cardboard box to deliver to his grandmother.

His home was as clean as his office. When his parents died, it had taken weeks to empty their house. Hours of sorting, gallons of tears. Not so much his—he'd been a stoic fifteen-year-old—but his sisters, his aunts, his grandmother. So much stuff—what to do with the dishes, the clothes, the furniture, the knickknacks, the paintings hanging on the walls? The souvenirs from his parents' twentieth anniversary trip to Paris, the letters home from summer camps, the carefully saved kindergarten artwork of seven children, the sports trophies and certificates of achievement and prizes earned in busy lifetimes cut much too short?

He hadn't wanted anyone to have to do that for him, and so he'd made it easy. Some clothes, a few books, electronics… and one potted plant. He hadn't even been willing to have a pet. It wouldn't have been fair.

But he hadn't died.

He shook his head, trying to shake the thoughts away, and picked up the box of crayons. Kenzi hadn't moved. She was still standing, stiff and silent, in the center of his office.

"Ya want to sit at my desk?" he asked her, keeping his tone light. "Pretend you're the sheriff?"

He set the box of crayons down and picked up his notepad, closing it and tucking it into his pocket, before crossing to the filing cabinet he'd pointed out before. He had some recycled paper there, saved for just this purpose.

As he turned back around, paper in hand, a sudden flash of memory stilled him. Kenzi, crouched above him in the whirling light from his car. She'd been scared, but she hadn't run. She was a child, but she'd tried to help him. And she had, hadn't she? Her hands on his chest, a golden light, an all-encompassing pain.

"What happened?" His words were too abrupt. She stepped backward, moving away from him, body telegraphing wariness. "Last night, I mean." He gentled his voice, but he could see it was not enough. "When you found me."

Her eyes flickered sideways, glancing at the door as if measuring the distance to run.

Colin crouched, putting himself at her height. "I don't remember what happened on the road very well. I remember my chest hurt. And I remember waking up." He glanced at the doorway where Nat had disappeared. He remembered kissing Nat, the taste of her, the smell of her, the feeling of being absolutely present in his body, his heart pounding, his nerve endings sizzling. But between the pain and the joy, what had happened? "Between that, though, it feels like a dream. But you were there. In my dream, you were there. You did something, didn't you?"

Her lower lip trembled before she pressed it tight against the upper. For all that she was speechless, her face communicated worlds. Fear, defiance, a stubborn pride in the face of perceived danger.

"I think you brought me back to life," he said. "I think you healed me."

Her gaze didn't flinch. She stared at him steadily. But it was the look of a prey animal trapped by a predator, afraid to even quiver.

"I'm not complaining."

Her eyes looked as if they were filling with tears. Was it emotion or a physiological reaction to her fixed stare?

Colin's mouth twisted, a corner lifting in a wry smile. "If we were Wookies, I'd owe you a life debt," he told her. "Do you know what that is?"

He waited. She blinked, and then blinked several more times, incipient tears disappearing. And then, with the tiniest possible movement, she shook her head, barely an inch in either direction.

Solemnly, Colin said to her, "A life debt means that because you saved my life, I have a sacred obligation to you. If we were Wookies, for the rest of my life, I would have to protect and serve you."

Her nose twitched. She couldn't have expressed her skepticism better if she'd scowled.

Colin couldn't help chuckling. "All right, sweetheart. Paper, crayons, go wild." He held the paper out to her. Still eying him with suspicion, she accepted it gingerly.

Before she could take a seat, Joyce, the office manager, knocked on his doorjamb. Thrusting two slips of paper at him, she said briskly. "The hospital called. They want to know if you've made any progress finding next of kin for that drug dealer. They're talking about removing life support. I told them to call the FBI, but if you know anything you haven't told me, you should call them back."

Colin grimaced. That would make four dead from that fuck-up of a drug raid. The next time the Feds showed up in his town, he was confiscating all their weapons.

"I also rescheduled your budget meeting with the accountant about the fiscal year close, but he wants you to call him about the overtime numbers," Joyce continued. "And the psychologist has arrived. She's setting up in the interview room."

Behind her, Nat and Carla, the caseworker from DCF, appeared. Nat looked troubled, her lips pursed, fine lines appearing between her brows. He shot her a questioning look, but she didn't acknowledge it. Taking the phone messages from Joyce, he stuffed them into his pocket absently, trying to read Nat's face.

For a moment, he was tempted to ask Joyce to take Carla and the girl to the interview room so he could talk to Nat in private, but one glance at Kenzi and he let that idea slide away. If she'd looked poised to run before, now she looked ready to fly away, her eyes flitting rapidly from one face to the next. As the four of them walked down the hall, Nat talked to her in a low voice but Kenzi still hadn't relaxed as they entered the interview room.

Colin extended a hand to the psychologist, assessing her automatically as they exchanged greetings. Probably in her mid-forties, she had the type of trim figure that suggested a diet of yogurt and lettuce and a daily hour on the treadmill. She wore a plain, off-white button-down shirt paired with a straight brown skirt that extended beyond her knees. Tiny gold dots at her ears, a discreet cross dangling from a gold chain around her neck, and a gold wedding ring completed her professional look. Still, she had a faintly frazzled air about her, as if her day had started too early.

She obviously had experience with children, though. She'd pushed the table and chairs to the walls of the room and spread out a colorful cloth on the floor. A selection of toys—stuffed animals, dolls, even a few toy cars—were arranged on the cloth.

After introductions all around and a few moments of conversation, Colin, Nat, and the caseworker left Kenzi with the psychologist, retreating to watch the interview from the adjacent room.

"She looks familiar," Carla said, as the psychologist knelt on the floor across from Kenzi. The young caseworker was frowning, her brown eyes intent on the little girl.

"You think you've seen her before?" Colin felt a surge of optimism. "Any idea where?"

Carla shook her head. "I'm not sure. And I could be wrong. She's definitely not one of ours, I'm positive about that." She smiled at the sheriff apologetically.

Colin's optimism deflated like a flat tire.

Carla excused herself to make some phone calls, so Nat and Colin were left to watch the interview alone.

"You look worried," Colin said immediately. "What's wrong?"

"It's nothing," Nat answered, but the fine lines between her brows deepened.

"Tell me."

"Really. It's not important." Nat stared straight ahead into the room where the psychologist was trying to interest Kenzi in a stuffed bear.

That might be true, but Colin still wanted to know what had put that look into her eyes. "Nat. Let me help."

She gave an exasperated sigh. "You haven't changed a bit, have you?" But her tone held no anger, only resignation.

He touched her upper arm, feeling the softness of her cotton sweater under his fingers. "Tell me."

She didn't move away, but she shrugged off his hand as she spoke. "The psychologist. I'm not sure she's the best person to work with Kenzi."

"How so?"

Nat stepped closer to the glass that separated the observation room from the interview room. Putting a hand on the glass, she said, "She seemed... well, apparently she usually interviews clients in her office." She shot him a quick glance and a twist of a grin. "And she made it very clear she prefers it that way."

Colin shrugged. "Yeah, I heard about that, too. But taking the kid into Gainesville when we might find her parents any minute didn't make sense to me."

"No," Nat agreed. "But she felt... I think... She might not be..." She looked away from him, back into the interview room.

"Did you see something? A premonition?" he prompted after a moment of silence.

"No." Her voice was firm.

He paused, but when she said nothing further, he made the suggestion. "Why don't you try?" Nat's views of the future were reliable. He would trust any information she was willing to give him. If, that is, she was willing to share it. She'd always been reluctant to use her gift, but last night she'd been adamant.

She didn't look at him but she pressed her lips together, before saying, "I don't seem to be able to today."

"Able to?" He blinked, startled.

"My foresight appears to be broken."

"Broken?" His eyebrows shot up. Her foresight was part of her, as much her as her eyesight or sense of smell. How could it break?

She shook her head, dismissing the question. Turning away from the glass, she said, "It's not important. I'm being silly. The psychologist's a professional and I'm sure she'll do her job well."

Colin shoved his hands in his pockets and rocked back on his heels. Message received. She didn't want to talk about her foresight or her worries. Still, he'd take her concern to heart.

"I should go," Nat continued.

"Don't you want to watch? Or at least say good-bye?"

"Grace bought her a doll online so I told her I'd see her again and bring her the doll. But this is a job for professionals now. I'm glad I could help. And that I was there last night." The words were a dismissal, but Colin wasn't ready to be dismissed.

"Speaking of last night…" Quickly, Colin stepped in front of the door. "We need to talk about it."

"There's nothing to talk about." Nat lifted her chin into the air, her eyes meeting his squarely.

"Sure there is. I was supposed to die. And I didn't. Aren't you the least bit curious?"

Nat spread her hands. "Congratulations. I'm glad you survived. Now…" She shrugged. "Now I don't ever want to speak to you again."

"Nat," Colin protested. Surely she could see she was being unreasonable.

"You made your choice a long time ago. Freedom, remember? Space?"

Colin opened his mouth to argue. He'd said that, sure, but it had always been bullshit. She had to know that. Yes, he'd broken up with her—dumped her, as she'd so bitterly said at the time—but it was for her own good.

Before he could speak, though, Nat continued, "I don't know why you're alive but I know it doesn't matter to me that you are. I don't care about you anymore, Colin." Her voice was edged with the same bitter fury of a decade ago.

Colin took a deep breath, paused and let it out on a low, slow exhale. Nat had always been a lousy poker player. He knew she was lying. If nothing else, the fact that she was still so angry meant her feelings weren't dead and gone. But debating with her would do nothing but strengthen her resolve. He needed a better approach. A plan. Maybe even a way to earn her forgiveness.

Stepping aside, he wordlessly gestured to the doorway, before taking the three steps forward that brought him next to the glass. He might have no choice but to let her go, but he wasn't going to watch.

Staring ahead blindly, he tried to focus on the scene in the interview room, but until he heard the soft snick of the door shutting behind Nat, he couldn't make his eyes see what was happening.

When he finally did, he saw that Kenzi had backed herself against a wall and was looking as frozen as he felt.

Damn.

Looked like nobody was going to be doing much talking today.

✑ CHAPTER SIX ✑

Natalya slid into her father's favorite booth at Maggie's bistro, her back to the door. She'd spent the short walk from the sheriff's office talking herself down from her own irrational anger, but she could still feel the edges of it against her skin, a low-grade irritant like a mosquito bite on a humid day.

It made no sense to be angry, she told herself. Not at Colin, not at the world. Despite her words to him, she was glad the moment she'd dreaded for so long had finally come to pass and he'd emerged unscathed.

But Colin had had too much of her for too long—too much attention, too much love, too much anger. He wasn't getting it back, no matter what he wanted. He'd broken her heart. Trampled her feelings into the dust. Been a callous, heartless, selfish bastard.

Still, it was a long time ago. She was over it, she reminded herself, trying to let go of the memories and the feelings they stirred. She took a breath, forcing her mind to one of the calming exercises she liked.

Let the thoughts drift away, like clouds in the sky, she told herself. Just clouds, just drifting.

Over the years, she'd grown adept at shoving him out of her mind and she intended to keep doing so. The status quo worked: she'd spent two years in Tassamara barely acknowledging his existence. She wanted to go back to that polite coolness. If only she could stop scratching at the thoughts. Why the hell was he alive?

And who was the girl? Leaving Kenzi behind at the sheriff's office felt wrong. What choice did she have, though? The psychologist would interview her. DCF would take responsibility for her. With any luck, she'd be home by nightfall. The only task left for Natalya was to deliver the doll Grace had promised.

It still felt wrong. The psychologist had been abrupt, harried. She'd made it clear driving to Tassamara was an inconvenience. She'd probably planned to spend the day at home with her own family. Natalya hoped she wouldn't rush the interview or jump to easy conclusions. Kenzi needed patience, kindness, a gentle touch. Natalya knew and liked the counselor who worked with the local agency. It was a pity she was out of state for the holiday.

"What's wrong? You look upset." At the sound of her father's voice, Natalya twitched, startled. She'd been scowling down at the table surface, so lost in thought she hadn't seen him arrive. He seated himself across from her, frowning, his brows drawn down over his bright blue eyes. "Are you all right? What can I do?"

She forced a smile then felt it soften into a real smile at the sight of the worry in his expression. Maybe it was her own anxiety about Kenzi driving the thought but she couldn't help realizing how lucky she was. No parent was perfect. Max could be overprotective and managing, sure he knew best and wrong about that. But he loved her unconditionally. He'd do anything to keep his children safe and happy.

"I'm fine. You just startled me."

Max's frown grew deeper. "I did what? You don't startle easily."

Natalya's smile grew wider. "Interesting, isn't it?"

And then there was her foresight to consider. Where had it gone? All morning long, she'd been reaching for knowledge and finding it absent. It was like having a missing tooth. She couldn't resist poking at the spot where she ought to find solid matter and instead finding only empty space. "My foresight is gone."

"Gone?" Max's brows shot up in alarm. "Gone how? Is that even possible?"

"Apparently it is."

"Were you hurt? Did you hit your head?"

"No, no." Natalya waved her hand, dismissing that idea.

"What happened?" Max asked.

Natalya paused. Colin was a sensitive subject between them. But she knew her father would learn the whole story eventually. Grace knew, Colin knew, she knew, and in Tassamara, what three people knew had a way of spreading through the entire town like a virus.

"Hey, Max, Natalya." Akira joined them, dropping herself onto the seat next to Natalya without waiting for a response.

Her future sister-in-law would have to switch to maternity clothes soon, Natalya noticed. Her casual black t-shirt stretched tight across her rounded stomach and she was wearing a skirt instead of her more typical blue jeans.

"I hear you had an adventure last night, Nat. How's the little girl?"

Akira continued.

Okay, like a highly contagious virus. How had Akira heard? "Grace called you?"

"No, Rose told me."

"Rose?" Natalya repeated, trying to place the name.

"You know," Akira reminded her, voice patient. "The ghost that lives in my house. She was babbling about it this morning. Not making a lot of sense, actually, but I think I got the gist."

"Oh, of course." Natalya thumped the table with a closed fist. "The girl in costume Colin mentioned. I should have guessed." She'd suspected last night that Colin's story wasn't a dream. "Colin thought she was a shina... something or other. Some kind of spirit guide."

"Spirit guide?" Max leaned forward, laying his hands flat on the table.

"Hmm, I wouldn't call her that. Not exactly." Akira's mouth tilted up at the corners in a mysterious smile.

"What happened to Colin? Why did he think he needed a spirit guide?" The lines of worry in Max's forehead deepened.

"So did you find out who the little girl is and how she got lost?" Akira asked at the same time.

"But what was Rose doing?" Natalya asked Akira. The road leading to her house was miles from town. Why had Rose been wandering so far from home? Did she have some sort of connection to Kenzi? But if she did, wouldn't she know who Kenzi really was? "How did she even get there? Do ghosts go for hikes?"

"Natalya." Max interrupted, speaking in the firm, fatherly tone he used to use to send her to bed or tell her to stop fighting with her sister. "I'm worried about you, not ghosts. Please tell me what happened."

Natalya smiled an apology. "Sorry, Dad. It was..."

She paused. What were the right words? The moment she'd dreaded for years? The night that changed her life long before it happened? Her nightmares finally come true? "It was my vision," she continued at last. "You know the one. The dark night, Colin, the side of the road. The whole thing. Except it didn't come true. Colin wasn't dead, just unconscious."

She glanced at Akira. Akira hadn't lived in Tassamara a decade earlier. She wouldn't know what Natalya meant. But Natalya found herself reluctant to explain. It was old news. To tell the story—the whole story—would mean reliving the pain.

"Is Colin all right?" Max put his hand over Natalya's, squeezing it gently. "Are you all right?"

"He's fine." Natalya pressed her lips together. The sympathy she heard in her father's voice brought unexpected tears simmering up in the back of her eyes. She had nothing to cry about, though. Nothing at all.

"And are you all right?" Max's voice was gentle as he repeated the question, his hand tight and warm on hers where it lay on the table.

She turned her hand up and squeezed his, holding on to him, and nodded before letting go, blinking back the prickling in her eyes. "I'm fine, too," she said, keeping her voice even. "He wasn't dead. I took him to GD and ran a scan on him and saw nothing to indicate ongoing health problems. I don't know what happened, or how it happened, but he's healthy. He's not going to die. Or at least not the way I saw him dying."

"Are you sure?" Max asked. "Could it have been the wrong night?"

The corner of her mouth lifted up. "Me stumbling over his body by the side of the road in the middle of the night always seemed like a one-in-a-million chance. To have it happen twice would have to be more like one-in-a-billion. No, I think... I think my foresight was wrong."

"Oh, I have to talk to Rose again." Akira almost bounced in the seat, as if resisting the impulse to get up and leave immediately. "She didn't tell me anything about the sheriff. Well, ah, that is, not anything much about the sheriff. Nothing about him dying, anyway."

Her eyes met Natalya's and Natalya knew immediately what Rose had told Akira. The tingle of tears was entirely gone as a flush of embarrassment surged into her cheeks, only to be replaced by resigned amusement. If ghosts carried the news, no wonder gossip spread so quickly in Tassamara.

"Your foresight was wrong," Max mused, as the teenaged waitress approached their table. "That doesn't happen much."

Emma's blonde hair was tipped with purple and she wore matching purple eyeliner in heavy streaks around her eyes. She carried a tall glass of icy sweet tea and a spinach salad. Without bothering to greet them, she asked, "You on breakfast or lunch?" as she placed the food in front of Natalya.

"Breakfast," Max said quickly before Akira had a chance to respond.

"Not you." Emma dismissed him. She lifted her chin in Akira's direction. "Maggie told me to ask you." She glanced over her shoulder in the direction of the kitchen, before adding in a hushed whisper, "She didn't seem real happy about it."

Max sighed. "Do you know what she's making for me?"

Emma patted his shoulder sympathetically. "Grilled chicken and roast vegetables. The veggies are a winter squash mix, with fresh rosemary and sage. You'll like it, I swear."

He looked resigned, although he muttered a complaint under his breath, something about women holding grudges. Maggie, the owner and cook at the town's only real restaurant, maintained a menu of casual favorites. It was diner food with a flair—pancakes stuffed with wild Maine blueberries, burgers with sweet potato fries, meatloaf topped with a barbecue sauce glaze that gave it a spicy kick. But the menus were only for the tourists. For the locals, Maggie cooked what she pleased. Most often, it was exactly what they wanted.

A few weeks ago, though, the bistro temporarily shut down because of electrical problems. Maggie blamed Max for the trouble. Ever since, she'd been taking revenge via food, cooking him meals that were not his favorites, although they were still better than anything he could make for himself or get elsewhere.

"Got it." With a cheerful finger wave, Emma headed toward a neighboring table.

Akira leaned against the cushioned back of the bench, one hand resting on the curve of her belly. "Henry and I don't seem to share taste in food," she said with a worried frown. "We're confusing Maggie. I hope this doesn't mean he's going to be a picky eater."

"How many times am I going to have to apologize?" Max grumbled. "It's not as if it was even my fault. I didn't ask that ghost to show up. And I got the building inspector out here the very next day." He stared at the kitchen for a moment, before standing in resolve.

"I'm just going to go talk to Maggie," he said. Absently, he patted the back of Akira's hand. "Don't worry, dear. Zane didn't eat anything but hamburgers, french fries, and white rice until he was ten or so. It didn't hurt him."

"Oh, why does that not surprise me?" Akira's frown turned into a reluctant chuckle as Max moved away from the table.

Maggie hated people coming into her kitchen while she was working. If Max wanted forgiveness, interrupting her wasn't the way to get it, Natalya thought. But she didn't stop him. She wanted to talk to Akira alone.

"Speaking of Zane," she said, reaching up with a nervous hand to squeeze the pressure points at the base of her skull, "did you happen to mention…"

Akira bit her lip. "Sorry. It was a surprise. I didn't know…"

Natalya sighed.

"You and the sheriff?" Akira asked, her tone a little plaintive, a lot amused.

"It's a long story," Natalya muttered, pressing harder. Her impending tension headache was going to be a doozy. She needed to get to Zane. Order him to talk to no one. She'd need to bribe him somehow. Or maybe blackmail?

"Zane was rushing out the door, though. He was late to a lesson with Dave. He didn't say much, just blinked a lot. Maybe he didn't hear me?"

Natalya let her hand slide from the back of her neck to cover her eyes. Great. If Zane was spending two hours in a plane with Dave, she'd already lost her chance to shut him up. And Dave talked to everyone. By tomorrow morning, she'd be fielding questions from half the town and all of Colin's sisters. She dropped her hand and picked up her fork.

"I think I'd better savor this salad," she said. "I may be hiding out in my house for the next few months."

"Seriously?" Akira looked dismayed. "The sheriff's not married. He's cute. Why can't you fool around with him if you want to?"

Natalya's smile was rueful.

"You shouldn't let other people dictate your sex life," Akira said earnestly. "Your body belongs to you. It's nobody's business what you choose to do with it."

"We have history." Natalya took a bite of salad.

"Oh." Akira fell silent, but Natalya could see the question in her eyes.

Reluctantly, she finished chewing and told the story. "Growing up, he was Lucas's best friend. I was the little sister. You'd think, boys being boys, they'd have treated me like the pest I probably was. But it was never like that. Colin treated me—well, not like a little sister. Like a pet, maybe. A much loved pet."

The memories were flooding back. Colin helping her climb into their treehouse, dragging her along when the ice cream truck drove by, pausing to wait for her when the boys' longer legs let them go faster on their bikes. Swimming in the springs, cheering at one another's Little League games, helping her with her math homework—he was there in so much of her past, a second big brother. The time she broke her collarbone, he was the one who walked her home and held her hand when she cried.

"When he was fifteen, his parents died. Drunk driver. He was so sad. So quiet. He's got lots of family, so he wasn't alone, but I was the one he talked to. He was still Lucas's best friend, but he was my best friend, too. I went with him to his senior prom. Just friends. By my senior prom, everything changed. He was my world."

She stabbed her fork into a piece of spinach. The salad dressing was unexpectedly warm, rich with flavors of bacon and caramelized onion. It was delicious, but she'd lost her appetite. She let the fork drop.

"We were engaged. I'd graduated from college and he'd finally gotten the job he wanted as a deputy sheriff in Tassamara. And I had a premonition. Of his death. Or rather, of finding his dead body by the side of the road."

"Oh, Natalya," Akira murmured. "I'm so sorry."

Natalya forced her lips into an expression resembling a smile. "It was a long time ago." She went on, keeping her voice steady. "I recognized the uniform, so I wanted him to quit his job. I knew it would be near a forest. We could have moved away, lived by the ocean, maybe the desert. We argued. And argued, and argued. And then we broke up."

Positioned side-by-side as they were, it took only a slight motion of her head to turn her face away from the sympathy in Akira's eyes. But she could feel her presence, warm and comforting, and it compelled her to add the truth. "Not really. He dumped me. Told me we were through and I should move on with my life. He didn't want to see me any more."

She took a sip of tea. Her head was throbbing now, a pained tempo beating in time with her pulse.

"He wasn't willing to try to stop himself from dying?" Akira sounded incredulous.

"I like to say the future I see is a possibility. That our choices are our own. That we make our destiny. But when I see the future, it comes true." Natalya could hear the bitter undercurrent in her own voice. "I try to make changes sometimes. It doesn't usually work. One way or another—sometimes because of what I do—the future always happens as I see it." She looked back at her future sister-in-law and added, "At least until last night. Funny timing, isn't it?" Her chuckle held no amusement.

"That sucks," Akira said, as Max returned to the table. He set a plate containing grilled chicken and roasted vegetables down as he slid into his seat.

"I didn't hear yelling," Natalya said, keeping her voice light.

Max snorted, but his expression was glum. "She says she's cooking what her inspiration tells her to cook and if I don't like it, I can order off the menu like anyone else."

"At least she didn't tell you to get out of her kitchen."

"Oh, she did that, too."

"But what good is it to see the future if you can't do anything about it?" Akira ignored the interruption, sounding irate on Natalya's behalf.

"Ha," Max responded.

"Excellent question." Natalya pushed her salad bowl away.

"Nat and I have differing opinions on this," Max said, poking at the chunks of roasted squash on his plate. "I see it as an early warning system, a chance to prepare."

"I see it as the ruin of every birthday surprise and twist ending." Natalya tried to infuse her tone with humor. She didn't want to stir up old arguments with her father about the usefulness of their foresight. He was comfortable using his ability, while she thought she'd done her best to ignore hers. It was disconcerting to discover how much she relied on it.

Max snorted. "The strength of your ability does come with disadvantages, my dear."

"Every twist ending?" Akira asked. "You mean you always know how movies will end?"

"I've got a brain filled with spoilers," Natalya said dryly.

"How do you know them, though?" Akira asked. "I assumed you had visions. Or maybe precognitive dreams."

"I use the word vision sometimes, but for me, it's closer to memory," Natalya answered.

"What I have is more like extremely good intuition. I've learned to trust it," Max responded. "Generally, I see possibilities. Likely futures, potential outcomes. Usually they're related to hard facts. Semantic memory, conceptual in nature. Natalya sees what will be. Her signal comes in much clearer than mine, if you will."

"How does that work?" Akira's eyes narrowed, her intellectual curiosity clear.

"Ask me again in a few more years." Natalya shrugged. "I spend a lot of time looking at brain scans, but I haven't solved the puzzle of how our minds work. Yet."

"But your foresight is like memory?" Akira prompted.

"I remember the future the way most people remember the past," Natalya explained.

"Does that mean you know the next thing I'm going to say, the next person that's going to walk in the door?"

Before Akira even finished her question, Natalya was shaking her head. "I'm not experiencing the future. I just remember it."

"I don't get it."

Natalya gestured at the door behind them. "Do you remember the last person to walk in?"

Akira turned and let her gaze skim over the patrons at the restaurant. The booths that lined the walls were three-quarters full, mostly with families or teenagers, while the smaller tables held couples. A few middle-aged men sat together at the long counter, while a younger man sat alone at the other end.

"No idea," she admitted as she turned back. She tilted her head in the direction of the counter. "I said hi to the guys from the quantum teleportation project when I came in so I know they were here, but otherwise I didn't notice."

"Right. It's called selective attention. Memory requires three steps—we experience, we record, we retrieve. What you don't notice, you can't remember."

"Most of us can't remember much of anything," Max pointed out. "We forget what we had for breakfast, much less every conversation we have."

"I remember experiences that haven't happened yet as if they were memories," Natalya continued. "Sometimes vague or fuzzy, sometimes without the context that would help me understand what I'm seeing, but only ever when it's something I would have remembered anyway."

"But can you see anything you want to? If I asked you a question, something like—"

"Don't!" Natalya interrupted Akira sharply. As Akira drew back, looking startled, Natalya repeated herself in a gentler voice. "Please don't. I try not to see more than I have to." She forced a smile, rubbing her temple. The tension was turning the pounding in her head into shooting pains running up her jawline. "It causes a lot more trouble than it's worth."

"But you know everything about your future?" Akira still sounded doubtful. One hand curled around her abdomen protectively, as if she were considering the advantages and disadvantages.

Natalya shook her head. "No. My foresight gets triggered. Something—a smell, a feeling, a thought, a question—brings the memory to my conscious mind. But it's not all encompassing. Or constant, thank God. My worst nightmare is to develop hyperthymestic syndrome."

"Hyper-thy-mes-tic?" Akira sounded the word out. "From the Greek? Speed memory?"

"Vast memory, I think. It's a neurological condition, possibly caused by a defective frontostriatal circuit. It's characterized by an enlarged temporal lobe and caudate nucleus, which affect—" Natalya paused at the blank look on Akira's face. Right. Akira had a PhD and a fondness for science, but she wasn't a medical doctor. "People with it remember every detail of their lives. Random actions can trigger a flood of memories. One patient described it as living life with a split-screen, always half her attention caught by her memories of the past."

Akira wrinkled her nose. "That doesn't sound fun."

"Not so much, no." Natalya tipped her head from side to side, trying to ease the tension in her neck.

With a loaded plate in one hand, a coffee pot in the other, Emma swung by their table. As she slipped the plate in front of Akira, she glanced at Max. "I don't mean to be rude, Mr. Latimer, but Maggie's not mean. Well, maybe a little mean. But not, like, mean-mean."

"She's torturing me," Max complained. "I wanted bacon and eggs."

"Yeah, but it's not like she plans what to make for people, you

76

know?" Emma said. Max frowned but Akira gave Emma a nod, and, encouraged, Emma continued. "When she doesn't know what to make she gets cranky, but with you, she does know. It's good stuff, too, not like that time with the turkey sandwich. That time, she was mad. It was, like, symbolic, that turkey."

Natalya looked at her father's plate and her eyes narrowed. Emma had a point. Max's food looked and smelled as delicious as everything else Maggie cooked, despite its simplicity. Okay, maybe not quite as delicious as Akira's blueberry waffles, but still quite tasty.

"But that's not turkey," Emma finished. With a satisfied nod, as if she'd said what she wanted to say, she headed off to refill the next table's coffee cups.

"When did you last have a checkup, Dad?" Natalya asked. Maybe there was a subliminal meaning to the heart-healthy, low-sugar food Maggie was feeding Max.

"A checkup?" His gaze slid sideways. "Oh, it's been a while."

"How long a while?" she asked as he turned his attention to his plate.

"Let me see." Busily, he sliced into his chicken, working with more precision than strictly necessary. "I suppose, uh, I suppose it would have been before your mother passed away."

"Dad!" Natalya protested. Her mother had died several years ago, and her father was fast approaching his sixties. "Regular checkups are basic self-care."

"She scheduled that stuff for me," he said, hunching his shoulders like a scolded schoolboy. "I guess I should do that, huh?"

"I guess," Natalya answered, a touch of sarcasm in her voice, before frowning. This conversation should have stirred up foreknowledge for her. Mentally, she poked at the hole in her memory again.

"What is it?" her father asked. His eyes went vague and unfocused for a moment or two and then he shook his head. "I don't see anything. Did you just—"

"No," Natalya interrupted him. "Nothing. But my foresight isn't working, I told you that. You should still schedule a checkup."

"You know, the longer I live here, the more I realize why no one gets too bothered when I see ghosts," Akira said, cutting up her waffle. "Do you really think Maggie is somehow psychically choosing a diet for Max based on data she couldn't possibly have?"

Natalya lifted one shoulder in a shrug. "Why take chances?"

Max cut off a bite of his chicken. "I suppose she'd give me bacon and eggs if I insisted. But I like being surprised by my food."

"Does Maggie surprise you?" Akira asked Natalya.

"Not usually," Natalya admitted. "It's hard not to think about eating when you sit down at the table. With such an immediate experience my foresight is—well, was—quite clear."

"Was," Max repeated. "Where did it go?"

"No idea." The ice was melting in her tea, the water condensing on the sides of the glass. Natalya drank a little more of it, wondering how long it would take her to get used to the loss. Would it be permanent? Was her foresight gone forever? As she set her glass down, the corner of her mouth quirked up. If only she could see the future...

Akira said thoughtfully, "I wonder..." before letting her words trail off and putting a bite of waffle in her mouth.

Natalya tilted her head, waiting for Akira to finish her thought. In the purse by her side, her phone buzzed. Sliding her hand into the purse, she touched the phone's plastic, and then gave a sigh when she realized she didn't know who was calling.

"Do you mind if I get this?" At her father's shrug and Akira's head shake, she pulled her phone out. She didn't recognize the number, so frowning, she answered it.

"Nat, good. I'm glad you picked up."

A little jolt of recognition shot down her spine at the sound of Colin's voice, followed by a flush of heat. If she'd known who was calling, would she have answered? She didn't know, and the uncertainty put bite in her tone as she asked, "How did you get this number?"

"Your brother."

"Which brother?" Natalya needed to know who to scold. If she wanted her ex-boyfriend to have her unlisted number, she'd give it to him herself.

"Lucas. Apparently Zane called him?" His tone held a question.

Natalya closed her eyes. What had Zane told Lucas? She supposed it depended on what Akira had told Zane, and what Rose had told Akira. If her father wasn't sitting across the table, she'd ask, but that wasn't a conversation she wanted to have under her father's interested eyes.

"I managed to talk him out of flying home to kick my ass without pulling out my badge, but just barely. You might want to give him a call."

She managed to bite back a groan with an effort. Clenching her teeth, though, sent tendrils of tension pain spiraling into her head.

"But that's not why I'm calling. Where are you?"

"At Maggie's," she answered automatically, distracted by her headache. Then, "Why?" she asked suspiciously.

"Excellent. I need you. Can you get back here?"

"You need me?"

"Yeah. No," he corrected himself. "Kenzi needs you."

"What's going on?"

"Just get over here. Please."

"What's happening?" There was no answer. "Colin?"

But the line had gone dead.

❧ CHAPTER SEVEN ❧

Shifting from foot to foot, Colin knocked on the front door of Nat's cottage. As he waited for her to answer, he realized what he was doing and, disgusted, forced himself to stand still. He'd knocked on doors to serve divorce papers and foreclosure notices, evict tenants, break up domestic disputes and arrest violent criminals. It was ridiculous to feel nervous. Nat wasn't going to shoot him, after all. But when she yanked open the door, he wasn't so sure.

"Anything?" she demanded, not bothering to greet him.

"Not a clue," he admitted.

"It's been three days." Nat kept her voice low, but her accompanying glare was heated.

"I know." For seventy-two hours, ever since he'd persuaded her to rescue Kenzi from the system, he'd been reassuring her. Give it a day. One more night. Just a little longer. But it was getting increasingly difficult to pretend a confidence he didn't feel.

"What are you doing about it?"

"We're trying, Nat." He ran a hand through his hair. "I've had deputies running the plates of every car at the campgrounds and recreation areas, searching for one that's been abandoned. We've had people scouting all the back roads, all the trails. By now the rangers must have shown her photo to every registered camper in the area, looking for someone who recognizes her. But we've got nothing."

"Registered campers?" Nat recognized the caveat immediately.

"The squatters are tougher to find."

Nat glanced over her shoulder before opening the screen door and stepping out onto the porch. The night was cool, but not cold, and she didn't bother with a jacket. She looked up at him under the glow of her porch light.

He let his gaze drop to her mouth, wanting to taste her, wanting to tug her into his arms and feel her against him. She must have recognized the look, because her chin tilted up—unfortunately, not in the "kiss me, now, you fool," way but with a narrowed eye expression that said, "touch me and I'll smack you, jerk."

"What next?" she asked.

"We've been trying to get her picture on the news," he answered. "It may be our best chance of finding someone who recognizes her."

Nat wrinkled her nose. "No one in Tassamara is going to like having reporters in town."

"We've had no luck so far. Apparently a pop star got caught with a prostitute. The television stations don't have time for anything else.

Nat's scowl deepened. "You'd think a little girl lost in the woods on Christmas Day would be more important."

"You'd think," he agreed, his frustration adding an edge to his tone, before he changed the subject. "You're sure she doesn't speak Spanish?" He'd asked the question before. It was wishful thinking to hope the answer might be different.

"She doesn't speak anything," Nat responded with a snap. "She doesn't speak at all." He looked at her silently and she sighed, before adding, in a more reasonable tone. "My Spanish isn't great, but she doesn't show any indication of understanding it. English is no problem. Why?"

"Illegal immigrant parents might have an excuse for not searching for her."

It was Nat's turn to fall silent. For a moment, they stood together in shared worry, Nat looking up at him, and then her gaze fell. She stepped away and dropped down to sit on the porch steps. Absently, she swept the wood floor with her hand, grimacing at the dust before brushing her hands together to wipe it off. "I should sweep."

Colin sat down next to her. Their shoulders brushed, but Nat made no move to scoot away.

"If nobody's looking for her..." Nat said softly. "You're thinking Hansel and Gretel?"

"No Hansel," he answered. He looked over his shoulder at her neat cottage with its trim blue and white paint. "And your house lacks the requisite gingerbread." He paused. Trying to make a joke of it didn't help. "But yeah. Her parents might have abandoned her."

"I still don't think she's autistic." Nat stared out into the darkness as if she could see into the trees. "Or even truly emotionally disturbed. She's been through a trauma, that's clear, but when she thinks she's alone, she relaxes. She seems like a perfectly normal child. She plays, she draws."

The psychologist had been quick to give up on interviewing Kenzi, and as quick to decide the girl displayed symptoms of autism and should be placed in a residential facility. Colin was no expert, but he didn't think a cursory non-interview with a lost child was the right basis for that diagnosis or that decision. Nat agreed. After a confrontation with the psychologist in which the woman stiffly asserted that she'd done what she could, the stalemate was resolved when Carla, the caseworker from the foster care agency, suggested Kenzi stay with Nat. For a little while longer, until her parents could be found.

"She watches television." Nat pulled her hair over her shoulder and started twisting a lock around her finger, winding it tighter and tighter. "Too much television, probably. She watches it as if she's hypnotized. It's the Disney channel, but I'm not sure it's good for her."

"Is that what she's doing now?" Colin asked.

Nat nodded. "I was cooking dinner."

As if in response, his stomach rumbled. He put a hand on it. "Sorry. Long day, not much food."

She pressed her lips together for a moment before letting the words slip out. "There's plenty if you want to stay."

Colin didn't grin but his lips twitched. If he gauged her mood correctly, her ingrained southern hospitality had overridden her anger, and she was already regretting the words. Still, he would grab the opportunity with both hands. "I'd appreciate that, thank you." A muscle flickered in her jaw as if she were gritting her teeth so he added easily, as if it were the only reason he was staying, "I'd like the chance to spend some more time with Kenzi."

"Watching her watch television isn't fascinating." She'd wound her dark hair so tightly around her finger that the tip was turning red

"I want to ask her a few more questions."

Nat tugged her finger free. "You think she'll talk to you?"

"Nah." He shook his head. He'd been too busy over the past few days for more than fleeting interactions with Nat and Kenzi, but he'd seen the girl's body language when Nat returned to the sheriff's office. Her muscles relaxed, her breathing slowed in relief and trust. When Kenzi talked, it would be to Nat, he was sure. Still, given that she hadn't yet spoken, they couldn't count on that. "But her reactions could give us some clues to her background."

"I don't want you scaring her." Nat turned to face him. "She's been scared enough."

"Nothing like that." He put up a hand, fingers spread wide.

"She frightens easily." Nat's mouth twisted. "Yesterday…"

"What?" Colin prompted when she fell silent.

"After I got off the phone with you, I couldn't find her," Nat said reluctantly. Their eyes met and Colin winced at the guilt in Nat's gaze. "It took me a while to track her down. She was hiding in the bathroom closet, squeezed into a space that should have been way too small for her."

Colin wished he could put a comforting arm around her shoulders and hug her close. The previous day, his sister Jenna, the one closest in age to him, had dropped by Nat's house with an armload of hand-me-down clothes from her youngest daughter for Kenzi. It would have been a nice gesture, but she'd been bubbling over with delight about his survival and the future, a future she assumed would include Nat. Nat hadn't been pleased. She'd let him know about it—at a higher than average decibel level—the moment Jenna left.

"I won't say anything that would scare her," Colin promised. "I'll be careful."

"Avoid asking about her parents. She shuts down when you bring them up."

"Voice of experience?"

Nat spread her hands. "Just casual questions. Does your mom make you breakfast? Are your dad's eyes blue like yours?"

Those were exactly the sorts of questions Colin hoped to ask. He should have known Nat would be trying the same thing.

"She's locking her secrets up in silence. I've been looking for the key," Nat continued. "It's not parents, it's not home, it's not her own toys. It's not favorite foods or television shows. I don't know what it is yet."

"We'll find it," Colin said. "Seven-year-olds aren't noted for their ability to keep secrets."

"She's doing pretty well so far," Nat answered, her voice dry. It softened as she added, "It's too bad that Lucas isn't here. He could tell us what she's thinking."

Nat's brother, Lucas, was telepathic. Unlike his siblings, however, he didn't spend much time in Tassamara. He'd been in town for a few weeks, but on Christmas Day he and his girlfriend, Sylvie, had flown to North Carolina to spend some time with her family.

"Could you call him?" Colin asked.

Nat tipped her head to the side, a movement part nod, part shake. "I did, but he and Zane got called in on some government case. They flew to Japan the day after Christmas. He said they'd try to get back to town as soon as possible, but they're tracking some high-level security leaks and it might take a while. Kenzi's not in any danger, so I can't say it's urgent."

"Is there anyone else at GD who could help?" Colin suggested. The company Nat's family owned had an eclectic staff, many of whom had unusual abilities.

"Maybe, but we're closed until after New Year's," she answered. "We're on our own until then."

Colin rubbed his chin, feeling the stubble he needed to shave away. "Maybe we could pick up some clues about where she's from based on her behavior."

"Like what?"

"Table manners?" he suggested. "I don't imagine squatters camping in the forest devote much attention to teaching their kids how to use silverware."

Nat arched a brow, but her look was thoughtful, not doubting.

"I'd like to take a look at her drawings, too."

"Hoping to find the deep psychological undercurrents hidden within them?"

"Well..." Put that way, it sounded stupid, but Nat shook her head.

"I've been looking, too," she admitted. "Developmentally, they seem appropriate. Rounded human shapes, a step up from stick figures, with all the body parts one might expect, including facial expressions. She's using colors, a baseline, traditional symbols. I'm no expert, but I'd say she's a pretty good artist for her age."

"A baseline? Traditional symbols? That sounds like expertise."

"Well, art." Nat gave a shrug, as if her words were a complete answer. She stood, brushing off the seat of her pants. "For psychological analysis, though, we'd need her to explain her drawings. To tell us who the people and places are, her feelings about what she's creating."

"Can't you tell from looking at them?" Colin asked as he stood and followed Nat up the steps.

She glanced over her shoulder at him as she reached the door. "No, not really. Although... well, I'll let you see for yourself."

On that cryptic note, she opened the door and went inside.

❧ CHAPTER EIGHT ❦

Letting Colin stay for dinner was a terrible idea. Polite, maybe, but why had she let her mother's manners overrule her common sense? The more time she spent with him, the more conversations they had, the easier it was to fall back into their old patterns.

She and Colin thought alike. In the old days, they could finish one another's sentences. They'd never shared interests: he liked comic books and football, she preferred novels and art exhibits. But their companionship ran bone deep. It would be much too easy to get used to having him around again.

And she didn't want him around. She didn't want him in her space. She didn't want to have to remember him here, to picture him sitting on her comfortable couch, his long legs outstretched. When he was gone, she didn't want to hear the sound of his quiet chuckle in the silence or smell the scent of his laundry soap in the air.

So many of the memories of her past belonged to him. Her childhood, her adolescence, her college years—all were stamped Natalya plus Colin in the scrapbooks of her mind. She'd spent years missing him as if his absence was a hole carved out of her life, and now that her life was whole again, she didn't want to give him any part of her present or future.

At the thought of the future, Natalya searched her mind, hoping to shake loose a premonition, any premonition. Nothing came to her. It was maddening, like not being able to remember her name or her birthday. She was clenching her teeth, she realized, and forced herself to relax.

Enough thinking. Exist in the now, she reminded herself. The past couldn't hurt her and the future would be what it would be. Thoughts were just leaves on water, clouds in the sky, floating away.

Kenzi was still planted on the couch, watching television with hypnotized eyes, the doll Grace had given her tucked against her side. Natalya wasn't sure whether she'd let it out of her sight once since it arrived. Behavior. What did it mean that Kenzi was so fascinated with television, so attached to her doll? It wouldn't surprise Natalya to learn the doll was the nicest one Kenzi had ever owned. Grace hadn't skimped on quality. But that would be true for most children, Natalya suspected.

The television, though—was it her usual babysitter? She certainly watched with the glazed concentration of an addict, but she'd never once moved to turn on the box herself or even change the channel.

"That's beautiful." Colin's voice was hushed with awe. Natalya glanced at him in surprise, but he was looking past Kenzi, at the painting of her mother she'd hung over the couch.

Natalya had painted it from a mix of photograph and memory. The original photo had given her the shape of the nose and the cheekbones, the angle of the neck, the amber gold of the hair. But the stubbornness in the set of the chin and the light of laughter in the eyes—those had come from Natalya's memories of her mother.

The curve of the mouth had taken forever. Natalya had wanted to capture a very specific smile. Not a single photograph—not that there were many, given that her mom was usually the one behind the camera, rarely in front of it—had the exact look of exasperated affection her mother had worn so well. It had taken weeks of trial-and-error, of scribbled-out sketches and consultations with her brothers and sister for Nat to get it right, but she had in the end.

It was probably the best piece of work she'd ever done.

"You painted it?"

"Yeah."

"It's incredible. That's not watercolors, though."

She should walk away, go finish dinner. Letting him into her house didn't mean letting him into her life. But her art was a subject near to her heart and hard to resist. "No, it's oil. I started using oil pastels in med school because I didn't have a lot of time, and they were easy to carry around. And then I switched to oil paint a few years ago. I tried acrylic but it dries too fast."

"Aren't oil paints supposed to be difficult?"

Natalya made an equivocal gesture with one hand. "Slow to dry. But flexible. I love the translucency."

"Is that what gives her skin that light?"

Damn it. Every member of her family and several friends had seen the portrait of her mother. Every single one had admired it. Her brother Zane had asked for one of her preliminary sketches and it was hanging, framed, in his office. But Colin was the first to express interest in how Natalya had done it.

"Yes." She kept her answer short. "I should go finish dinner."

She took three steps away and was almost at the door to the kitchen when Colin spoke again. "She wasn't mad at me, you know."

Natalya's chin went up as she turned back. "She never got mad at you. You were the golden boy."

Colin chuckled, but his eyes were on the portrait. "Well, the whole pitiful orphan deal was good for a pass on most stuff."

Natalya pressed her lips together. Colin might make light of it now, but his parents' deaths had been devastating. He'd wound up spending almost as much time at her house as his after that. Not because he didn't have relatives who wanted him—he did. But he'd bounced around from house to house, family to family, as situations changed.

His aunt got pregnant and he moved to a sister's. The sister got a new job with a longer commute and he wound up with his brother. He failed chemistry and his grandmother decided his brother wasn't responsible enough to be taking care of a teenager, so he moved to an uncle's. The love and family support had been consistent, but still, her house was as much his own as any of the places he'd spent the night.

"That wasn't it, though," he continued. "She thought I did the right thing."

"She—" Natalya snapped, her voice hot. And then she paused. Kenzi was looking at her now, face unsmiling. Natalya took a deep breath, released it, took another, and when she spoke again the heat was gone. "She was wrong."

"You were unhappy. She saw that. She wanted what was best for you."

"I was perfectly capable of making those decisions myself." Natalya's words were even, her tone calm.

"But you wouldn't. You would have just waited it out."

"Colin?" Natalya waited until he looked at her instead of at the portrait. "Cut it out or you're going hungry."

A corner of his mouth turned up and he looked back at the portrait. "I miss her still."

Natalya opened her mouth and then closed it again, the words unsaid. Unfair, unfair, her brain protested. One short conversation and the solid wall of her resistance to him, the one that should have been made out of impenetrable steel, had melted into something more like flimsy wood.

Maybe she should forgive him. Not get back together with him. That was definitely out. But let go of being angry at him? Stop holding onto a grudge that didn't do much except tie her stomach into knots?

"I'm going to finish dinner," she said brusquely and headed into the kitchen.

Not much needed finishing. The chicken enchiladas had five more minutes on the timer and the salad was the rip-open-the-bag-and-toss-it-into-a-bowl kind. But she wanted the moment of solitude.

He'd shut her out of his life, she reminded herself as she lifted plates out of the cupboard and set them on the counter. He'd chosen to live without her, she thought as she pulled silverware out of the drawer and set it atop the plates. He hadn't wanted her, as she found the salad tongs.

But she sighed as she tugged open the bag of lettuce. Knowing he would die, waiting for him to die, and never knowing when had been hell. Those months were the worst of her life. When she'd gone away to medical school, she'd buried herself in her work, but every minute she'd been away from Tassamara, she'd known she was safe. He was safe.

The best months were the winter months. The tree-lined road in her premonition could have been many times, many places, but not a northern winter. She'd hated the cold, though. Snow was fun the first time and thoroughly unpleasant on every subsequent experience. Why didn't the romantic Christmas specials ever mention that snow burned when you touched it?

And she'd missed home. Living in the outside world meant always guarding what she said, always avoiding revealing her foreknowledge. Working in a hospital made that close to impossible, and she'd had to learn to accept the peculiar looks and whispers. In the end, tired of fighting fate, she'd come home.

She stared down at the salad bowl, not really seeing it. Thinking about the past wouldn't get her anywhere. She needed to focus on the present. Kenzi. That's who she should be thinking about. What could they discover about Kenzi without words? What did she already know about her that she hadn't realized she knew?

She didn't hear any conversation coming from the living room, so she crossed back to the archway leading to the other room. Colin still stood where she'd left him, his gaze on the girl. Kenzi ignored him, but she was holding her doll a little tighter.

"Kenzi?" Natalya wasn't sure if this would work. Seven. What did parents expect from their seven-year-olds? When Kenzi looked her way, she said, "The sheriff's going to be staying for dinner. Would you come set the table, please?"

Without hesitation, the girl hopped off the couch and joined her in the kitchen. Natalya watched as she looked around the room, spotting the plates and silverware on the counter. Trying not to look as if she were attending to Kenzi's every move, Natalya turned to the oven, finding a mitt and taking the enchiladas out.

Carefully, Kenzi set her doll on the seat she'd been using at previous meals, then crossed to the counter and reached up for the dishes. Back at the table, she left the dishes stacked as she climbed up on a chair and took table mats from the pile in the center of the table, then distributed the mats, plates, and silver. That answered that, thought Natalya, grabbing a serving spoon out of the container set by the stove.

"Interesting," Colin said quietly from the doorway.

"She makes her bed every morning," Natalya answered, equally quietly. "It's what made me think of it."

"Huh." Colin cocked his head to one side. "We might have to consult an expert or two, but I think that could be considered unusual."

"Little pitchers," Natalya cautioned, but she knew exactly what Colin meant. How old had she been before she made her bed every day without maternal prompting? Twenty-five? Twenty-six?

As they ate, Colin chatted as easily as if his companions were responding, but Natalya was as silent as Kenzi as she turned over her interactions with the girl in her mind. Kenzi definitely wasn't autistic, she decided firmly. The psychologist had seen her lack of eye contact, her refusal or inability to speak, her social withdrawal—all of which were potentially symptoms of autism. But she hadn't seen the fuller picture.

"Nat?" Colin's voice interrupted her reverie. "Earth to Nat."

She blinked at him, brought back to her surroundings. "Lost in thought. Sorry."

"Great enchiladas."

"Thanks." Her eyes narrowed. Was he going to start reminiscing about their past? That she'd had enchiladas in the oven was pure chance, but they'd shared a fondness for Mexican food during their UCF years. The first few times she'd made them at home, he'd been her appreciative and tolerant test audience.

"I like the kick." His words were polite, but the minuscule tilt of his head in Kenzi's direction was loaded with meaning. Natalya followed his gaze.

Kenzi's shoulders were slumped as she eyed the food on her plate with all the misery of a prisoner contemplating the firing squad. As Natalya watched, she took a bite. The wince and shudder as she swallowed were subtle, but unmistakable.

"Oh, honey, I'm sorry. You should have..." She stopped herself before letting the words slip out. Kenzi could have told her, but she should have paid more attention. Or at least been more thoughtful. "You don't have to eat that."

Kenzi stared at Natalya. Her gaze darted to Colin's face and back again, but she didn't push her plate away in relief or even put down her fork. If anything, she clutched her fork tighter.

Natalya pursed her lips before exchanging glances with Colin. With a raised eyebrow, she silently asked him what he thought. He lifted a shoulder, then reached across the table and took Kenzi's plate. "I love enchiladas," he said cheerfully, scraping her tortillas onto his plate. "But maybe Nat can find you something less spicy."

"Toasted cheese?" Natalya asked Kenzi. The little girl's eyes were bright as she nodded.

After the cheese sandwich was made and duly consumed, Natalya suggested to Kenzi that she show Colin her drawings. As Natalya cleared the table, she could hear Colin admiring Kenzi's work in the front bedroom. A reluctant smile curled her lips at the sound of his voice saying, "Interesting use of color. You must have worked hard on that one." It sounded as if he hadn't forgotten her lectures on what an artist wanted to hear.

She separated the leftovers into multiple plastic containers. Usually she got a week's worth of lunches out of a pan of enchiladas, but not this week. But as she looked for space in the crowded fridge, she sighed. She wanted to stir up the embers of her anger against Colin and it got harder by the minute. But he'd made the choice to push her away, to shut her out, and there was no going back from that.

"So…"

She jumped at the sound of his voice right behind her, sending the last container skidding onto the floor. "Damn it."

His eyes glinted with amusement. "If her first words are damn it, we'll know who to blame."

She scowled at him. He bent down to pick up the container as he grinned back at her. "I didn't mean to sneak up on you." He handed her the dish. In his other hand, he held a few pieces of papers—selected drawings, she assumed, from the pile Kenzi had created in the past days. "Have you seen these?"

She finished storing the leftovers, craning her neck to see which drawings he held. "Yeah. Or at least the top one."

He took them to the table and spread them out. "What did you think?"

She joined him, standing by his side. "I assume you're not asking for my opinion as an art critic?"

"This…" He tapped the first drawing. The picture showed a house and several figures against a background of pine trees. In some ways, it seemed like a typical child's drawing. The house was a square box with a triangle roof and the trees were angled lines drawn away from a central stem. The figures were only slightly more elaborate than stick people. But the house was colored completely black, with none of the doors or windows of a traditional house. And the figures were all different sizes, all different places. "This has to be meaningful, right? Not too many black houses around here." Colin sounded optimistic, as if he were ready to start searching for a house of that description immediately.

Natalya wrinkled her nose as she shook her head. "Think metaphor," she suggested. She glanced over her shoulder, wondering if Kenzi was close enough to overhear them.

"She's drawing me a picture to take home with me," Colin said. "I closed the door to the bedroom."

She could still be listening, so Natalya kept her words cautious. "If this represents a real location, I think it's safe to say it's not a good place. But I don't think you can assume the actual house looks anything like this."

Colin grimaced. "And the people?"

"I'm sure she doesn't know anyone who's as big as a house," Natalya replied, touching the largest figure. "Or as small as this one," she added, tapping a tiny figure at the edge of the paper, shorter than the bottom branches of the pine tree it stood under.

"What do you think is going on here?" Colin asked, pointing to a central grouping of figures.

"That's... troubling," Natalya said cautiously. One of the shapes appeared to be lying down. Kenzi might have meant the red scribble across its chest as writing on a t-shirt. Or spilled juice, perhaps? But blood seemed painfully likely.

"Could she have witnessed a crime?" Colin asked.

Natalya shrugged. "Maybe. But I don't think we can make any assumptions."

"Yeah, it's not a lot to go on." Colin agreed. He shuffled the first picture to the side and pulled the next one closer to him. "What about this one?"

"Huh." Natalya hadn't seen this one before. Three figures stood side-by-side. One had long dark hair and wore carefully filled-in blue pants and a blue shirt, much like the blue jeans and sweater Natalya was wearing. The next, much smaller, had brown hair in wild curls, with pink pants and a blue-and-white shirt. The third had blonde hair, a wide smile, and a pink dress.

"That's got to be you, right?"

"This must be what she was drawing when I was painting this afternoon." Natalya eyed the image thoughtfully. "Why did you pick this one out?"

When she'd brought Kenzi back to her house after the disastrous meeting at the sheriff's office, she'd had no idea what she was going to do with the girl. With the company closed for the holiday week, she didn't need to go into work. But she hadn't spent extended time with a child in years. When her college friends were getting married and having babies, she'd been immersed in medical school and residency. What did seven-year-olds like to do exactly?

But Kenzi was easy. Natalya didn't have crayons, but she had oil pastels and colored chalk. That and a pile of scrap paper had kept Kenzi busy for hours. With the television, her doll, a few old board games Nat had stashed in a closet, an occasional trip into town or friendly visitor, and a daily walk by the water, they'd managed to spend their time together quite contentedly. Natalya suspected most children wouldn't be so complaisant, but she wasn't complaining.

"The girl in the pink dress," Colin answered.

"Grace, you think?" Grace had dropped by every day. She seemed to have set a personal goal of making Kenzi laugh. She hadn't succeeded yet, but she'd gotten Kenzi's cheeks to dimple with restrained amusement.

"No, I don't think so." Colin pulled the next image over. This one was again of a girl in a pink dress but this time she was outlined in yellow.

"Hmm, interesting." Natalya picked up the drawing. The yellow was more than a simple traced line. Kenzi had carefully shaded the color around the body, setting the figure against a background of light. "It's almost like she's glowing."

Colin's voice was taut with tension. "I think it's the girl from my dream."

"Oh! Rose, of course!" Natalya wished Kenzi had advanced beyond basic figures. She would have liked to know what the ghost girl looked like. "So she must be able to see her, too. I wonder if Akira knows that. I wonder if Rose knows that."

"What?" Colin stared at her as if she'd sprouted another head.

She raised an eyebrow. "Rose? The girl from the other night? The ghost you saw when you were, well, dead?"

"What ghost?" Colin sounded completely confused. "What are you talking about?"

"Akira didn't tell you?"

"Tell me what?"

The Tassamara gossip loop had fallen down on the job. Natalya had expected the details to be all over town within twenty-four hours. But perhaps since Colin was involved, no one had shared the story with him?

"The girl you saw the other night is a ghost. She lives with Akira and Zane. Her name is Rose."

"A ghost," Colin repeated. He blinked and shook his head as if trying to kick-start his brain. "Okay, right. I knew... A ghost? Really?"

Natalya bit back her smile. Colin had always been more skeptical than the average Tassamara resident. Maybe it was being the youngest in a big family. His siblings had teased him with stories about the town, true or not. It might have been why he'd followed in his father's footsteps and become a police officer.

"We need to question her."

Natalya blinked. Somehow that hadn't been what she expected him to say next. "How do you want to do that?"

"I don't know. A séance?"

"Those don't work. We tried back when Dad was convinced the house was haunted." Her father had been right that their house was haunted, but until Akira moved to town, the mediums and séances and ghost hunters had all been a big waste of time and energy.

"She must know something, though. Why else would she have been there?"

Natalya paused. If Rose knew any helpful information about Kenzi, wouldn't she have told Akira? And wouldn't Akira have relayed it? But maybe Colin was right. Maybe they needed to talk to Rose.

❧ CHAPTER NINE ❧

"Yay!" Rose clapped her hands with delight.

"Akira doesn't like being asked about ghosts. Zane asked us not to bring them up." Tiny lines of worry creased Natalya's brow.

"Pfft." Rose waved her hand to dismiss that concern. "She won't mind talking to me."

She spun in a circle in the kitchen, not caring that her energy passed through the oblivious living people. She didn't mind keeping the little girl company—especially not since they'd started watching television—but it would be nice to be able to talk again. To someone who could hear her, that was.

"Under the circumstances, I think she can make an exception." Colin said, voice firm.

Natalya lifted a dubious shoulder as Rose paused in her twirl. Firm was the wrong tactic to take. Akira got stubborn when she felt pushed.

Colin glanced at his watch. "It's early still. I'll go visit her. It's the old Harris place, right? Off Millard?"

"Yeah. But are you sure Rose will be there?" Natalya set down the drawing she'd been holding and picked up another one, her expression thoughtful.

Rose peeked over her shoulder. It was the one Kenzi had drawn earlier that day, of the three of them together. Rose didn't think the likeness was anything to write home about, but she appreciated the thought.

She hadn't known how clearly Kenzi saw her. In the forest, the little girl had followed Rose through hours of hiking and miles of wooded terrain. She'd never complained, never cried, just persisted, one step after the next. But since then, the little girl hadn't seemed to recognize when Rose was with her except for the occasional moment when she'd stop and stare or quickly turn her head as if she'd caught a glimpse of Rose out of the corner of her eye.

Little kids often could see ghosts. Babies were the best. Rose would play with them, tickling their toes and making silly faces, hoping to catch a smile or even better, a full-fledged giggle. The older

97

they got, though, the less likely it was they'd acknowledge her. Toddlers could mostly see her, but they couldn't feel or hear her anymore. And a child Kenzi's age shouldn't have seen her at all.

"Doesn't she live there?" Colin asked.

"Technically, I think the term you want is reside," Natalya murmured. "Or possibly haunt, if that's not rude."

Colin snorted, as Rose laughed. "I don't mind," she said generously. "Not anymore." Back when she'd been trapped in her house, before Akira came and set her free, she hated people saying the house was haunted. It meant fewer and fewer visitors over the years and Rose loved company.

"But more seriously," Natalya continued, "don't you think she might be here?" She tipped her chin in the direction of the picture. "Kenzi's obviously seen her. There's no setting on this drawing, no house or forest to give us a sense of place, but she's put the three of us together. That's got to be me, her, and Rose, don't you think?"

"Yeah."

"So maybe Rose is with us."

Rose twirled again, delighted by the direction of the conversation. "Oh, I am, I am."

"Huh. Interesting idea." Colin rubbed his chin, looking around the kitchen. "What do you suggest?"

Natalya looked thoughtful for a moment, then said, in a louder voice, "If you're here, Rose, can you give us a sign?"

"Help Wanted?" Colin suggested.

Natalya's lips twitched, but she didn't smile. "Trespassers will be shot?" she offered tartly.

"Now how hospitable is that?" Colin drawled, his grey eyes alight with amusement.

Rose looked from one to the other, her lips curving up. She couldn't read minds and she hadn't spent long enough with the sheriff and Zane's sister to fully understand their relationship, but she knew that crack about trespassers hadn't been directed at her. The sheriff knew it, too.

"If you're here, Rose, you're welcome to stay," Natalya said. "But please let us know whether you are."

"What are you expecting her to do? Start banging cupboard doors? Make objects fly around the room?"

"Dillon sends text messages," Natalya told him, referring to her ghostly nephew.

"Oh, that's so hard," Rose protested. She'd tried, she had, but she'd never succeeded in replicating Dillon's skill at controlling cell phones. Still, Natalya had only asked for a sign. Maybe Rose could manage some other feat? She was good at switching channels on the television, but only when the magic pointer was positioned correctly. Natalya kept hers in a drawer. It had been very frustrating. Rose didn't mind the Disney Channel, but some Cartoon Network would have made a nice change.

With a pout, not really wanting to do what she was about to do, Rose stepped into Natalya. Standing on top of her, her legs lost in Natalya's body, she thought of the worst, saddest, bleakest thoughts she could.

It took her a minute. Death, the obvious tragic thought, just didn't scare her anymore. Not hers or anyone else's. Sure, it would have been sad if the little girl died in the forest, but the spirit who'd sent Rose to find her was probably waiting for her somewhere. And Colin, why he'd practically been looking forward to seeing his parents again. No, death wasn't scary.

Loneliness, though, that had power. Rose imagined herself still tied to her house, but without Henry, without the boys in the backyard, without Dillon or Akira or Zane, without music or television or visitors.

Natalya shivered, tugging the light cardigan sweater she wore closed, and tucking one hand into a fist by her neck.

"Is your phone ringing?" she asked Colin.

He shook his head. "Not a quiver." He slipped it out of his pocket and thumbed it on, glancing at the screen. "Nothing."

"Huh," she said. "Well, maybe she's not here."

Annoyed, Rose tried harder, concentrating on the thought of a completely silent, completely empty world. Why, it was such a miserable idea she almost wanted to cry herself. Natalya couldn't possibly miss that.

Natalya shivered again. "I might need to turn the heat on tonight. The weather must be changing."

"A cold front came in," Colin confirmed with a nod.

"Cold front! I'm not a cold front." Rose stepped out of Natalya, shaking her head. "Ask for a sign, then totally ignore it," she grumbled. What else could she do?

"Maybe we should ask Kenzi if she's here." Colin sounded dubious, even as he made the suggestion.

"Oh, don't do that," Rose protested, but Natalya was already shaking her head.

"Not a good idea," Natalya said. She didn't bother to explain herself, but Rose nodded in relief. Kenzi might be scared at the idea of a ghost haunting her and Rose didn't want to give the poor kid nightmares. Colin and Natalya exchanged a long look before Colin dipped his head in acknowledgement, not questioning her decision.

"In fact…" Natalya glanced in the direction of the living room. "Let's discuss this after Kenzi goes to bed."

"All right." Colin started to slip his phone back into his pocket before pausing. "I'll call Akira, though, and see if Rose is with her. If she's not, maybe Akira can come over, see if Rose is here, and translate some ghost for us. "

"I'll call," Natalya said.

"I don't mind." Colin tapped at his phone screen, head bent. "She knows me." Natalya shot him a look, but he didn't seem to notice. "I know I've got Zane's number in here somewhere," he muttered.

Natalya reached over and tugged the phone out of his hands. Rose chuckled, saying, "Ooh, decisive."

"Hey," Colin protested, as he let it go.

Natalya pressed the button to turn it off and handed it back. "I'll call," she repeated.

"What's the big deal?"

The look Natalya gave him was the same as the one Rose's math teacher used to give her when she hadn't done her homework: a steady gaze, head tilted, both reproachful and annoyed.

"Ah." A slow grin spread across Colin's face before he smothered it. Rose thought he might be biting the interior of his cheek to hold it in as he said, "Should I not be inviting people to your house?"

"In fact, you should not," Natalya said. Her tone grew exasperated as she added, "In actual fact, I'd prefer it if no one knew you were at my house. Not my family, definitely not your family, and not the rest of the town, either."

"Don't think of it as a visit," he suggested. "I'm following up on a case. That's all. Of course, most witnesses don't feed me dinner. I guess if I mention how delicious your chicken enchiladas are…"

He let the words trail off at Natalya's glare. Pointing over his shoulder at the living room and the bedroom adjacent to it, he said, "I'll just go, ah, check on how that drawing's coming along, yeah?" Natalya didn't answer as she picked up her own phone to call Akira, but as he turned, Rose heard him chuckle softly.

Natalya's frown smoothed out when Akira answered. She took only a moment to get to the point. "Is Rose with you?"

"Hello, Akira," Rose called from across the room. She didn't think Akira would be able to hear her, but it couldn't hurt to try.

She paused as Akira responded. Rose couldn't hear Akira's side of the conversation, but as Natalya began to smile, Rose drew closer to listen in.

"Ghosts disappear. They do. They're around and then they're not and that's how it goes. But three days. And she didn't say good-bye, she didn't leave a message—not that I know how a ghost could leave a message, it's not as if she could write a note. But the television's never on, the house is quiet. It's spooky. People think haunted houses are spooky, but a not-haunted house is so much worse."

"She's here, I think," Natalya finally interrupted Akira.

"With you?" Akira's surprise was clear, but she almost immediately added in a calmer tone, "Oh. The little girl. The one you're still taking care of. That should have occurred to me."

"We," Natalya started before correcting herself, "that is, I'd like to ask her some questions and see what she knows."

"I'm not sure how much help she'll be." Akira sounded doubtful. "Rose can be mysterious."

Rose snorted. She would so be helpful. And she was not mysterious. But then her nose wrinkled as she thought about what she knew. Not a name. Not an identity. Not an address. And she wasn't even sure she wanted Colin and Natalya to find Kenzi's home. They might think their job was to return her, but Rose wasn't convinced that was a good idea.

She was still puzzling over the question of what she would tell them after Natalya got off the phone and while she and Colin had a low-voiced argument about whether he could stay. Natalya wanted him to leave, promising to relay any useful information, but he insisted it was bad enough not to be able to communicate directly with a witness without playing telephone. Reluctantly, Natalya conceded the point.

Colin took a seat in the living room and waited for Akira to arrive as Natalya put Kenzi to bed. Rose perched on the arm of a chair and watched the expressions crossing his face as the two of them listened to Natalya talking to the little girl, first about pajamas and clean teeth and clean faces, and then the soothing up-and-down lilt of a bedtime story.

He looked sad, Rose decided. She wondered why. She'd only met him once—in the brief moments after his death—but she'd seen him around town many times. She'd watched when he arrested Dillon's mom with a smooth and quiet calm, and when he sternly admonished a texting teenage driver on the street in front of her house. She'd witnessed his casual charm, the smile with which he greeted customers at the bistro, the warmth in his laughter when they joked about the weather. Sad didn't seem to fit.

A quiet knock on the door interrupted her thoughts. Rose didn't pause to give Colin or Natalya time to answer, rushing straight through the wood and into Akira.

"Ooh," Akira protested, shivering, as Rose's energy passed through her.

"Sorry, sorry!" Rose spun around. "I've missed you!"

Akira turned, too, and held her hands out as if she would take Rose's in hers. "You need to learn to use the phone."

"I need Dillon to come home so he can do it for me. That'd be so much easier."

Akira laughed in response as Colin opened the door. "Oh! Well." A glimmer of a smile spread over Akira's face. "Hello."

"Thanks for coming," he said easily, beckoning her inside.

"They haven't kissed again," Rose reported from over Akira's shoulder as she followed her in. "Natalya yells at him, though."

"Really?" Akira sounded entertained. "Yelling? She always seems so calm."

"What's that?" Colin asked.

Akira shook her head. "Just something Rose said."

Colin looked at Akira, his eyes narrowing and then a corner of his mouth lifted. "Grace used to call my ability to piss Nat off in two minutes or less my secret superpower."

"Not the most useful gift," Akira responded as Natalya emerged from the front bedroom, pulling the door closed behind her.

"Not really, no," he agreed.

Natalya looked between them and sighed. "Colin is here working on a case, and that's all."

"She gave him dinner, though. Chicken something. It looked good," Rose told Akira.

Akira didn't say anything, but she looked amused as she took a seat on the couch. "So how can I help?"

"Rose was the first person to find Kenzi," Colin answered readily, sitting in the chair across from Akira. "Anything she can tell us about where Kenzi came from or how she found her could be useful information."

"Aw, how sweet." Rose ran her hand through Colin's tawny hair, her touch not disturbing the short strands. "He called me a person."

"Rose," Akira said, a warning in her voice.

"He's cute. Not really my type, though. But they make a pretty couple, don't you think?" Rose gestured at Natalya who still stood by the door.

"Rose," Akira repeated, the warning tone a little clearer. Colin shifted in his seat, turning his head as if hoping to see what Akira was looking at.

"She should be nicer to him. He did die, after all." Rose slipped away from Colin and joined Akira on the couch.

"Did he?" Akira asked, interest replacing the reproof in her voice. Colin relaxed as Akira's gaze followed Rose's movement away from him.

"Oh, yes," Rose reported. "Dead as a doornail."

"But he's not now. Did you have something to do with that?"

"Hmm." Rose blinked. "Maybe. I'm not really sure."

Akira crossed her arms, looking exasperated. "You know, I warned Natalya you liked to be mysterious."

"I do not," Rose protested. "I don't know what happened." Akira might not believe her, but it was the truth. She and Colin had been having a pleasant conversation after his death. Maybe she'd been flirting a little, but she didn't have many opportunities to flirt these days. And then the little girl did something and Rose's energy went all shivery. Next thing she knew, Natalya was there and Colin was sitting up. She told Akira the story.

"Huh," Akira said thoughtfully.

"What's she saying?" Colin asked.

Akira shook her head as if to say it was nothing important. He opened his mouth as if to object, and she said hastily, "Tell me about the little girl, Rose. How did you find her?"

Rose sighed. Although she felt reluctant to share the details, she could tell Colin wouldn't give up. He was going to find the little girl's parents one way or another. She might as well give him what help she could, but she shared her reservations with Akira as she told her about the spirit at the hospital. Akira relayed the information, warnings and all.

Natalya and Colin exchanged a long look. "Not Hansel and Gretel, after all," Natalya said. "More like Snow White, I suppose. Or maybe Bluebeard."

"Yeah," Colin agreed. The single word held a weight of sorrow.

Natalya glanced over her shoulder at the closed door to Kenzi's bedroom. "She's asleep, but..." She stepped away from the door, moving to perch on the arm of the couch next to Akira. "We should keep it down. I don't want her to wake up."

Colin's expression was grim as he nodded.

Rose flitted up and off the sofa. She stuck her head through the wall into Kenzi's bedroom, near her bed. The girl's eyes were closed, her breath even. Rose popped her head back out and reported to Akira cheerfully, "She looks sound asleep to me. I'll keep checking."

Akira thanked her and then asked, "Was the spirit her mother, do you think?"

Rose shrugged. "Maybe. Probably, I guess."

"Poor kid," Akira muttered. "Seven is..."

"...too young," Natalya finished the thought and put a hand on Akira's shoulder, before moving to sit next to her. Both women had lost their mothers.

Colin turned in his chair to address Rose, but the direction of his gaze was off by a solid two feet. "Did the spirit give you a name?"

"Oh, look how polite he is," Rose said approvingly. "Trying to talk right to me." She sidled a few steps closer to the door so she could pretend he was looking at her.

"A name, Rose?" Akira prompted.

"She didn't say." Rose shook her head, Akira following suit.

"Can you describe her?" Colin asked.

Rose tried, but after a rattle-fire series of questions from Colin—height, weight, hair color, eye color, skin color, age—she could tell she was disappointing him. But she truly hadn't noticed much beyond the woman's desperation.

"Do you have any idea how the woman died?" Colin asked.

Rose thought back. The living people in the hospital had been talking, sometimes shouting. Could she remember any of their words? Nothing came to her, and she spread her hands helplessly. "No," she admitted.

"I'll check on all the deaths at the hospital," Colin said, pulling a small notepad out of his pocket and making a note with a frown. "There can't be too many in the right timeframe. We should be able to find her." He tucked the notepad back in his pocket. "What about the spot in the forest where you found the girl? Was it near a road? Any houses around?"

Rose brightened. "I bet I could take you back there. We walked a long way, but I think I'd be able to find it again."

"Great," Colin said with enthusiasm, but Akira looked noticeably less excited.

"How exactly do you plan to follow a ghost through the woods?" Natalya asked Colin, arching an eyebrow.

"Ah…" He looked closer at Akira and winced. "I guess you haven't been taking too many long hikes, huh?"

"I'm pregnant, not disabled," she told him, putting one hand on her rounded belly.

"Would you be willing to give it a try?" The question was tentative, as if Colin was unsure whether he should ask.

"Sure." Akira shrugged, but Natalya's brows drew down.

"What's wrong?" Colin asked immediately.

"I—" She shook her head without saying any more.

"Are you seeing something?" "Is it dangerous?" Colin and Akira spoke over one another.

Again, Natalya shook her head. Restlessly, she stood and paced across the room. "No, it's not my precognition. And medically, there's no reason a healthy pregnant woman can't hike a reasonable distance. " She turned back, facing them, crossing her arms over her chest. "But I'm worried. Something feels wrong."

"Could it be Rose?" Akira asked.

"Hey!" Rose protested. There was nothing wrong with her.

"What do you mean?" Natalya asked, her hands relaxing but her arms not dropping.

"Some people are more sensitive to the presence of spirits than others," Akira explained. "Ghosts can make rooms colder. Those temperature drops are a measurable physical reality."

"Ha. Now you tell them." Rose bounced on the sofa. "Tell them not to ignore me next time."

Akira's lips curved up. "I guess you experienced that already. But people who are sensitive to ghosts also sometimes have an emotional reaction to their presence. Sometimes it's uneasiness or fear. Sometimes it's warmth or a sense of peace. Rose is worried, too." Akira gestured in Rose's direction, even though the others couldn't see her. "Maybe you're picking up on that."

Natalya didn't look reassured, but Colin said, "We'll be careful. We need to trace her family, but we won't just hand her over to them."

"Yeah, you better not," Rose said with an emphatic nod that set her blonde curls to bobbing. "Because if anything happens to her, you better believe I'm gonna be haunting you for the rest of your life."

❧ CHAPTER TEN ❧

"I'm not going to ask him that, Rose."

Colin suppressed his grin as he pushed a branch that Akira had passed under with ease out of his way. "I don't mind."

Akira glanced over her shoulder at him, her cheeks pink with the cold but her eyes bright. She'd been toughing out their walk through the forest with impressive energy. "You don't know what she wants to know."

He lifted a shoulder. "We've already established I don't watch nearly enough television, my musical tastes are sadly narrow, and ghosts can't read books unless someone turns the pages. Shouldn't we be on movies now? How does she feel about *Star Wars*?"

When he'd met Akira at the parking lot Rose deemed closest to her entry point to the forest, he'd handed her a bright orange vest and suggested they talk loudly. It was still hunting season, and over-eager hunters had been known to hear scuffling in the leaves and shoot first, look too late.

The conversation had been stilted initially. Colin had met Akira before, of course, but casually, and knowing they were walking with an invisible person only she could see or hear was unsettling despite his desire to accept her ability with his usual calm. For the first half hour or so, Akira herself had seemed uneasy, reluctant to say more than pleasantries about the weather, the climate, and her upcoming wedding. But when Colin had made it clear he didn't mind talking to Rose through her, the conversation had gotten much livelier. Rose appeared to be insatiably curious.

Akira listened, and then reported, "She doesn't like the one where the kids die, but she doesn't want to talk about movies. She wants to know…" She paused and glanced back at him again. As they'd walked, they'd been passing through scrub pine growth, mostly narrow trees with grey trunks and sparse boughs, but they were nearing the edge of the tree line.

"What is it?" Colin took a few extra steps and fell into place next to her as they left the trees for a white sandy path on the edge of the prairie, trees on one side, tall grasses on the other.

107

"She wants to know why you didn't try to stop yourself from dying."

Colin blinked. He hadn't expected that. "You mean the other night?"

"At all. The other night or any time in the years since Natalya's premonition. Why didn't you—oh, I don't know. Move to New York City and become a big-city cop? Give up police work and move to Antarctica? Most people fight death with everything in them. You let it happen." Her words could have been accusing, but her expression held no challenge, only interest.

Colin raised an eyebrow. Should he mention she hadn't waited for Rose to speak? Rose might have asked the original question but it was obvious Akira wanted answers, too. "I'm a Florida boy and a cop's kid," he said. "Never wanted to be anywhere else. Never wanted to do anything else." His chuckle was rueful. "If I could go back now, I'd do it different. But at the time, staying made sense to me."

"Why?" Akira asked without hesitation.

Colin stuffed his hands in his jacket pockets and hunched his shoulders. He could tell her it was none of her business. But a part of him wanted to talk about it. And someday—someday if he got lucky—she'd be a relation, his brother-in-law's wife, so technically his sister. Maybe he'd start treating her like one a little ahead of schedule. "Nat's knowledge doesn't come date-stamped. I didn't know when I'd die, just that I would. I thought it'd be soon, probably real soon."

Her voice softened as she said, "That must have been hard."

Colin's lips quirked in a wry smile. Hard wouldn't have been his first choice of description. Horrifying, maybe. Devastating. He'd had plans and they'd all come crashing down around him.

"Mostly when she sees something clearly, it's because it's about to happen. Take finals. She could tell me an hour before a final how I was going to do, but a week before, nothing. It's not exactly helpful to know you should have studied harder when you're out of time."

"Interesting."

"And she never had been able to figure out our future. We both wanted a big family, lots of kids, but she'd never seen them. Never seen the wedding, never seen the honeymoon."

"Those do seem like moments she'd remember." Akira kicked at the sandy ground, staring down at it, not looking in his direction.

Colin could feel the sympathy emanating from her. He went on steadily, saying, "Sometimes her foresight caused the problem. This one time, she was all upset. She wouldn't let me drive to school, because she knew I'd crash the car. I got a ride with my friend Jake and he crashed his car. She still got the phone call saying I'd been in an accident, but it wasn't what she'd expected it to be."

"She mentioned something along those lines. That sometimes her actions created the future she remembered."

"If I'd driven that day, I would have gotten to school on time."

"But you didn't think she was wrong about your death?"

"I knew what she saw would happen the way she saw it. Maybe she didn't understand exactly what it was or maybe she had some of the details wrong, but running away wasn't going to change anything. We argued about it, over and over again."

Akira bit her lip. "Is that why you broke up with her? Because you couldn't stand the arguments?"

"No, of course not," Colin protested, but Akira was looking at the path ahead of them, her head angled as if she were listening to Rose. "What's Rose saying?"

Akira acknowledged the question with a quick smile, dimples flashing. "She says she thinks you like to argue with Natalya. Or at least to tease her."

"Making up always made it worth it," Colin said, his own lips tugging up at the corners.

"So why?"

Colin's smile faded. "She deserved better. A husband who'd grow old with her, kids who'd have a father."

Akira snorted. "I don't think she agreed with you."

His hands, still hidden inside his pockets, tightened into fists. "No. No, she didn't."

Damn it, how could he have screwed up so badly? Had it all been inevitable? But if so, what did that mean for the future? His future? Their future?

"I wonder if quantum physics can explain her ability," Akira said. "Maybe it's like Schrodinger's cat. The rest of us have to wait until the box is opened to know whether the cat lives or dies, but Natalya knows once it happens. But not until it happens. Like a wave function."

Colin made a noncommittal hum. He vaguely remembered

something about a cat and physics but he had no idea what a wave function was.

"Or maybe more like a human tide table," Akira went on, sounding dreamy.

"A tide table?" Colin shot a startled glance in her direction. He wasn't sure whether to laugh or take her seriously.

"Imagine time is an ocean." Akira waved her hand in front of her in an up-down pattern, simulating waves. "We're swimming in it. Individual waves are unpredictable, but the tide's not. It's part of a pattern, controlled by the moon. Natalya and Max, they can see the pattern."

"I don't think Nat sees patterns," Colin said cautiously.

"No, no, not like that. Obviously what she has is a perceptual ability, in some sense, like vision or hearing. But time could be predictable in the way that oceans are predictable. Natalya sees the currents, the tides. Not everything, but the path in front of her, even as her own actions create it."

"Hmm…" Colin's brow furrowed. Did Akira's ideas fit with his experience of Nat's foresight? Maybe.

"I'm not making sense, am I?" Akira smiled at him apologetically. "Sorry. I just love the scientific possibilities inherent in the things we don't understand. It's real mind candy, so fun to contemplate."

Since leaving college, Colin hadn't spent much time thinking about science. Certainly not for fun. But the reminder of school brought back a distant memory. He squinted, making an effort to recall the exact words, and then offered, "There is a tide in the affairs of men?"

Akira's eyes narrowed. "And women, too. Did you just quote somebody at me?"

"You obviously didn't have Mrs. Martinez for eleventh grade English." The words were flooding back to him. Clearing his throat, he gestured widely with one arm in the direction of the prairie, and spoke. "There is a tide in the affairs of men which, taken at the flood, leads on to fortune; Omitted, all the voyage of their life is bound in shallows and in miseries. On such a full sea are we now afloat; and we must take the current when it serves, or lose our ventures."

"Shakespeare?" Akira hazarded a guess.

"Yep. Julius Caesar, Act 4, Scene 2. One of the many speeches Mrs. Martinez made us memorize. I could probably do all of 'To be or not to be' and 'But soft, what light through yonder window breaks,' too."

"I never liked Shakespeare. Too confusing."

Colin scratched his head. "Wave functions? Dead cats?"

Akira laughed. "Fair point. But do you even know what the speech you quoted means?"

"Sure," Colin responded. "Fate versus free will. An opportunity exists—that's fate—but taking it is up to us. Free will."

He frowned. In a way, he'd done the opposite. He'd believed in fate, so much so that he'd given up his opportunities. He'd gotten trapped in the shallows, in a life emptier than the one he would have chosen. Damn it, if he'd known Nat's prediction might not come true, he would have lived his life very differently. But her predictions had always come true before, always.

"Nice," Akira said. "And pretty much what I meant. Our choices do matter. But there can also be an inevitability about the future, like the tide coming in on time every day."

"But I didn't die."

"An earthquake hit," Akira replied promptly.

"An earthquake?"

"Rose-shaped." Akira paused for a minute and then laughed again. She must have been responding to something Rose said as she added, "All right, so earthquakes don't have shapes. But an earthquake can cause a tsunami, changing the tides."

"Not permanently, though." Colin's lips tightened. He wanted to believe he'd been given a second chance. An opportunity to live out his life and die in a peaceful old age. But if he was fated to die young...

"Sometimes permanently," Akira corrected him. "If a quake changes the geography of the land, the tides adapt. They flow around the new surfaces."

"So fate's fluid? Despite's Nat's ability to see what the future will bring?"

"Yes." Akira gave a firm nod. "When you run into an ange—erm... into a spirit like Rose, all bets are off."

"Into a what?" Colin asked.

Akira put a finger to her lips and then grimaced, squeezing her eyes shut as if she were responding to being scolded. She hunched up her shoulders like a guilty little girl. "I know." A pause. "I'm sorry.

Yes, of course I heard you."

Colin tried to puzzle out what she'd said. When you run into an angerm? An ang—erm? And then his eyebrows shot up as he realized what Akira had almost said. A what? His memories were fuzzy, but he was pretty sure Rose had looked like a normal girl to him. But then what did he know about angels?

"I know," Akira repeated. "No halo, no wings, no harp, not an angel, got it. But Rose…" She fell silent again.

In his front pocket, Colin's phone vibrated. As Akira continued to listen to Rose, he pulled it out and glanced at the display. Joyce. He should take it.

With a laconic, "Yep?" he answered the call.

"Where are you, Sheriff?" Joyce's voice held an impatient edge.

"Damn fine question," he answered her. They'd been hiking for at least four or five hours. How far had they gone?

"Damn lousy answer," Joyce muttered. "Did you forget your meeting with the accountant?"

Colin winced. Oh, hell. He'd thought his schedule was clear. He wasn't supposed to be on duty today, which had meant a fine opportunity to follow up on a lead he had no intention of sharing with anyone in the office. It was Tassamara so folks were tolerant of the unusual, but he had a reputation for skepticism he intended to maintain. Talking about ghosts wouldn't do it. "Ah…"

"How fast can you get back here?" she interrupted him.

"Not fast. I'm in the middle of nowhere." They'd headed south, deep into the forest, before reaching the trail leading along the prairie. Within minutes, if they stayed on the trail, they should be headed back into forest, this time the deep, tropical growth that flourished around the springs and lakes. A road shouldn't be too far away. Still, he'd need to call a deputy to pick them up. Their cars were miles behind them. "At least an hour, probably more."

Joyce's sigh held a wealth of exasperation. "As sheriff, you have responsibilities—"

"I know, I know," he interrupted her in turn. He could recite Joyce's responsibility speech by heart. He heard it every time he didn't finish his paperwork as promptly as she would like. Distracting her was the only way to defuse her. "Have you checked the hospital records yet?"

"Of course." She sounded smug, but less satisfied when she

added, "But there are no deaths fitting the description you gave me."

"None?" Colin didn't understand how that could be possible. It was a hospital. People died at hospitals.

"You said female, aged between twenty to fifty, deceased within the last week. No one fitting that description has passed at the hospital this week."

Could he have gotten the wrong hospital? The wrong age? "Anyone dead on arrival?"

"Not that I was told." There was a pause before Joyce added, "I assume the administrator I spoke with would have been intelligent enough to tell me if so."

"Let's not assume that." He glanced at Akira. He could interrogate Rose again, at least to check on the hospital, but he'd rather not do so while Joyce waited impatiently on the phone. "Check the clinics, too, and forget the age range. And expand our timeline. Make it ten days instead of a week. I want to know about every recently deceased woman in a thirty mile radius since before Christmas. I don't care how many calls it takes."

"How about I start with one call? The local health department will have death certificates on file for all deaths that occurred at least seventy-two hours ago."

"Good, start there."

"All right," Joyce sounded agreeable, before she asked pointedly, "What do you want me to do about the accountant? He's waiting in your office."

Colin paused and thought. It ought to be a straightforward meeting. The budgets weren't complicated. "Take the meeting for me. Let me know if there's anything I need to know. Leave the paperwork on my desk and I'll sign off on it when I get back to the office. You can do that, right?"

"Of course I can. I know the budget better than you do."

"Yep," Colin agreed cordially, ignoring Joyce's tone. Getting her involved in all aspects of his job was one of the ways he'd prepared for his death. When the day came that he never made it back to the office, Joyce would have made the transition to a new sheriff seamless. "I'll call when I know my schedule."

He tapped off the phone call and stuffed his phone into his pocket. He'd been right about where Rose was headed. They'd entered the deep forest, one of the richly verdant areas scattered around the national park. Spanish moss draped from oak trees like grey shrouds over the deep green of the undergrowth.

Akira stopped. "Okay, we're here."

Colin looked around them. "Here?"

No distinguishing features separated this patch of trees from any other patch of tropical forest.

Akira nodded. "Rose says yes."

Colin pulled out his phone again, calling up an app to check the GPS coordinates of their location. The numbers meant nothing to him. He frowned down at the screen, pulling up the map. Nope, still meaningless.

"Does Rose have any idea which direction Kenzi came from?"

Akira paused before shaking her head. "How did you find your way back here, Rose?"

They'd taken the ghost girl at her word that she could retrace her steps through the forest, but for much of the way, she hadn't followed anything as obvious as a trail.

Akira blinked and her eyebrows arched upward, before pulling down as she asked, "Are you teasing me?"

Rose must have said yes because Akira smiled. "Seriously, though, how?"

"What did she say?" Colin asked.

Akira waved a hand. "She said she followed a rift in the space-time continuum."

Colin chuckled.

"She doesn't really know, though. She felt pulled here and then pulled to where you found Kenzi. She could take us there if we wanted."

"Why did you take her all the way there, Rose? There's a much closer road to the south." Colin crouched, eyeing the ground for signs of tracks or indications of human presence.

"She says that's where Kenzi needed to be," Akira reported. "Also to look under that bush over there. That's where she first saw her."

Colin followed the direction of Akira's pointing finger and stood, crossing to the bush in question. No evidence leaped out at him. He looked down at his map again, sliding to enlarge it. Which direction would Kenzi have come from? To the east lay water, one of the ponds that dotted the forest, and to the south, a road led to the town of Sweet Springs. To the west, there was nothing but more prairie until the land turned back into pine scrub, and they'd come from the north.

The best bet was probably to head for the road and check out the area. Maybe she'd come from one of the closest houses. But he found his feet turning toward the east. The undergrowth to the south was tangled and dense. To the east, overgrown saw palmettos and cabbage palms clustered close together. A small child could have walked between the eastern trees easily, unlike the path to the south.

He ducked under the sharp-edged leaves of a palmetto, scanning the scenery, looking for anything that might provide a clue to Kenzi's original direction. Nothing jumped out at him as he walked forward. The trees were much denser than the scrub pine landscape but typical of the tropical forests found around water.

Except... His eyes narrowed.

Those plants weren't ferns.

Oh, hell.

He stilled, putting up an abrupt hand to stop Akira. She was still chatting to Rose, her light voice clear on the cold breeze.

"Hush," he ordered in a harsh whisper, eyes searching for signs of movement, evidence of life.

Akira took a few steps forward, joining him. "Don't we want to let the hunters know we're coming?" she asked in a whisper of her own.

Colin pointed. "Not hunters who might be guarding their illegal crops." Talking would make them easy targets if one of the drug dealers responsible for the patch of marijuana plants growing around them was nearby.

The forest wasn't quiet. Colin could hear birds, jays yelling and the musical trill of sparrows or warblers, and leaves rustling in the wind. But nothing that sounded like human beings moving through the woods.

"Wait here," he told Akira, planning to take a closer look at their surroundings. "Don't get shot."

Akira snorted, a sound suspiciously like a chuckle. "Better idea," she suggested, putting a hand on Colin's arm before he could move away. "We both stay here and let Rose explore. She'll tell us if there's anyone around and it's tough to shoot a spirit."

Colin glanced at her in surprise, feeling his lips relax into a smile. "Ghostly reconnaissance? Handy."

"Rose," she said, voice hushed. "Could you—okay. She's on her way."

The two stood together in silence for several minutes, Akira frowning as she stared in the direction Rose must have gone, Colin scanning their surroundings in quiet tension.

Akira's sigh of relief was the signal Colin needed.

"Good?" he asked.

She nodded. "No sign of anyone. Rose found a campsite down by the water, but she says it looks abandoned."

Colin didn't let himself relax. "I'll call this in to the rangers. They'll send a team out to clear up the site and collect any evidence." Shelby answered on the first ring. He filled her in, providing her with the GPS coordinates, before finally closing his phone.

Akira stood by, waiting for him to finish. When he did, she gestured toward the water. "Can we go take a look at the campsite or would that be like disturbing a crime scene?"

"Any dead bodies down there?" Colin asked, only partially serious. He hoped Rose would have mentioned anything along those lines before he called for help.

Akira shook her head.

"I think we can take the risk, then."

The two of them walked through the marijuana plants, Akira in the lead. Colin would have preferred to be on point himself, but since he couldn't see Rose, he took rear guard, inspecting the territory around them and behind them as they moved.

The plants were tucked under the trees, relatively far away from the water. The patch wasn't huge, only thirty-five or forty plants. The growers might not be pros, just locals taking advantage of the forest's relative safety. Growing pot in national forests was big business, but Ocala historically had less of that activity than other regions. Meth labs were sadly more common.

Colin paused at the edge of the field. Examining the sandy soil without touching it, he kicked at the ground until he found the irrigation system he expected. The growers were using a simple hose set-up to shunt water from the pond to their field. Nothing elaborate, but effective enough in the Florida climate.

Hurrying to catch up to Akira, he paused at the edge of the campsite Rose had found. He understood immediately why she'd decided it was abandoned, instead of simply unoccupied at the moment. Something about it reeked of desolation. Maybe it was the two-person tent, ties flapping in the wind, middle drooping like a tired old man. Maybe it was the scattered trash and personal belongings. Or the lone sock caught in the roots of a tree, as if someone had rushed to pack up without looking behind them when they left.

"Do you think Kenzi was living here?" Akira's eyes were troubled.

Colin rubbed his chin, thinking. Slowly, he shook his head. "She makes her bed. She sets the table. She eats what's put in front of her. If she was here, it wasn't for long. She's not a kid who's been living rough in the woods."

Akira looked reassured, but there was a queasy feeling in the back of Colin's throat. A memory itched at him, a thought he couldn't quite grasp.

Marijuana growers.

A lost girl.

Could they have something in common?

CHAPTER ELEVEN

Natalya worried. She hated it, but she couldn't seem to help herself, and she hated that, too.

Seeing the future had never been as useful as one might imagine. Oh, sure, she'd probably saved a few lives with her gift. When a seemingly healthy patient walked into the emergency room complaining of a headache, the knowledge that she'd be scrambling to lower his dangerously elevated blood pressure in the near future meant she moved him to the front of the line. But that incident and others like it led to uncomfortable questions and odd looks.

And the silly stuff never worked out. She didn't know the lottery numbers, probably because she never won so they weren't important enough for her to remember. She still forgot to bring an umbrella on rainy days. Sports were boring when the winner was never in question and card games lost all their appeal when every turn of the deck was predictable. Not to mention no one she knew would play with her.

No, her precognition had always been more of a curse than a blessing. But losing it left her feeling like she was standing, blindfolded, at the edge of a chasm, where one false move would send her tumbling over the edge.

She stared at the blank canvas in front of her. The underpainting was done and dry, waiting for her to start sketching. A sampling of her drawings of her father was pinned to the wall. The blinds were up, letting in the clear natural light of a wintry Florida day. She had no reason not to get to work.

But her studio didn't feel right.

Nothing felt right.

It wasn't because her studio had become Kenzi's bedroom with startling rapidity. She didn't mind that she'd had to put most of her paints into boxes to make room for a small dresser to hold the clothes the little girl was accumulating. Or that she'd had to do the tone coat on the canvas outside, so Kenzi wouldn't have to sleep surrounded by the smell of linseed oil. And sketching while Kenzi played contentedly with the over-the-top dollhouse Grace had brought by that morning ought to be easy. Kenzi was peaceful company most of the time.

But the feeling of foreboding was like ants crawling on the back of her neck, a prickling sense of danger, danger, danger. Without conscious thought, her hand started to move. Quick, light strokes. Fine lines, shading, charcoal angling smoothly across the burnt sienna surface of the canvas. Darker lines, deeper, heavier, almost a scribble of black curves until the charcoal snapped from the pressure and she stepped away from her easel. What the hell?

She glanced at the sketches on the wall. In them, she'd caught her father's warmth, his lively curiosity, the quality of focus he gave to his conversations as if nothing could be more important to him than the person he was with. It was in his eyes.

This man's eyes were cold.

She hadn't drawn her father. But who had she drawn? She'd never seen him before.

"What. The. Hell." She spoke aloud, oblivious of the little girl a few feet away.

Behind her, Kenzi yelped. It was a squeak of fear, and the first vocalization Natalya had heard her make.

Natalya spun as the dollhouse crashed to the ground, toppling over from the weight of the little girl scrambling over it in her rush to the door.

"Kenzi, no," Natalya called out to the girl's back. "I wasn't—I didn't mean—"

She sighed and said in a voice she knew the girl couldn't hear. "I wasn't swearing at you."

She set down the charcoal, wiping the dust off her fingers and onto her paint-splattered shirt. She should have been more careful. She didn't think her tone sounded angry, but Kenzi didn't handle anger well. And then Natalya's eyes narrowed. She glanced from the easel to the door and back again.

Oh, damn, she was stupid.

Natalya hurried after Kenzi. Her eyes swept the living room, a quick check to see that the girl wasn't hiding under the tables before she headed straight to the bathroom closet. Kenzi wasn't buried in the back of it as she had been before. Frowning, Natalya checked the tub and behind the door, then more slowly, went back to the kitchen. The back door was closed, deadbolt locked. Her eyes scanned the room, but there was no place to hide. She checked the linen closet on her way to the bedroom, then her bedroom closet, but Kenzi wasn't on the shelves or crouched in the back behind her clothes.

She looked around her room.

Where could Kenzi be? Her house just wasn't large enough to have many hiding places. She crouched to look under the king-size bed, despite knowing the little girl couldn't possibly fit because of the boxes stored under it. A pair of small feet tucked up at the top revealed that she was wrong.

Natalya knelt for a moment, wondering what to do. Crossing to the other side of the bed, she lay down flat on the floor. From this position, Kenzi was totally hidden. If Natalya had looked under the bed when she came into the room instead of after checking the closet, she would never have seen her.

"You're not hiding because I said a bad word, are you?" she asked, her voice gentle. She waited for a response, but wasn't surprised not to get one. The carpet felt scratchy against her cheek and her nose itched as if the dust might make her sneeze but she ignored the discomfort. "Do you think you know the man in my drawing?"

Still no response, but the silence felt frozen, as if Kenzi was holding her breath.

"I don't know him. I just drew a picture that came into my head. But that's what scared you, isn't it?"

Still no response.

"I'm scared, too." The words slipped out without forethought.

Immediately, she cursed herself silently. What the hell kind of grown-up tells a troubled child that she's afraid? What an idiotic thing to do. But a rustle from under the bed told her Kenzi was pushing a box aside.

In the shadows, Natalya couldn't see much but there was enough light to let her see Kenzi's searching gaze.

"I am," Natalya repeated herself. "I don't know why. I don't know what there is to be afraid of. Do you know?"

Kenzi didn't answer her.

"We're safe here," Natalya told her. She slid her arm under her cheek, hoping to get more comfortable, but her discomfort wasn't caused by the hard floor. It was the surge of dread rising in her throat at her own words. "You don't think so," she whispered. The words weren't quite a question.

Kenzi shook her head.

Natalya stared at her, trying to put the pieces together.

Her gift was back. Not completely, not like it used to be. But the nightmarish feeling, the sketch—those were premonitions, not random.

"Do you recognize the man in my drawing?" she asked Kenzi, keeping her voice steady with an effort.

Kenzi turned her face away, burying her expression in the darkness under the bed.

"Kenzi, I can keep us safe," Natalya said. "Colin is the police. He can keep us safe. I promise you, he can. But not if you don't tell us what we should be afraid of."

Kenzi took a gasping breath, the kind of shaky inhalation presaging tears. But she didn't say anything and she didn't start crying.

Natalya reached under the bed and touched the top of Kenzi's head, feeling the smooth silk of her hair under her fingertips. What could she do? How could she comfort the girl? Kenzi must have scoped out this hiding place earlier in the week, maybe right after Natalya found her in the bathroom closet. What must her life have been like if she searched for hiding places as a matter of course?

"I want to help you," Natalya said softly. "But sweetheart, you need to help yourself, too. I know…"

She paused. She had deliberately sheltered Kenzi from their conversation with Rose. Little girls didn't need to know about ghosts and she'd been worried about the long-term consequences if Kenzi started talking to outsiders—like that psychologist—about her experiences. But what did Kenzi know already? "You drew a picture of a girl in a pink dress," she said, voice cautious. "You saw that girl when you were lost in the woods, didn't you?"

Silence from under the bed.

"Her name is Rose."

A scramble as boxes shifted. Natalya rolled away, pushing herself up as Kenzi pulled herself out from under the bed and stared at her, eyes wide. The little girl opened her mouth as if to speak and then closed it again, pressing her lips together as if the words were struggling to fly free and she fighting them. She swallowed hard.

Natalya reached out and stroked a bit of hair out of Kenzi's face. "Someone told you not to talk," she said. "Someone told you to run,

122

to hide, not to say a word. And you're trying so hard to do what you were told, aren't you?"

Her lips stayed tightly pressed together, but her chin wobbled. Natalya could see the answer in Kenzi's eyes. What now? She wasn't about to tell Kenzi her mother was likely dead—that job was reserved for a time when the knowledge was sure and certain, not speculation. But how could she reassure Kenzi enough that the little girl would tell her the truth?

The doorbell rang.

Suddenly, the dread was back. Natalya's stomach churned as she glanced over her shoulder.

It was broad daylight.

She was in her own home.

The doors were locked.

She had no reason to be afraid. But she was. The fear felt almost like a living thing, grabbing her and twisting. She put a hand on her abdomen, pressing against it, and looked back at Kenzi.

"Sweetheart," she said, "I'm sure this is nothing. But you go ahead and hide again." Kenzi's lips parted in surprise but Natalya nodded at her, gesturing toward the bed. "Quickly, go on now."

She waited until the girl obediently slithered under the bed again and then helped her position the boxes, feeling her heartbeat pulsing at her throat.

Leaves on water, she reminded herself, trying to calm her racing thoughts. It was probably Grace at the door, bringing more furniture for the dollhouse. She'd promised to come by again after the afternoon mail delivery.

Undoubtedly, Natalya was being ridiculous.

Of course, she was being ridiculous.

But telling herself so didn't calm her pounding heart as she walked toward the front door. Leaves on water, she told herself again. Leaves on water. Why the hell was calming meditation so hard?

At the door, she called out, "Yes, who is it?"

She never did that. It was Tassamara, home. She knew her neighbors. She knew every person who would drop by. The doorbell rang and she opened the door. That was how it worked. But not today.

She pressed herself against the door, trying to hear a response. Grace's voice, she told herself. It will be Grace... except Grace never bothered with the doorbell, she just let herself in. So maybe a delivery guy? A package she needed to sign for?

"Excuse me, ma'am, I'm sorry to disturb you."

Natalya's brows drew down. That sounded like a boy. A young boy, maybe in his early teens.

"I was wondering if I could use your phone? My grampa and me, our car's broke down."

Natalya pulled away from the door.

She stared at it. A car breakdown. On her dead-end road?

"Where were you going?" she called out.

The answer was slow to come. "Fishing, ma'am. On the lake."

In the middle of the day?

Natalya's heartbeat was so loud in her ears she almost missed a muffled aside as if the boy were whispering to someone else.

She closed her eyes and pressed her hands against her face, trying desperately to think. Okay, two people out there. One of them, maybe, the scary man Kenzi feared. One of them, a young boy. She could send him on his way easily enough, but what then? If they'd found Kenzi and were lying to get to her, they'd be back. And the boy might need help as much as Kenzi did.

But maybe she was being ridiculous. Maybe that was just a young boy, going fishing with his grandfather, experiencing car trouble, nothing to worry about.

She snorted, a sound audible and louder than she expected, and then rubbed her hands across her face, shaking her head in decision. No one went fishing in the middle of the day. The car breakdown was bad enough, but fishing was a stupid lie.

"Hang on, I'll get my phone," she yelled through the door, keeping her voice steady.

She'd call Colin. He might still be out marching around the woods with Akira and Rose, searching for Kenzi's starting point, but he'd send help. And a nice police officer, preferably in uniform, joining the two people on her doorstep would make everything so much simpler.

She retrieved her phone from the kitchen. Standing in the archway between the kitchen and the living room, she found Colin's number in her caller ID and pressed the call button. Eyes on the front door, she waited for him to answer.

Her heart was pounding, she realized. His phone only rang twice before he picked up, but the time stretched out like saltwater taffy. What was the boy doing? Was he waiting patiently? She hadn't exactly been welcoming, but did he believe she was going to open the door to him?

"Nat? Everything okay?"

The sound of Colin's familiar voice, the warmth and the worry, sent a rush of relief flowing down her spine.

"Colin, good, you're there," Natalya said, keeping her voice as calm and steady as if she were issuing orders in the emergency room. "I need you to send a deputy to the house—one in uniform."

"A deputy? What's going on?" His tone sharpened, instantly concerned.

"Someone—I think—I can't tell..." Natalya inhaled and then exhaled as slowly as she could bring herself to. She should have organized her thoughts instead of worrying about what the boy was up to. "I think my foresight's coming back. There's a boy at my door, maybe with company."

"And you think he's trouble?"

"He's connected to Kenzi, I'm sure of it. But he claims his grandfather's car broke down while they were on their way to fish on the lake. He's asking to use my phone."

"Fishing? This time of day?"

Natalya felt her lips turning up. She loved the way Colin jumped to the same conclusions she did. Back when they watched television together, they'd always liked guessing the culprit in their favorite shows. "That's what I said."

"All right, I'm going to need to put you on hold to call in. But stay on the line. Don't hang up and don't let go of the phone."

"Got it," Natalya answered.

"And don't open the door," Colin ordered.

Natalya rolled her eyes. Did he think she was stupid? She had no intention of opening the door. But as the line went quiet, she heard a jangle of breaking glass followed by a crash as the glass fell to the ground from the room behind her.

Natalya whirled.

A thin arm was reaching through the window of her kitchen door, feeling around for the interior lock.

Natalya yelled, "Don't you dare!"

She lunged for the knife block next to the stove, grabbing the

125

smooth handle of her biggest chef's knife. She didn't know what she'd do with it—it wasn't as if she would slice up a kid, not even one who smashed her window and tried to break into her house—but maybe she could scare him off. Him and the grandfather she had yet to see.

But as she spun to face the door, the kid screamed. "Oh, shit. It hurts, it hurts. Mac! Mac! Travis, help me!" His hand withdrew from the window as abruptly as it had appeared.

Nat dropped the knife and the phone. The red on the shards of glass still caught in the frame told the story. Without hesitating, she leaped to the door, fumbling with the deadbolt, finally yanking the door open.

"You idiot," she scolded him. "What did you think you were doing?"

His left hand clutched his right forearm, blood spurting from between his fingers. She took it in with one quick glance, then darted back inside and grabbed a clean dish towel from the drawer by the sink. She hurried back out again.

"Sit," she ordered, pushing his shoulder until he folded onto the porch steps. "Arm up."

He was moaning, rocking slightly, muttering "oh, shit, oh, shit," under his breath. He didn't move to obey her, still holding his arm, so she crouched in front of him.

"Arm up," she repeated herself. "Elevate to slow the bleeding, pressure to stop it. You're going to be okay. Let me help you."

He blinked at her, brown eyes framed by dark lashes looking imploring. "I need Mac."

"Is he around front? I'll get him, but let's get the bleeding stopped first." Natalya lifted his arm gently. He'd hit the radial artery. Fortunately, the laceration wasn't long, although it was deep. She pressed the dish towel against his forearm, holding it firmly in place even as he winced away.

"Not a he," the kid said.

Natalya barely heard him, most of her attention on his arm. She'd need to check if he'd gotten glass in the cut. They'd need to clean it out. He should get a tetanus shot and maybe stitches. "Are your vaccinations up-to-date?"

"My what?"

"Shots?" she asked him. "Does your mom take you in for

checkups?" His clothes were well-worn, t-shirt faded and blue jeans dirty. For plenty of families in Florida, routine health care was a luxury item.

"Ain't got a mom." He sniffled. Natalya guessed he was trying hard not to cry, and estimated his age a year or two downward. Eleven, maybe.

Thudding footsteps sounded from the side of the house. Natalya glanced that way as another boy rounded the corner. This one was older, a teenager, maybe sixteen or seventeen. He had the lanky look of a boy spurting into adulthood, with long legs and arms that looked too big for slender shoulders to carry.

"Mitchell, what did you do?" The boy skidded to a stop next to them.

"Learned how stupid it is to try to break into people's houses," Natalya said with a bite in her voice, as she rose, bringing the younger boy's arm up and over his head.

"Never hurt myself before," Mitchell protested.

"Oh, you make a habit of this?" Her fingers pressed tighter on the towel and the boy yelped. "Sorry," she said, loosening them slightly but still keeping the pressure on. Blood was seeping through the towel, a stain slowly beginning to grow.

"Shut up, Mitchell." Worry put lines on the older boy's face that belied his age. "Did you find Mac?"

"Didn't get a chance. She was on the phone." The jerk of his head at Natalya made it clear he was referring to her.

"We gotta find her and get outta here." The older boy moved as if to shove past them and up the steps.

Natalya shifted to block him. "Oh, no, you don't."

"Lady, you don't want to get in our way." The grimness in his voice, like the lines in his face, didn't belong there.

"Your friend here needs to go to the hospital." Natalya stood firm, but she couldn't resist a glance toward her bedroom window. Mac? Could they be talking about Kenzi?

"My brother," the boy corrected her, touching the younger boy's shoulder with a possessive hand.

Natalya's eyebrows rose. She supposed it was possible they were related, but they didn't look much alike. Maybe half-brothers? Or loyal step-brothers?

"He'll be fine as soon as we find our sister," the older boy continued.

Natalya's lips parted in surprise—could Kenzi be related to these boys?—before she pressed them together and scowled. "He'll be fine as soon as he gets stitches and a tetanus shot. Where's your grandfather?"

The older boy grunted, but Mitchell gave a quiet whimper.

Natalya put her free hand on his cheek to comfort him and said, voice gentler, "It'll only hurt for a minute or two." The stain on the towel didn't seem to be growing any bigger. The blood must be clotting, the bleeding slowing.

"Not if he catches us," Mitchell mumbled, his eyes down. A tear clung to his eyelashes and then trickled free.

"Yeah, which means we need to get outta here." The older boy tried to stare Natalya down but she didn't budge.

She only had to delay these boys another ten minutes or so. A deputy would be on the way. And since she'd dropped the phone, a whole slew of them might be on the way, lights flashing and sirens blaring. Colin would be doing his version of freaking out, which probably still meant barking orders and moving fast.

"Mac! Mac!" The older boy abruptly bellowed, loudly enough that Natalya flinched, tugging the younger boy's arm. He groaned.

"Quit yelling," she snapped at the older boy, annoyed at her own reaction. "You're not going anywhere."

For a second, his hands clenched into fists and his shoulders hunched up as he glared at her. Then his shoulders dropped and his fists uncurled. "I'm real sorry about this, ma'am," he said with unexpected politeness, one hand sliding behind his back.

The gun he was holding when he slid it back out looked ridiculously large.

❧ CHAPTER TWELVE ❧

Hell.

Natalya's heart was pounding again. Here it was, the danger she'd been anticipating. She had a momentary flash of realization—she didn't much care if this boy killed her, but it would break her heart if he hurt Kenzi and she could have stopped him. The thought was clarifying. She didn't shift her position.

"The police are already on their way," she said, keeping her voice soft. "Killing me will destroy your life. There's no way you'll get away with it. And it won't help your brother."

"I don't want to kill you," the boy said, his voice much too steady, his hands too tight on the gun. "I just want my sister."

The back door flew open and Kenzi burst out, her arms stretched in front of her as if she were going to hug the boy. Or push him off the steps, Natalya realized, as Kenzi skidded to a stop next to her and glared at him, making a shoving motion with her hands without touching him.

"Mac!" Both boys exclaimed at the same moment, the younger one with relief, the older one with surprise.

They spoke over one another, as the older boy said, "We're here to rescue you," while the younger one said, "I got cut, Mac. It's bad."

Natalya couldn't let go of Mitchell's arm. The bleeding might start again. But she put her other arm out, blocking Kenzi from going any farther. "Go back inside," she ordered, her throat tightening with fear.

The little girl stamped her foot and shook her head, making wide motioning gestures with her hands.

The older boy relaxed, a half-smile lightening his stern look. He let the gun drop to his side. "Ya gotta talk someday."

Kenzi stamped her foot again.

"Yeah, whatever." He nodded toward the younger boy. "Fix him up, we gotta get outta here."

Natalya didn't move, her mind racing. Kenzi had a name, a weird one, more appropriate for a truck. Kenzi had brothers, apparently, although genetics had played some odd games if they were full blood

129

relatives. But what in the world did they think they were doing?

She kept her eyes steady on the older boy as she licked her lips. Directing her words to him, she said, "Seriously, your brother needs to go to a hospital. He hit an artery. He's lost a lot of blood already."

Kenzi pushed under her arm as she spoke. "Kenzi, please go inside," Natalya added, voice almost a whisper. If the boys were here for Kenzi, they wouldn't shoot her, she hoped, but as long as that gun was in the boy's hands, the potential for accidents existed.

Kenzi ignored her, her small hands reaching up to touch Mitchell's arm. Natalya's gaze flickered down at her, then straight back up to the older boy. Priorities. She didn't know what the little girl was doing, but she had to focus on the kid with the gun. For the moment, he posed the biggest risk. "I'm a doctor. I can help him if you let me, but you need to put the gun away first."

"A doctor?" He lifted his brows in surprise, before lowering them in calculation. "A real one? Not the book kind?"

"Book kind?"

"You know." He waved the gun impatiently.

Natalya couldn't help flinching, her muscles twitching. She wished she knew more about guns. Did it have a safety? And was the safety on?

"The ones in schools. That write stuff," he explained.

"I'm a medical doctor. The kind that takes care of injured people." Technically, she was the kind that looked at pictures of injured people, but the boy didn't need to know that.

Below her, Kenzi whimpered, a tiny gurgle of pain, as Mitchell sighed. "Thanks, Mac," he said.

"Hey, hey," Natalya protested as Mitchell tried to tug his arm out of her grasp. "You're going to start the bleeding again. Stop that."

But Mitchell was standing, pulling away from her, and she couldn't step forward to follow him without tripping over Kenzi. Natalya looked down as she tried to hold onto the wiggly boy. Kenzi was swaying, her face white, lips almost blue. Startled, Natalya relaxed her grip and Mitchell broke free.

"Put pressure on his arm. Quickly," she snapped at the older boy, crouching, her arms encircling Kenzi. "Kenzi, sit, honey. Put your head between your knees. What happened?"

Part of her attention was on Kenzi as the girl followed her instructions, but the rest was on Mitchell as he peeled the bloody dish towel away from his arm and dropped it to the ground. Natalya swallowed hard to stifle her gasp. Her arms tightened around Kenzi.

The gash on Mitchell's arm wasn't gone. But it had scabbed over, pink around the edges, as if he'd injured himself days instead of mere minutes ago.

Kenzi was breathing fast, taking in deep gulps of air. Her skin was cool to the touch, slightly moist. Natalya slid her hand down the girl's arm, fumbling for her pulse as if she hadn't taken a pulse hundreds of times before. Heartbeat fast, but no faster than that of the average seven-year-old.

Vasovagal syncope, a cool, calm part of Natalya's mind diagnosed. Fainting at the sight of blood. Not too uncommon. If the girl lost consciousness, she'd need to lie flat to prevent a seizure caused by lack of blood to the brain. Nat should get her off the porch to avoid the puddles of the red stuff Mitchell had left behind.

A less calm part of her brain said, ha. The girl's a psychic healer. And an amazingly good one. That explained Grace's lack of burns and Colin's survival.

Kenzi had her head down, but Natalya could feel her trembling. "Shhh." She stroked a hand down the curve of her back, feeling each tiny vertebra under her fingers. "Shhh. It's okay. Do you need to lie down? Shall we go inside?"

"Good job, Mac. But we gotta get outta here," the older boy said brusquely. "Come on."

Natalya felt Kenzi tense under her hands. She rested them on the little girl's shoulders. "Kenzi's not going anywhere."

Kenzi lifted her head. Looking at the boy, she shook it, a firm no.

The boy stared at her, his brown eyes showing a hurt that made him look suddenly younger.

"She doesn't know, Travis." Mitchell poked at the scab on his arm as if testing how much it hurt. "She thinks we're going home. Back there, I mean."

The older boy—Travis, Natalya realized—took a deep breath and started talking at top speed. "We ran away. All of us. He beat up Jamie, locked him in the basement, 'cause he wouldn't say where you and Mary was. But we need you. Jamie's hurt bad. Real bad and we can't help. And if he finds you, he'll take you, you know it."

"No one is taking Kenzi anywhere," Natalya said automatically, but the dread was back, the chill closing off her throat. She looked down at the top of the little girl's head. She'd promised to keep her safe.

"You can't stop him," Travis said with disdain.

"What's he going to do, point a gun at me?" Natalya retorted.

"Ha." The boy scowled, but didn't raise his weapon. "Lawyers, more like. Social workers. Judges. They'll say no proof, need evidence, best place for you, man's got rights. End of the road, kid." Bitterness etched his voice and the lines drawing down his mouth.

Natalya blinked at him, her breath stopping.

This boy was in the system.

That was the only explanation.

Carla had said she thought she recognized Kenzi. But Kenzi couldn't be a foster child—she would have been reported missing. They would have identified her. It made no sense. She looked from one boy to the other and then back at Kenzi again. It made no sense, but there were others. The names he mentioned—Jamie, Mary. At least one injured, maybe badly.

If she delayed them until the police got here, would they be able to convince the boys to say where the others were? Not Travis, he wouldn't talk any more than Kenzi would. But Mitchell? He might not know. And the man they were talking about must be the face in her painting, but who was he? Was he dangerous? A shiver ran down her spine, giving her an answer of sorts.

"All right," she said slowly. If the children were related, Zane ought to be able to find the ones who were hidden when he got home. But there were no guarantees with Zane's gift. Well, not many—he'd always been able to find any of his own relatives, no matter how distant they were.

"All right?" Travis's eyebrows shot up. "Not trying to convince you, lady, just her," he said, shaking his head.

"Put the gun away." Natalya tightened her hands on Kenzi's shoulders. "We'll both come with you." Kenzi looked up at her, eyes wide, and Natalya gave her a smile she hoped looked reassuring.

Travis stepped back, his expression not quite horrified. "No way, lady."

"Doctor. Not lady, doctor," Natalya corrected him. She smiled, feeling an adrenaline surge replace the chill that had come over her. She was clearly insane. Colin was going to be furious. "Kenzi was white and shaking after healing a minor laceration. She's obviously got a special gift, but if your friend is badly injured, you might need something more." She spread her hands wide. "That's me."

Kenzi reached up and clutched Natalya's open hand. Natalya tightened her fingers around the little girl, as Kenzi nodded at the boy who called himself her brother, her smile lighting up her face like the rising sun.

Travis sighed. He ran the fingers of his free hand across his short, close-cropped dark hair, seeming to think.

"Car," Mitchell said abruptly.

"Police?" Travis's hand tightened on his gun.

Mitchell shook his head. Natalya tried to follow his gaze, to see what he was seeing, but the angle of the house was wrong. From her position on the porch, she could see the lake, the oak trees shading her yard, and patches of grass and shrubs, but nothing of the front of the house or the road.

"All right, we go." Travis shook his head in apparent disgust, stuffing the gun into the back of his pants. "Come on, lady doctor. I'll figure out what to do with you after we get Jamie fixed up."

❧ CHAPTER THIRTEEN ❧

Fuck.

Colin studied the blood on the porch. Spatter by the door, a trail across the painted wood planks, a puddle on the steps, a bloody dishtowel discarded in the grass.

He was trying to stay detached, professional, but he would have liked to put his fist through the wall. Or through someone's face.

"You okay?" Akira's quiet murmur interrupted him. Startled out of his thoughts, Colin glanced in her direction. She nodded toward his hands and Colin realized he was opening and closing his fingers compulsively.

He stopped himself and forced a grim smile. He should order Akira away. Civilians and crime scenes were a bad combo. But he didn't. "Yeah. Pissed off, that's all."

The corner of her mouth lifted although her dark eyes stayed serious. "I know what you mean. This is... worrying."

"Does Rose know anything?"

Akira shook her head as if she'd already asked. "She's been, um, vociferous since we got here."

Colin rolled his eyes. She wasn't the only one. The moment he'd realized Nat was no longer on the phone, he'd scrambled into action. He sent out a priority one, code three alert to his dispatcher, while Akira contacted General Direction's security team.

After a frantic trek to get to Nat's house, aided by Shelby, the ranger who'd been on her way to investigate the marijuana patch, they'd arrived to find Colin's deputies smugly arresting the GD security guards. Vociferous wasn't the word. His deputies' ears would be burning for a good long time.

Akira studied the blood on the floor. "What do you think happened here?"

"I think your future sister-in-law was an idiot," Colin replied with some bitterness. Akira's eyebrows arched upward and Colin felt himself flushing. "Sorry," he muttered, spreading his fingers wide in apology, "that was totally unprofessional of me."

Akira's smile was real this time. "I won't tell her you said so. But why do you think so?"

Colin gestured at the scene in front of them. "Nat said it was a kid and his grandpa at her door. Maybe, maybe not. But look what happened here. The window was smashed from the outside. The glass falls into the house. The perp reaches in…" Stepping carefully to avoid the blood, he got closer to the door and pointed out the blood on the shards of glass left in the door. "…and he cuts himself on the glass. Not the hallmark of a criminal mastermind."

"That's a lot of blood," Akira replied. She glanced away. Colin couldn't tell if she was uncomfortable with the sight or listening to Rose until she added, "Rose wants to know if it's enough to have killed him."

Colin shook his head. "I don't think so, but we'll have to get a crime scene tech out here to say for sure. Still, I'd say he hit an artery." Colin turned and nodded toward the dishtowel in the yard. "And Nat, instead of staying on the damn phone and getting me to send an ambulance, comes out here to help him with the bleeding."

"You think that's her towel?"

Colin was sure of it. The yellow under the deep red and brown bloodstains matched the sunny walls of Nat's kitchen.

"Maybe he grabbed it from inside," Akira suggested. "Or his partner did."

Colin's deputies had already searched the interior of the house, finding no sign of Nat, Kenzi, or evidence of a struggle. "Not him." Colin shook his head. "He would have left traces. There's no blood in there. As for his partner, maybe, but with Nat standing right there? No, they stayed outside and Nat came out with a towel. Why would she do that when she felt threatened?"

"The Hippocratic oath," Akira said. "Gotta help the injured."

"Yeah, maybe," Colin agreed. "Still, all the signs read that this was not a professional abduction. These weren't kidnappers targeting Nat for a pay-off. We won't get a ransom demand." Colin probably shouldn't be talking to Akira so honestly, but after their day spent hiking, she felt like an old friend.

"You don't say that like it's a good thing." Her eyes were worried.

"No." Colin stuffed his hands in his pockets and rocked back on his heels. "Rose told us the ghost she met said someone wanted Kenzi dead. But if that was the goal, we should have arrived to an uglier scene." The thought made his stomach churn.

"God." Akira shuddered. "That's a horrible image."

"Understatement," Colin muttered.

"But it didn't happen." Akira sounded uncertain, as if she wanted to reassure him but couldn't trust the truth of her words.

"No," Colin said simply, not wanting to share his darker thoughts.

Nat's gift didn't keep people safe, even when it worked. She'd sounded calm on the phone, but she would have left a message or picked up her cell again if she could have. She would have known he would worry. That her family would worry.

He didn't understand the scene at the house. Nat's behavior confused the hell out of him. Why had she gone outside? Why weren't there signs of a struggle? How would she have simply let someone take Kenzi? He had his deputies and the GD security team out canvassing the area and searching the nearby woods, but if Nat had taken Kenzi and hidden, why hadn't she returned when she heard the sirens?

He stepped off the porch and crouched next to the towel, examining it without touching it. As Akira had said, there was a lot of blood. Without moving, he began scouting Nat's grass, eyes scouring the blades for traces of color. "Huh," he said thoughtfully. "Where's the blood trail?"

"I don't see one," Akira said after several seconds.

"Me neither." Colin straightened, glancing at the porch again. He rubbed his chin, eyes narrowing as he thought.

"Tell me," Akira asked. "What are you seeing?"

"This wasn't a quick mop-up and run. They took the time to stop the bleeding. More than a couple of minutes."

"So?"

"The timing doesn't add up. I was off the phone with her for a minute to call it in, no more than that. As soon as I realized she wasn't on the line, we had people on the way."

He was going to stay annoyed about the slow response from his deputies for a good long time, but even though they'd let the GD security guards beat them here, they'd arrived within fifteen minutes of his second call.

"And?"

"But the road's two miles long, no turns off, no other route out of here. Even if my guys were late, the guys from GD should have passed their car. No way around that."

"But they didn't?" Akira asked. "Could they have missed it?"

Colin shook his head. "They're pros. All of them would have been alert to a departing vehicle. And none of them saw anything." He'd checked within minutes of his arrival. If they'd gotten a description, they could have used the Amber alert system for Kenzi. Without more information, though, an alert would be close to useless.

"I called Zane," Akira told him. "He's catching the next flight home. He'll find her."

"Did he—" Colin paused. He'd met too many fake psychics to trust them automatically, but he knew Zane and he knew how Zane's gift worked. Zane could find anything—except for the dead.

"He's too far away. He couldn't get a read on her." Akira bit her lip, worrying it nervously. "Do you think…" She let her words trail off.

"I don't know," Colin answered. "But we can't wait for Zane. I need to run this investigation like any other abduction. We'll get roadblocks on the main roads. Dogs out here to track the direction they headed. Alert the media, the FBI." After the last time they'd been in town, Colin hated the thought of bringing the Feds in, but he didn't have the resources or the manpower to run an operation as big as this one ought to be. A lump in his throat—could it be fear?—felt tight and hard.

"If there's anything I can do…" Akira offered with a wan smile, but then her smile brightened. "Or more practically, anything General Directions can do. Max is on his way here, but I know he'd want me to make that offer."

"I'll take him up on it," Colin answered, already planning how to use the extra manpower. But his eyes narrowed as he saw the way Akira was rubbing her side. This stress, on top of hours of hiking, was probably not the healthiest activity for a pregnant woman. "Why don't you go sit in the car?" he suggested. "Rest for a while. I'm going to search the house again, see if there's anything my guys missed."

Akira nodded. But before Colin could turn away, Akira put a hand on his arm, stopping him. Colin waited, despite his impatience to get started.

"You and Nat," Akira finally said, eyes searching Colin's face. "It's been a long time. And it didn't end real well."

"I love her," Colin interrupted her. "I've always loved her. And I am not going to let anything bad happen to her."

Akira's silence spoke louder than words. Colin sighed. That probably wasn't the answer to the question Akira hadn't asked. Professionalism and his feelings for Nat didn't mix well. "What did you want to know?"

A funny little smile was playing on Akira's mouth as she shook her head, and answered, voice gentle, "No, we're good. I'll go wait in the car."

Colin began his search at the back of the house. Mindful of Nat's words about Kenzi hiding, he was careful to be more thorough than his deputies might have been. In her bathroom, he pushed towels out of the way to confirm that Kenzi wasn't hidden in the closet. Nat's towels were dark green and lush. He ignored the mental flash of what she would look like, stepping out of the shower, wrapped in one of them, her dark hair wet and drops of water still clinging to her skin.

He flipped open the top of the wicker hamper and glanced inside. A sky-blue shirt with skinny straps where shoulders should be lay almost on top. Nat's. She'd been wearing it the previous day under a deeper blue cotton sweater. It would do for the dogs. He bagged it, not letting his hands brush against the lacy bra sitting next to it or his memories turn to other days, other lacy bras.

In her bedroom, he tried to pay no attention at all to the king-size bed, the fluffy comforter, the sleek cotton sheets. He refused to let himself think about what it would have been like to be with Nat here. But he spotted the box sticking out from underneath. Nat wouldn't have left it that way. His eyes narrowed as he crouched down. To his disappointment, Kenzi wasn't under the bed. His deputies wouldn't have missed her if she was, he knew, but he'd had a moment of hope. Nat's actions might have made more sense if Kenzi were safe inside the house.

The living room held no hiding places, nor was anything in disarray. Nat's house was as tidy as his own office. But Colin paused in the doorway to the front bedroom. A dollhouse lay tipped on its side, furnishings scattered on the floor. Apart from the broken glass in the kitchen, it was the only sign of mess. Colin stepped into the room, wondering. Had Kenzi knocked the heavy toy over? Or had Nat? And why?

Nat's easel stood in the fading light by the window, a canvas propped on it. Colin glanced at it and then blinked in surprise.

Photos of Max Latimer tacked to the wall in front of the easel suggested Nat should be painting a portrait of her father. But the charcoal sketch on the canvas didn't look like Max. His eyes narrowed as he studied it. It was just a simple line drawing. Maybe the likeness would get better as she worked? But no. The eyes were wrong and so was the mouth. The nose—eh, maybe. But the whole structure of the face looked off to him, too angular, too stern.

How long did it take to do a sketch like this? Had Nat seen the man at the door from the window? Thoughtfully, he looked back at the dollhouse. Kenzi wouldn't have been frightened by a knock at the door, but maybe...

Pulling out his phone, he photographed the sketch and tapped out a quick text to Joyce as he sent it. It was a long shot, but if she passed it around the department, someone might recognize the man.

As he stepped out of the house into the twilight, mentally he was making lists: people to call, orders to give, the next steps he should be taking. But part of his brain couldn't help puzzling over the pieces. The broken glass, the blood on the porch, the spilled dollhouse, the box out of place, the portrait—Colin felt like he was missing something obvious. Something so obvious it was going to hurt when he realized what it was.

The sun was setting over the lake. Colin grimaced. Full darkness arrived early during the winter. Another couple of hours of daylight would have been useful, given him more time to get a full-fledged search underway. And then he stopped moving, standing absolutely still as he looked at the reflection of the light on the water.

Time.

Every clue he'd found added up to time, to seconds turning into minutes—minutes during which his deputies and GD's security team rushed to the scene. How had Nat's kidnappers escaped? They shouldn't have. They couldn't have.

But they had.

Little threads were starting to weave themselves together into a map inside his head—a map pointing straight to the lake.

❧ CHAPTER FOURTEEN ❧

Natalya regretted the Christmas trifle. Also the Christmas cookies. Also the two plus years since she'd practiced yoga regularly, in an actual studio, with an instructor who'd push her to work harder. In fact, it felt as if she was finally paying for every one of the extra pounds she'd shrugged off over the years.

"A canoe? Who uses a canoe for a getaway car?" she muttered, as she dipped her oar into the dank water of one of the small canals connecting one lake to another.

She glanced over her shoulder in time to catch the disgusted look Travis shot her. He was in the stern, steering. Mitchell and Kenzi—Mac, Natalya mentally corrected herself—huddled in the middle. Natalya had the bow. It had made sense at the time, as much as anything about this whole experience made sense. Travis knew where they were going, Mitchell was injured, and she was far stronger than Kenzi. But her arms ached with the exertion and the canoe was so low in the water from their combined weight that each sloppy swing brought a little more water into the bottom of the boat.

"He don't know how to drive," Mitchell volunteered.

"Shut up, Mitchell." The words were automatic, as if Travis said them as a matter of routine. "I coulda figured it out if we had a car. But we don't."

Natalya kept paddling. The light was going. It was getting darker and colder and she really hoped their destination wasn't too much farther away. But Travis had refused to answer any questions about where they were headed. He hadn't been threatening about it—the gun had disappeared into the back of his pants as if he'd forgotten it—but she didn't want to alienate him by pushing.

Not yet, anyway.

She suspected the boy didn't have a plan. He was ricocheting from one emergency to the next. Running away with his injured brother, finding his missing sister, keeping his family safe. Did he have any idea what his next move would be? Pulling a gun on her would have been disastrous if the police had arrived sooner.

Still, maybe he hadn't done so badly. Even in semi-darkness,

Travis navigated as if he knew exactly where he was going. "How did you find us?" she asked impulsively.

He grunted. "Got lucky." He looked toward Kenzi and grinned, a smile that warmed his eyes, his expression practically doting. "Real lucky."

"Okay." Natalya paused to swat at an errant mosquito. Didn't the damn bugs know it was midwinter? She slid her paddle back in the water. "But how?"

"Went on a food run, heard people talking." Travis sounded positively cheerful.

Natalya frowned. What people? And what had they been saying? "Where was that?" she asked, trying not to sound as annoyed as she felt. Apparently she and Kenzi were out in the dark and cold and wet, getting munched on by bugs, because people couldn't keep their big mouths shut.

"There's this real little town, like two streets big."

"Tassamara. I know it." The town was much bigger than its tiny downtown area would suggest, but Natalya didn't feel the need to explain that to Travis. If he didn't know as much, they probably lived closer to one of the other nearby towns.

"Weird place. But if you go to the restaurant there and order the special to go, you get a big bag of food, big enough to feed all of us. Good stuff, too. Like last time, she gave us soup and turkey sandwiches and muffins and these huge chocolate chip cookies, big as your head almost." The thought of food was making Travis positively loquacious.

Mitchell's stomach rumbled loudly. He pressed a hand to it. "I'm hungry again, Travis."

"Aw, man, Mitchell. Not yet," the older boy protested.

"I can't help it." Mitchell sniffled. Kenzi pressed herself against him, looking up into his face with worry.

"Jamie didn't eat the soup last time," Travis said, sounding worried. "You can have that when we get back. And maybe there's some of those crackers left."

"Okay."

The resignation in Mitchell's voice made Natalya want to reach out to him and ruffle his hair, right before bringing him back to her house and feeding him a huge pot of spaghetti. Instead, she pressed her lips together to stop herself from pointing out the obvious to

Travis. She and Kenzi were going to need to eat, too. He'd multiplied his problems by adding two more mouths to feed. But it wouldn't kill her to go hungry for a night and she was sure Zane would find them as soon as he got home.

"How long have you guys been on your own?" she asked instead.

"Not long," Travis said briefly, as Mitchell said, "A long time."

Travis sighed. "Hang on." He put up a hand, signaling Natalya to stop. With relief, she rested her paddle across her lap. In front of them, the over-hanging trees were opening up, as the winding stream reached one of the small lakes or springs that dotted the area.

Slowly, Travis steered them forward. He paused, paddle motionless. In the stillness, Natalya could hear the lively buzz of insects, a few chirps of sleepy birds, and the occasional splash of water on rock. But no sounds of cars or people. She tried to map out the geography in her head: they'd headed west from her house, then north, so they could be nearing Dirt Lake or Lake New, maybe Lake Deer. But they'd paddled into a small stream off her lake, crossed another small lake, headed up a canal, passed through one of the springs and kept going, and she'd quickly lost track of the direction in which they were moving.

She had no idea where they were, she admitted to herself. She was familiar with the area around her house and some of the nearby recreation areas, but she'd never simply headed into the wilderness the way Travis had. She hadn't even realized so many of the lakes connected. She knew, in the abstract, that there were over six hundred lakes in the area, but most of them were so small they barely had names.

"All right," he said. "Fast now."

With sure, strong strokes, he headed straight out into an open body of water. Natalya didn't protest, just tried to match her pace to his. Her muscles were groaning by the time they reached a short dock extending into the water. And it was full dark, a darkness lit by a rising moon and thousands of stars. A building loomed before them.

Travis held the canoe steady as Mitchell and Kenzi scrambled out. "Go on up to the house," he ordered them. "Jamie's hurting bad. We'll put the canoe away."

"Hang on," Natalya protested. Her feet were soaked and uncomfortable and the cold, although it didn't bite, was unpleasant, but her discomfort wasn't why she stopped them. "I want to see him

143

before Kenzi does her thing."

"Why?" Travis sounded revolted, as if she were voyeuristic instead of worried.

"Lawyers, judges, and social workers, remember?" Natalya said with a snap. She shouldn't antagonize him, she knew, but her arms hurt, her shoulders hurt, her stomach muscles hurt, and she was hungry, too. "They like witnesses. Especially ones with Doctor in front of their names. I want to see his injuries before they're healed."

"That don't matter. We ain't never going back," Travis snapped back at her. "Never."

Natalya gritted her teeth, sliding her paddle into the canoe with a clatter. This kid was a pain in the ass. He so was going back—although not to the foster home he'd run away from, that was for sure. But they'd find him a new home, a better home.

Kenzi plopped down on the dock, crossing her legs as if she planned to stay for awhile.

Natalya bit back her smile. She had an ally—a very small, but very powerful ally. "Let's get this canoe put away, shall we? We'll all go up to the house together."

Grudgingly, Travis allowed that the canoe didn't need to be put away immediately. "I'll need it again later anyway."

Natalya's eyebrows lifted. The canoe was small enough that a solo paddler could manage it, but canoeing after dark sounded dangerous to her. One unnoticed spur of an underwater cypress or tree root and he'd be in the water. And the night was chilly. Hypothermia could be fatal at fifty degrees if he got wet.

But she kept her silence and clambered out onto the dock, trying not to get any wetter than she already was. Once she was safely out, Travis grunted, paddling forward to beach the boat on the sandy shore. Kenzi took Nat's hand as they walked together down the dock, Mitchell ahead of them. They met Travis at the foot of the dock.

In the dim light from the moon, Natalya looked up at the building in front of them. "What is this place?" she asked, voice hushed as if something about the night and the stillness made talking risky. It looked at least three stories high, a solid wall of darkness.

"Best squat ever." It sounded as if Mitchell gave a skip of happiness with the words.

"Shut up, Mitchell." Travis's tone was world-weary, resigned, as he turned to lead the way. "It's just a house."

"A really big-ass house," Mitchell chortled.

"Mitchell," Travis barked. Kenzi's hand tightened around Natalya's and then relaxed as Travis added, "Watch your language. No swearing around Mac."

"Sorry, Mac." Mitchell's apology was immediate and cheerful. "But it's way cool. It's got two swimming pools, one inside, one out. We can't swim, 'cause they're all gross and stuff, but there's like a ton of rooms and a tennis court and this one room, it's like a movie theater. It's got seats in rows and everything."

Natalya followed the boys into the darkness, her brain churning. Which one of the lakes had a lone mansion on its shores? If she'd been living in Tassamara during the housing boom, she was sure she'd know—every stage of construction would have been monitored in the local conversation. But she'd been away for medical school and her residency and since she'd returned, she spent more time in her quiet lab than she did in town. She didn't remember hearing anything about any abandoned McMansions.

They rounded a corner and Travis paused at a door in the wall. He shoved it open and waved them through, before pulling it closed behind them, lifting it up slightly as if it hung partially off its hinges. On the other side of the door, Natalya paused, Kenzi's hand tight in hers. They were on a patio. She could see from the reflected light of the moon that a swimming pool lay in front of them, but the water was dark and murky.

"This way," Travis said, brushing past them and heading to the left.

Natalya felt a shiver run down her spine. She'd been distracted by the ache of exertion, the chill of the air and the discomfort of her wet feet, but her sense of foreboding was back. She felt spooked by the house, reluctant to go inside.

Gritting her teeth, she followed Travis. Mitchell chatted happily to Kenzi but she tuned out the flow of his words as she tried to push her foresight into action. What was going to happen? But it was like a dream, a half-forgotten mélange of images and sensations: boys yelling; a blur of doorways and tiled floor; Kenzi glaring fiercely, an expression Natalya had never seen her wear.

Natalya took a deep, gulping breath, feeling shaky. Leaves on water, she told herself. You can't stop the future, you can only prepare for it. The reminder helped. She let the thoughts drift away, focusing on the present.

Bits of broken glass crunched underfoot.

"I see you were busy here, too, Mitchell," Natalya said, voice dry, as she stepped more carefully. In the dim light, she couldn't tell which window was broken.

Travis snorted. As he stepped through an empty doorframe, Natalya realized they were walking on pieces of a glass door.

"Not me," Mitchell said. "It was too hard. But it broke a lot better. No big pieces sticking out, waiting to cut ya." He sounded aggrieved, as if Natalya's window had attacked him instead of the other way around.

Natalya's lips twitched in a half-smile as she followed Travis through the door and into an echoing space. This must be the inside pool Mitchell had mentioned. It didn't smell of chlorine, though, but of mold and dead things. Natalya swallowed hard.

"Yeah, it stinks," Travis agreed, although she hadn't protested. He'd stopped moving and seemed to be kneeling, rummaging along the ground. "Ah," he said, sounding satisfied, and clicked on a flashlight. For a moment, the light was too bright. Natalya squinted until Travis aimed the beam at the ground in front of them, creating a small circle of warmth in the darkness.

"Isn't this cool?" Mitchell sounded bouncy again. "There's toads living in here, Mac. Lizards, too. Maybe even snakes."

Natalya felt a bubble of hysterical laughter rising. Snakes? Just what she wanted to hear.

"Shut up, Mitchell." Travis sighed, moving away. "Mac's a girl. Girls don't like snakes."

"Don't be sexist. Kenzi can like snakes if she wants to." Natalya corrected him automatically, before almost stepping on his heels as she hurried after him to get away from the potential reptile residents of the pool. Kenzi might like snakes, but Natalya definitely didn't.

Inside the house, the darkness was even deeper. Natalya paused, wary of running into doors or furniture.

"This way," Travis said, leading them to a wide flight of stairs. Natalya couldn't see much, but the floor under her feet felt smooth and polished. She hoped it was tile, but as Travis shone the light onto the steps, she could see they were made out of a beautiful hardwood. With an inward cringe at the thought of their wet and muddy shoes, she followed him upstairs, Kenzi and Mitchell close behind them.

They climbed up the switchback stairway to the top floor and into a wide open space. Travis let the light flicker around the room, touching on a kitchen separated from the main room by a bar. The moonlight shining in through the wall of windows provided enough light for Natalya to see two people, one sitting on the floor by the windows, the other lying down next to him.

"Come help Jamie, Mac," Travis ordered, setting the flashlight down on the bar.

"You found her," exclaimed Mitchell, scrambling to his feet.

Natalya blinked twice and then a third time, before glancing at the Mitchell who had come in behind her. Same dark hair, same brown skin, same skinny arms and big smile.

Twins.

Because the world needed two of Mitchell, of course.

She couldn't help smiling at the boy's jubilant welcome as he drew Kenzi forward, but as she grabbed the flashlight Travis had set down, her brain was ticking.

"Me first," she said. Twin boys. And a teenage boy. And maybe…

"Who's that?" The Mitchell double protested as she hurried across the room and knelt next to the prone figure.

The boy lying on the floor lifted feverish eyes to hers. The bruises on his face were unmistakable, deep purple and yellow stippling the tawny skin, but Natalya was more immediately worried by the cracked lips and sunken eyes. Gently, she lifted up his arm and pinched his skin. The skin tented up and only slowly dropped back into place.

"He's dehydrated," she said, keeping her voice calm. Severely dehydrated. The boys must not understand how dangerous his condition was. "Do you have water for him?"

"He throws up," Travis said. "Blood and gunk."

Internal bleeding, Natalya thought. Damn it, this boy needed a hospital, immediately.

Kenzi dropped to her knees next to Natalya. She reached for the boy's face but Natalya put a hand out to stop her.

"Wait," she said. "Do you know how you do what you do?"

Kenzi lifted her face, eyes searching Natalya's. She shook her head.

"He has serious injuries, internal injuries," Natalya explained. She lifted the boy's t-shirt, pushing it up and out of the way with steady hands. She shifted, moving over so Kenzi could see. His abdomen didn't look hard or distended, so the blood loss was a slow leak. Maybe his spleen, maybe somewhere else. If it had been faster, he'd be dead already, she knew with grim certainty. As it was, she couldn't be sure he'd survive, not without proper care. But Kenzi was what she had, at least for the moment.

"Do you know where it hurts?" she asked the boy.

"Everywhere," he rasped.

"Any place more than the rest?"

His hand lifted, hovering above the left side of his torso. Natalya nodded. She saw nothing so obvious as protruding bone, but his ribs might be cracked. "Right here, Kenzi," she directed the girl. "Touch him here and try to focus on this area."

The girl licked her lips and nodded. Gently, so gently, she put her tiny hands on the boy's side. Natalya watched but there was nothing to see, until she realized Kenzi was swaying, her body rocking back and forth, her eyes closing, her skin growing paler.

"Enough," Natalya said sharply, lifting Kenzi's hands off the boy. She'd only worked with a couple of psychic healers before but she'd read the literature. Most healers had only minor power, the ability to encourage the growth of healthy cells, to spur a metabolism into action. But a few in the historic record could pour their own energy into others. They tended to die young.

"You just okay with that?" Travis's voice interrupted Natalya's absorption.

"With what?" Natalya's eyes didn't leave Kenzi's face. The little girl was pale and shaky, lips parted, breathing hard as if she'd been running, but her hands still reached for the prone boy. "No more, honey, not yet." The whimper Kenzi gave in response was so quiet Natalya might have imagined it.

"With what she does?" Travis stood across the room from them, still by the bar, the expression on his face lost in the shadows. Mitchell and Other Mitchell were together, close enough to Kenzi to watch with wide eyes.

"What do you mean?" Natalya asked. The shadows already under Kenzi's eyes looked deeper, her cheekbones more pronounced. Maybe it was the light. But if healing used her innate energy, she didn't have a lot of it to spare.

Natalya glanced back at Jamie. His eyelids drooped over dark eyes, lashes dark lines against the bruises, but his face looked easier, more peaceful. She touched his cheek. He felt warm, but not as fevered as he'd looked before.

Kenzi reached for him and again, Natalya stopped her. "No, sweetheart. You don't have enough energy to heal him all the way." Kenzi looked at her, a question in the tilt of her head. Natalya stroked her hair, cupping her cheek. "You need to eat something, get some calories in you. What you do takes energy. You can't give it to Jamie if you don't have enough to give."

"You act like it's normal." Travis moved forward into the room, his motion abrupt, almost angry.

"Normal?" Natalya raised an eyebrow. Keeping her voice deliberately light, she said, "I've always thought normal was overrated."

Jamie chuckled, the sound a bare puff of air. "Wish everyone felt that way." His voice cracked, rough with thirst.

"Don't try to talk," Natalya said, automatically reaching back to him. "You need liquids." She frowned down at him.

What he really needed was an ambulance. A hospital. An IV. A complete scan to assess his injuries. Maybe surgery.

What she had was a canoe. And Kenzi.

"How did you get him here?" she asked, turning back to Travis.

He shrugged. "Canoe."

"You couldn't all have come here in that canoe," Natalya protested. Jamie wouldn't have been able to paddle, and the combined weight of the Mitchells plus the older boys would have been enough to swamp the small boat.

"Not in one trip," Travis answered. "I went back for Mitch and Mike. Promised I wouldn't leave 'em there."

"Where's there?" Natalya asked.

"None of your business." Travis crossed his arms across his chest.

Natalya's eyes narrowed. She waited for a memory to float to the surface, to tell her what the next minutes would bring, but her mind stayed stubbornly blank. She licked her lips. "The Thompsons?"

It was taking a risk. Maybe a big risk.

"How the hell did you know that?" Travis's arms dropped, his mouth falling open, before his expression changed to a glare. "No way did Mac tell you."

149

"You just told me," Natalya said. She put an arm around Kenzi, feeling the little girl trembling next to her. The twins were looking from Travis to her, their faces uncertain, their eyes worried.

"I did not." Travis took a step forward.

"Confirmed it, let's say." Natalya nodded toward the twins. "There aren't a lot of twins in foster care." She was far from intimately familiar with every kid in the local system, but she remembered the twins' story. No father in the picture, a mother who'd died in a car accident without a will. The state hadn't been able to locate an appropriate guardian and the boys had entered foster care.

"How did you..." Travis stopped. "It doesn't matter. We're not going back there."

"Of course you're not," Natalya agreed. "They're clearly not fit caregivers. You'll never go back to them."

"No one believed us before," one of the twins volunteered.

"You ran away days ago and they haven't reported you missing." She tried to make the words reassuring. "Believe me, that's not the sort of thing foster care agencies take lightly. At the very least, the Thompsons are neglectful. You won't have to live with them, not ever again."

Except, she realized, Kenzi wasn't in foster care. If she had been, they would have discovered her name days ago. Could she be biologically related to the Thompsons? Natalya tightened her grasp on the little girl. Keeping a biological child out of the hands of bad parents was a lot harder than moving foster children to a new home.

Still, there'd be a thorough investigation before Kenzi went anywhere. Colin would make sure of it.

"Right now, though, we need to get Jamie to a hospital," she continued. "Do you have a phone? We should call an ambulance."

"No." Travis was breathing hard, the rising and falling of his chest visible even in the dim light. "We can't. You don't understand."

"Explain it to me," Natalya said calmly.

Travis shook his head, his words abrupt. "I gotta go on a food run. Michael, you come with me this time. Mitch, stay here. Stand guard."

"Wait," Natalya protested, half-rising out of her kneeling position. "Where do you think you're going? You can't just leave us here. Jamie needs medical attention. Kenzi needs food and dry clothes."

Blankets, a bed, an IV line, a damn cell phone—the list of other things she wanted ran through her head but she didn't say them aloud.

"You're the medical attention, lady," Travis said bleakly. "Do your best. Jamie understands." He crossed the room to them and crouched next to the boy on the floor, squeezing his hand. Voice hushed, he spoke directly to Jamie, "Try to eat some soup, man. I'll be back as soon as I can," before rising without waiting for a response. He moved away, heading for the stairs. Both twins followed.

Natalya fumed, but let him go. He had the gun, after all. And her brother would be on his way home already. Zane would find her.

"There's some stuff over in the corner," Jamie said, voice a husky whisper. "You can see if you can find something for Mac to wear there. Won't fit, but better than nothing."

Kenzi had her face buried in Natalya's shirt, but Natalya stroked a hand down her back. Her leggings were damp, her socks wet. Natalya's own shoes were soaked.

"Kenzi, honey, do you see the clothes over there?" Kenzi lifted her head and Natalya gestured. "Go see what you can find that will fit you. Or be more comfortable than your wet clothes, anyway. And maybe find me some socks?"

Kenzi nodded obediently and trotted away. Natalya sat down on the floor next to Jamie and started taking off her wet shoes. "Tell me what you understand," she said to him. "You must know how sick you are. You need a hospital."

He blinked, his eyes tired, and then turned his head slowly to follow Kenzi's movement across the room. "Later," he said quietly. "I don't want to upset her."

Natalya's gaze followed his. She felt a surge of worry and pushed it away. It wouldn't help. "All right. How are you doing then?"

His lips turned up at the corners. "Better."

"Less pain?"

He nodded.

She reached for his wrist to take his pulse. It felt like a useless gesture, but any information was better than the none she was working with. His heartbeat was strong and steady, not as rapid as she would have expected with severe dehydration. Maybe Kenzi had helped with that, too.

Mitchell came bounding back into the room. "Travis says we can eat the soup. It's cold but still good. And we've got crackers." He rummaged around the bar area, before triumphantly coming forth with a large Styrofoam container and a handful of plastic spoons.

After Kenzi was dressed, with pants rolled up five times and a belt cinched tightly around her waist, the children ate. Natalya let Jamie sit up and risk a few bites. She watched him closely, but when he didn't start vomiting, she relaxed a little.

Kenzi and Mitchell shared the rest of the food between them. Although Natalya was hungry, she wanted Kenzi to have as many calories as possible. When they'd licked every last drop out of the container and swallowed every last crumb of cracker, Mitchell turned to Kenzi. "Want to explore, Mac? This house is way cool."

Kenzi looked to Natalya for permission and Natalya nodded at her. "Sure. Stay away from the pool, though." She handed the little girl the flashlight. "Here, take this."

Natalya waited until she could no longer hear the sounds of the children moving away, before turning back to Jamie.

He still sat, his back against the windowed wall, his eyes closed, but as if he felt her gaze, he opened them. His lips lifted in a half-smile, half-grimace. "It's a long story," he warned her.

"I seem to have plenty of time on my hands," she responded. "Start at the beginning."

"I guess it started when Mary came back," Jamie began.

"Who's Mary?" Natalya interrupted him.

"Mac's mom. She's the Thompsons' daughter. Real daughter, not a foster kid."

Natalya's head dipped. She wasn't going to tell this boy about the spirit at the hospital, not yet, maybe not ever. But she feared she'd just learned the ghost's name.

Jamie shifted restlessly. "It didn't use to be a bad place. They were okay people. Pretty strict, but not mean. Some stuff was kind of a drag. Chores and rules and Mr. Thompson would pray for like ten minutes before we could eat. But then there was always lots of food, plenty to go around. And Mrs. T, she's nice. I guess that made it harder when it got weird."

"What do you mean, weird?"

"Mrs. T, she was real happy when Mary came home. She'd run away a long time ago. And they didn't know about Mac, she was a surprise. But Mr. Thompson, he said stuff. Crazy stuff. He was worried about judgment day and how Mary was going straight to hell, she needed to repent and all that. It wasn't so bad at first. He wasn't around so much. Then he lost his job and he was home all the time."

Jamie stopped talking.

Natalya waited, but when he didn't say more, she pushed harder. "What happened?"

"Sometimes he'd get real quiet for a while. Lie on the couch all the time, not talk much. That was okay, except ya never knew when it was gonna end and he'd get all mad and weird. He thought Mac was like some symbol of evil. Proof of her mom's sinfulness. And any little thing would set him off. He'd yell and scream and then…" He fell silent again.

"Then?" she prompted.

"The first time was a while ago. It was dinner time and he was praying. And praying and praying. We all just wanted to eat. Mrs. T, she tried to interrupt him, but then it was like he was talking to God and hearing God talk back. It was creepy. So Travis said 'a good God would let folks eat before the food gets cold' and Mr. Thompson, he hauled off and smacked him. Knocked Travis right out of his chair."

"That sounds frightening." Deliberately, Natalya kept her voice soft, non-judgmental, hoping to ease the pain of the memories, but inwardly she was furious. That poor boy. Those poor children.

Jamie shrugged. "I guess. But he was real sorry after and Mrs. T, she cried and cried."

"You didn't tell anyone?" She made the words a question, although she was sure she knew the answer.

"No. Not that time." Jamie looked away, seeming uncomfortable.

"It kept happening?"

"A few times, yeah."

"You still didn't report him, though." Natalya kept her face and voice neutral.

"They would have taken us away," he said. "Split us up. Travis and me, we'd end up in juvie or a group home. No one wants teenage boys and I'm almost aged out. Only two months to go. The M&M's mighta been okay but they didn't want to leave either."

"M&M's?" Natalya felt her lips twitch into an unexpected smile. The nickname fit the bouncy twins.

"Yeah, Mary always called 'em that." Jamie's lips turned up, too.

"She liked to tell 'em they were made of chocolate, pure sweet all the way through."

"She sounds nice," Natalya said.

"She is. Real nice." Jamie's voice held a deep desolation. He closed his eyes, but not before Natalya saw the shimmer of moisture in them.

She waited again. The silence stretched between them but she made no move to break it.

Finally, Jamie swallowed and continued his story, his voice huskier. "Then, back in the summer, he hit Mac."

Natalya clenched her teeth together as tightly as she could, refusing to let the words that wanted to spill out of her escape. Why hadn't Jamie gone straight to his caseworker? The agency wasn't perfect, but allegations of abuse were always taken seriously. And with multiple witnesses, the children would have been pulled out of the Thompson house immediately. "What happened then?"

Jamie sounded almost dreamy as he went on, "I don't know when Mary knew about Mac. That she's special, I mean. She can make a hurt stop like it never happened. But we all knew by then. It made it better, easier. But Mac can't heal herself. So when he hurt her, Mary knew they had to go."

At last, a reasonable decision. Except, of course, it apparently hadn't been carried out. Natalya forced herself to relax her fingers. They wanted to clench into fists. "Why didn't she?" Her voice was still perfectly controlled.

"No money, no job, no place to go. Same reasons she was there in the first place. But..." Jamie stopped talking, seeming reluctant to say any more.

"But what?"

"She knew a guy," he muttered. "We... did a little job for him."

"A little job?" Natalya felt a lump dropping into her stomach like a cartoon anvil and no amount of relaxation training could keep all of the bite out of her voice when she asked, "Let me guess, a not exactly legal little job?"

He nodded, looking miserable.

"How bad is it?" she asked.

"I don't know," he answered.

"You don't know how serious the crime you committed is?"

"Oh, no, I know that. I just don't know what happened. I

think..." He stopped speaking and swallowed hard. "I think maybe Mary's dead. She would never have left Mac for so long. Not if she could get back."

Natalya pressed her lips together. She thought he was probably right, but she didn't want to say so. "Tell me the whole story," she said gently instead. He didn't answer right away and she leaned forward, putting her hand over his. "Let me help you," she told him. "All of you. Your brothers need help, Kenzi—Mac needs help, and you need help, too. I understand you're in trouble, but you can't get out of it by running away."

He let his head fall back against the window. "We needed money. A lot of it. Mary—well, I don't know what all she did while she was gone, but she didn't want nothing to do with meth or molly. But she knew this guy. A big dealer. At least that's what he said. He agreed to buy some weed from us. So we planted a patch in the forest and took care of it."

"Round Thanksgiving, Mr. Thompson really lost it. Mary'd been keeping Mac out of his way, keeping her quiet, eyes down, do what she's told, don't make no waves. But he went off on how she was the spawn of Satan and everything bad that happened was because of her, because of her cursed blood. Mary took Mac and left, hid out in the woods. We took turns bringing her food. Mrs. T, all she did was cry, but she knew we was sneaking stuff out. She didn't tell. But he figured it out."

Natalya shivered involuntarily. Jamie sounded old beyond his years, tired beyond endurance. "He beat you," she said flatly.

"To get me to tell where they were. And I did."

❧ CHAPTER FIFTEEN ❧

The bistro was packed with people. Half the town filled the tables, stood in the aisles, held quiet conversations outside the front door. A steady stream of them stopped by Max's booth, offering their words of concern and support.

"If there's anything more I can do..." Meredith, the local realtor, squeezed his hand before moving away. Max's smile of thanks didn't touch the worry in his eyes, but he nodded his appreciation. Meredith held a pile of flyers in her hand, featuring photos of Natalya and Kenzi. All of the searchers had copies and she was passing out more. Volunteers would be taking them to the nearest towns and campgrounds.

"Still nothing?" Grace asked him in the momentary quiet.

He shook his head, mouth drawn into a grim line. "I don't sense anything about her future. It's as if there's a blank space where my intuition about Nat should be. I don't like it."

She sighed and picked up her cell phone, then set it down again. She tapped the surface restlessly. "Probably shouldn't call Zane again, huh?"

This time his smile crinkled the laugh lines around his eyes. "Not unless you want him to hang up on you. You know he said he'd call the moment he felt something."

Grace looked away. "I know... it's just..."

"I know." Max turned to speak to another concerned friend.

"Oh, call him anyway," Rose suggested from the seat next to Max. "Or not," she added with a sigh when Grace ignored her.

Over the decades in which she'd been a ghost, Rose had learned to be patient. Time passed, events happened. There wasn't much she could do about it one way or another. Ghosts were watchers, trapped in time they could never change.

Rose had never minded. She liked people, watching them and listening to them and thinking about them, and she loved the stories they told and the music they made and the beauty they created. As far as Rose was concerned, television—especially now when Akira's magic box would let her see absolutely endless streams of interesting shows—was just as good as life.

Except she had changed this time, this series of events. The little girl had been safe because of Rose's choices, because of her actions. And now she wasn't anymore. Rose hadn't experienced the emotion she was feeling in so long she almost couldn't identify it, but it was unhappiness.

She didn't like it.

Her tie to the girl was gone as if it had never existed. It had been since the moment Kenzi crawled out of the darkness and into Natalya and Colin's company. But Rose had stayed with Kenzi out of curiosity and an affection that came from the hours they'd spent in the woods together. Now she bitterly regretted having left. If she'd been there... well, nothing would have been any different. Rose wouldn't have been able to do anything to stop whatever had happened. But at least she wouldn't have been left in the same dark as all the other worried people in the diner.

Akira slid into the booth next to Grace with a weary sigh.

"You okay?" Grace asked immediately.

"Tired," Akira said. "It's been a long day."

Rose pursed her lips thoughtfully. She glanced down at her hands, placed as they were in her lap. Akira didn't like to be touched by ghosts. Spirit energy coursing through her burned and sizzled. Yet when she'd passed through Akira the previous day, Akira had shivered, but not complained. Rose knew her energy felt different lately.

"That it has," Grace agreed. "Any word from Zane?"

Akira shook her head, eyes rueful. "He's on a plane already, but the flight is fifteen hours or so, and they'll have to stop to refuel. He'll let us know as soon as he senses her."

Grace nodded, her smile tired. She had all of that information already, Rose knew. She'd spoken to her brother no more than half an hour ago.

Across the restaurant, people were responding as Colin strode in. They called out greetings and questions and he lifted a hand to wave them all to silence. "No news," he reported. "But we need a few more volunteers for the search parties. We particularly need people with access to small boats. If you can help, please report to Deputy Jayne down on MacLarren Road." A dozen people immediately stood and headed for the door, as an anxious looking young woman entered followed by a teenaged boy.

Rose frowned at the new entrants. The woman looked familiar, although she couldn't place her, but the boy looked almost more interesting. Despite the crowd at the bistro, he kept his chin tucked into his neck, his head down, as he crossed to the cash register.

"Sheriff," the woman said with relief. "Joyce said you'd be here. Any word?"

He shook his head. "Not yet, Carla."

With the name, Rose recognized her—the caseworker from the foster care agency.

"I have to file a report with the state," Carla said, sounding apologetic. "Has Kenzi's information been entered into the National Crime Information Center database?"

"Yes, ma'am." The sheriff sounded impatient. "We did that immediately."

"I'm sorry, Sheriff," Carla apologized again. "I know you're busy. I don't want to interrupt you. It's just—well, you know what it's like. Ever since Rilya Williams, foster care agencies have to be hyper-vigilant about the possibility of children in the system going missing. The schools report absences to us, but..."

Carla kept talking but Rose had stopped listening. The boy, the one who'd been keeping his face hidden, had lifted his chin at Carla's words, his expression wide-eyed. Was he shocked or scared? Or both?

Rose slid through Max and out of the booth, eyes intent on the boy. Akira, who had been talking to Grace about their hike and the find they'd made in the forest, turned to watch her go.

"What is it?" she asked.

"Oh, nothing," Rose said airily, waving away Akira's curiosity. But then she paused. She was interested in the boy and wanted to see him from a closer perspective, but she had also wondered whether she might be able to help Akira. Maybe she should check that out. Feeling unusually shy, she said, "Ah, would you mind if I touched you?"

Akira flinched, her reaction clearly instinctive.

"Just... like an experiment," Rose said hastily. "Just... to see."

"To see what?" Akira asked. Grace and Max exchanged puzzled but accepting glances.

"To see if..." Rose started and then, impatiently, she reached out and put a hand on Akira's shoulder.

Akira's eyes widened and her shoulders dropped as the nervous tension that had been keeping her on her feet drained out of her. "Oh, wow," she breathed.

"Good?" Rose asked anxiously.

Akira arched her neck backward, tilting her face to the ceiling. "I think I could run a marathon. Or sleep for a week, I'm not sure which."

"But better?" Rose asked, still nervous.

Akira dropped her head and smiled. "Much, thank you."

Rose's relief was tinged with smugness as she moved away. She'd never deliberately infused someone with her energy before. It had happened inadvertently by the side of the road with Kenzi and one other time, but she'd never done it on purpose.

Of course, it probably wasn't a good idea to do it too often. Akira had all sorts of theories about spirit energy and inter-dimensional particle motion—none of which Rose paid the slightest bit of attention to—but Rose did have enough experience with other ghosts to know sometimes they faded away into nothingness. She'd prefer not to have that happen to her.

The boy was ordering dinner to go. "I'll take the special, thanks," he muttered, his head down again.

Rose slid up next to him, squeezing in without worrying about how she moved through the people nearby. "Well, aren't you a cutie," she said to the boy. He reminded her somewhat of her friend Henry when he was young, with the same dark skin and lanky body. But Henry had had a smile that could light up a room and this boy's expression was grim. He'd turned his face to her, so she had a chance to study him. But was he turning to her or away from someone else?

She looked over his shoulder to see who was behind him. Carla still spoke earnestly to the sheriff, who nodded, listening patiently despite the press of people waiting to speak with him.

Emma, at the cash register, said to the boy, briskly, "That'll be ten dollars even." He passed over a crumpled bill without looking at her.

Rose tipped her head to the side, examining him. He was looking straight through her, of course, but she didn't think he was looking at anything beyond her. From his expression, she thought he might be listening to the conversation behind him.

"I've talked to everyone who works at the agency and all of them swear they didn't reveal Dr. Latimer's address to anyone. It would, of course, have been completely against procedure if they had, but I have faith in our people. If someone had made that mistake, I think, given the gravity of the situation, they'd admit it so you could investigate." Carla's hands were clasped in front of her, her tension showing in the lines of tendon.

"I appreciate your thoroughness, Carla." The sheriff put a hand on her lower arm, giving her a warm smile, his southern drawl stronger than usual. "I admit, you've gotten out ahead of me on this one. You're absolutely right, though. If Kenzi was the target, the question of how she was found is vital."

The boy twitched, his eyes closing for a split second and his shoulders hunching.

"My, my," Rose said. "That was an interesting reaction." She crossed her arms and pursed her lips, before glancing back to the table where Akira sat. Should she mention him to Akira? But she hesitated.

She'd spent all the years of her brief life in Florida, in the 1940s and 1950s. She didn't remember the war years, she'd been too young, but she remembered what life was like when she was a teenager. Dozens of black-owned homes were burned and bombed in Florida during those years. One time, over in Groveland, they'd had to call out the National Guard to stop the lynch mobs.

Accusing a black boy of messing with a white woman and a white girl? Why, that would be a fast way to get him murdered. Times had changed, of course, but in this crowded room of anxious people, Rose didn't much feel like claiming a black boy was involved in a kidnapping just because of a nervous twitch.

Of course, she was also a ghost. It wasn't like anyone was likely to listen to her, anyway. Akira would take her seriously, but Akira hated talking to people about anything ghosts said. She'd do it, but she wouldn't like it.

"We do have one possible item of evidence," Colin was saying to Carla. His eyes scanned the room and he waved over one of his deputies.

As the man wove his way through the tables, Emma passed a large white shopping bag of food over the counter to the boy. "Here you go."

His eyes widened as he felt the weight of the bag and looked at the multiple containers within it. "That's—um—you sure?"

Max Latimer, he'd listen, though. Rose liked him. She'd watched him inviting ghosts into the diner one day—not real ghosts, but ghosts he thought might be there—and found it right friendly of him. He didn't usually realize it, but she often sat next to him while he ate and chatted to him. If she had even the slightest clue as to where his daughter was, she wanted to share it with him. But was this boy really a clue?

Emma's smile held a glimmer of mischief. "Maggie is. She decides what goes in a special. Gotta say, though, you're the first guy my age I've ever seen get spinach salad. Maybe she thinks it'll be like a Popeye thing."

He stared at her blankly.

Rose's eyes widened. Spinach salad? Could that be for Natalya? Could Maggie be providing this boy with what Natalya wanted to eat without even knowing it? She tried to peek into the bag, to see what else was in there, but he was already closing it up, bundling the bag close to his chest.

Behind the boy, Colin held out a piece of paper his deputy had handed him to Carla. "Do you recognize this man?"

She glanced down at it, mouth opening as if to immediately respond, before pausing, her mouth closing. "Well," she said slowly. "This looks a lot like Jack Thompson, one of our foster parents." She raised her eyes to Colin's.

"You know, like..." Emma bent her arm to show off her bicep to the boy, "super-strength?"

The boy shot a frantic glance over his shoulder, before grabbing the bag. "Um, thanks," he blurted out. He retreated through the crowd, backing away until he'd almost reached the door, before turning and bolting through it.

Emma sighed. "Way to scare off the cute guy, Em," she muttered to herself, before turning back to the next customer at the register.

"That little girl was not in our care before Christmas," Carla was saying to Colin. "We would have known, we would have recognized her, she couldn't have gone missing. We have procedures..." Her voice was rising, as Colin moved to reassure her.

"We don't have any reason to believe he's involved, ma'am. We'd just like to ask him a few questions, that's all."

Ah, drat. Rose had run out of time to be indecisive about whether to talk to Akira or not. With one last glance at the table where Akira sat, deep in conversation with Max and Grace, she darted out the door after the boy.

He was already rounding the corner. Rose hurried after him, wishing she'd learned Dillon's trick with cell phones. The boy moved quickly, not running, but striding along at a brisk pace. Rose had no trouble keeping up with him. If she'd been alive, she would have been complaining and out-of-breath within minutes, but ghosts didn't get tired.

"You sure don't look like a kidnapper," she told him. "Not that I've met many kidnappers, but I do watch a lot of television."

He ignored her, of course, but Rose didn't mind. She followed along, speculating on their destination, his relations, what subjects he liked in school, whether he had a girlfriend, his favorite television shows, if he enjoyed dancing or was one of those boys who just stood still while pretending to move, and anything else that popped into her head, as they wound their way out of town.

After they'd hiked for at least a mile along one of the main state roads connecting Tassamara to nearby towns, Rose said, "Your dinner must get pretty cold by the time you get home." She was starting to wonder whether she'd made a mistake. Anything could be happening back in town and she would be missing it. She'd feel a right fool if she got home and Natalya was sitting peacefully with Kenzi, explaining how the whole thing had all been one big misunderstanding. It could happen.

But when the boy came to a crossroads and ducked into the woods by the side of the road, Rose didn't hesitate to follow him. She stayed close to him, stepping on his heels unnoticed more than once as he wove his way through the forest. She didn't understand how he knew where he was going. The moon was high, but under the trees, the shadows were impenetrable.

Rose thought they were still deep in the trees when she heard a quavering voice, say, "That you, Travis?"

"Yep." Her boy's answer was laconic as he pushed his way through some ferns and Rose realized they'd reached a stream.

"Did you get the food?" The speaker was a younger boy sitting in the bow of a canoe.

"You know it." Her boy, Travis, leaned over and placed the bag of food by the other boy's feet. "She gave us a lot this time."

"Cookies?" The words were hopeful, the boy's eyes bright as he looked up at Travis, but he made no move to open the bag.

"Didn't check yet." Travis paused, looking down at the boy. "Anything happen while I was gone?"

The boy dropped his head. "No," he answered, but his voice was small.

"You okay, Mike?" Travis sounded surprisingly gentle.

"Oh, you're a sweetheart, you are," Rose said. She shifted around him so she could see his face, liking the way he talked to the younger boy.

"Heard a big splash, that's all. Got scairt." The last word came out in a mumble.

"Told you before, you're way too big for a gator. It's more scared of you than you are of it." Travis made no move to get into the boat.

"You saw that big one. Thirteen foot long, it was! I'd be, like, breakfast. And not a good breakfast, neither. Not bacon and eggs, I'd be like a bowl a' cold cereal."

Travis chuckled. "Well, it didn't get you," he said indulgently. "You go ahead and see what we got. If we got cookies, you can have one while we head home. But we gotta get there fast." On his last words, his voice lost its softness and his tone became grim. The light, now that they weren't under the trees, was enough that Rose could see his lips shaped into a tight line.

"A boat ride? Oh, how fun," Rose said with enthusiasm. As Travis positioned himself in the stern, she leaped lightly into the middle of the boat. The canoe was small and the floor was damp, but Rose sat down, cross-legged and spreading her skirts wide, ready to concentrate on the movement.

As a ghost, traveling in vehicles didn't always work out for her. More than once, she'd been left behind as a car started when the vehicle moved through her and away instead of carrying her along. Her friend Dillon never had that problem, but he'd spent most of his ghostly life trapped inside a car. She thought he perhaps had an instinct for it she lacked. In her limited experiments, though, paying close attention to the moment the motion began triggered her energy to stay with the car. She hoped it would work with a boat, too.

It did.

"Oh, yay," Rose said as Travis began paddling. She clapped her hands with delight as the boat moved through the water, gliding smoothly up the stream. She was almost disappointed when they reached a dock a short while later. She'd never gotten to take a moonlit boat ride before.

The younger boy hopped out first, reaching back for the bag of food. "You want I should leave this here while we put the canoe away?" he asked.

Travis shook his head. "I gotta go out again."

Mike paused. "Why?"

Travis ignored the question. "Go on, take the food up. I'll be right there."

Mike looked doubtful, but did as he was told, grabbing the food and scampering off. Rose waited in the boat as Travis paddled forward, beaching it on the shore. He swore under his breath as his foot splashed into the water as he got out and Rose tsked at his carelessness as she climbed out after him. Wet feet in this weather? He'd catch his death of cold.

She followed Travis into the house and up the stairs, wondering the whole while whether she'd been right in chasing after him, and crowed with delight as soon as she entered the wide open space on the top floor. Natalya and Kenzi and a collection of boys were clustered on the floor around the shopping bag, taking out the containers of food.

"I found you, I found you," Rose chortled, hugging herself. Now if only she had a way to reach Akira.

"Spinach salad?" Natalya said dubiously, holding a clear plastic container up to the light from the window. "Which one of you wants it?"

"Yuck," one of the younger ones said. "I'm not eating that. But we got brownies."

"Healthy food first," Natalya said, digging deeper into the bag. She handed Kenzi a white Styrofoam container. The little girl's face held a smile of satisfaction as she opened the container and tilted it up to show off the generous helping of homemade macaroni and cheese inside.

"Yum, Maggie makes great mac 'n cheese," Natalya said with approval as she handed out more white Styrofoam containers to the boys.

"How did you know about her?" Travis asked suspiciously.

"I live in Tassamara, kid. Everyone knows Maggie's," Natalya answered, pulling out another soup container.

"Not a kid," Travis muttered as one of the boys opened his container and announced, with a squeal of glee, "Pizza, pizza, I got pizza in mine!"

"I want some," protested his lookalike, a hint of a whine in his voice. "I got enchiladas. Pizza's better." Rose hadn't paid enough attention to his clothes to be sure which one of the two had been in canoe with her, but she thought it might be the one with the enchiladas.

"Share the pizza, Mitch," Travis ordered, sounding weary.

"Yeah, okay," the other boy said agreeably. "Enchiladas are good, too, though. Do they got the green stuff?"

As the twins compared food, Travis crossed the room to the small group, Rose right behind him. "How ya doing, Jamie?"

"Ate a little soup," the boy leaning against the windowed wall told him. "Didn't puke it up."

Rose frowned at him. Even in the shadowed room, Jamie looked terrible, deep bruises around his eyes and across his cheekbone, his face too thin, his eyes too bright.

"Good, good." Travis squatted next to him. "You gotta get well and quick." His eyes flickered over the group and his mouth twisted as if he were chewing on his words.

"What is it?" Jamie asked, pushing himself up.

Travis nodded toward Kenzi who was happily spooning up her macaroni. "Make sure she gets plenty to eat, okay? We need to get you healed and get out of here."

"Why? What happened?" Worry tightened Jamie's voice.

Travis pressed his lips together as if reluctant to speak, then spoke anyway. "We got a time limit. Turns out the school reports absences to the agency. They'll know we're missing pretty much as soon as break's over. We gotta be long gone by then."

"Aw, man." Jamie's shoulders sank. "How's that gonna work? Even if I'm better, Trav, we gotta be almost out of money by now. You can't count on making another score like..." He looked toward Natalya and fell silent.

"Breaking and entering, I assume?" she asked, spearing a piece of spinach with a plastic fork. "Let me guess, you found a stash of cash in one of the vacation houses over by Sweet Springs."

"Jesus, lady," Travis swore. "Who tells you this shit?"

Wordlessly, Natalya pointed her fork at Kenzi, sitting next to her, and raised an eyebrow.

"Mac don't talk," Travis complained. "She ain't said a word for weeks now."

Natalya waved the fork in a negative gesture. "No, no, I was referring to your language. No swearing in front of the children, remember? Kenzi—Mac didn't tell me anything."

"Why do you call her that?" Jamie asked. "It's the wrong way around."

"The wrong way... oh." Natalya ate a bite of salad, looking thoughtful. "So her real name is Mackenzie? That's interesting."

Rose was more interested in the condition of the boy. Could she help him? But she paused before touching him. If he was healed, and they moved on immediately, what would they do to Natalya? There must be a reason the woman had come with them.

"Don't say you guessed that," Travis protested.

"I'm a good guesser," Natalya said peacefully.

"You're spooky, lady."

She smiled at him, looking happier and more amused than Rose had ever seen her. Kidnapping must agree with her. "I told you normal was overrated."

Travis shook his head. "Don't matter, I don't got time for this." He turned back to Jamie. "We got one chance."

Jamie looked confused for a moment and then his expression cleared. "No way, man. You never wanted..." He glanced back at Natalya, and his voice dropped to a whisper. "You thought it was a bad idea to begin with. And without Mary—"

"Hush," Travis ordered. He, too, glanced at Natalya. "I'm gonna go get it now. We'll need a couple days, maybe more. But we gotta be outta here by next week and it'll be worth at least a couple thousand bucks, enough to get us to..." He fell silent again.

"Trav, it's not worth the risk." Jamie was shaking his head weakly, his face pained.

"Yes, it is," Travis whispered furiously. "You guys are the only family I've ever had. I'm not letting go. And we're not letting Mac get hurt. We owe that to Mary."

Jamie closed his eyes. Rose thought he looked like he was fighting the need to cry.

Natalya looked down. She ate another bite of salad, before

dropping the fork into the container and setting the container on the ground by her side.

"So let me get this straight," she said, her voice gentle. "You're going to go harvest the marijuana crop you planted. You're hoping you can find a buyer for the plants—they won't be properly cured, you know, so probably not worth much. When you do, you'll use the money to get all five of you to... someplace. Somewhere you think will be safer."

"Holy fuck, lady!" Travis jumped to his feet, his words a yell. "How the hell do you do that?"

She smiled, her eyes almost sad. "Go," she said to him. "It's not a great plan, but I understand why you're hoping it works."

❧ CHAPTER SIXTEEN ❧

The children were curled up on the floor like a pile of puppies, snuggled together, heads and bodies intertwined. One of them had the slightly stuffy nose that made for a gentle, occasional snore and gasp of breath.

Natalya wished she could follow their example. It was late. Really late. She didn't wear a watch, of course—who needed a watch in the era of cellphones?—but she suspected Travis had been gone for at least three or four hours. Her best guess was that it was well after midnight.

She shivered. Clouds crawled across the sky, alternately shading and revealing the full moon. When it was clear, the bright light shone through the windows, casting a glow across the carpeted floor, but no warmth. She'd spread all the extra clothes across the children and Jamie, but she would have given a month's pay for a space heater or an all-weather blanket. It wasn't freezing—none of them were in any danger—but it wasn't comfortable.

She picked up the flashlight sitting next to her and turned it on. Aiming it at the window, she clicked it on and off in a three quick, three slow pattern. She had no idea whether she was spelling O, S, O or S, O, S, but she hoped if anyone saw it they'd investigate even if she had it wrong. Not that anyone would. It was the middle of the night and she'd been signaling with the flashlight since the last of the children had fallen asleep.

Nothing was stopping her from waking up Kenzi and walking out into the darkness, of course. It might be a long hike, but the house had to be on a road that would lead somewhere eventually. But she couldn't leave the other boys behind, and even if she could convince the twins to come with her, Jamie was in no condition to walk for miles.

She felt slightly guilty about Travis. She'd let him go off to harvest marijuana in the middle of the night knowing his plan had no chance of success. But it was a way to distract him, to keep him busy enough not to think of another plan that might work better. Carjacking, ransom, bank robbery—if she could come up with those ideas, he could, too. That gun and his seeming willingness to risk anything for his family made a dangerous combo.

Instead every minute he spent in their illegal garden brought them another closer to being found by the authorities. He might think he had until the school break was over, but she knew full well he had less than twenty-four hours until Zane got home from Japan and directed Colin straight to her.

Unfortunately, it felt as if twenty-four hours wasn't going to be soon enough. Her gift was coming back and with it, her sense of foreboding. She felt like a deer trapped in the headlights. She didn't want to be an armadillo, though—jumping up to avoid danger only to crash straight into the bumper of the car that would have passed over her if she'd crouched in stillness. Waiting in the silence of the night felt like her best option, even as she strained her brain trying to kick her gift into action.

She clicked the light off and paused. Had she heard something? What was that sound? Pushing herself to her feet, she held the flashlight by her side as she headed across the room. Her heartbeat was louder in her ears than she wanted it to be, her breath too fast. At the top of the stairs, she paused. Holding her breath, she listened.

A muffled thunk.

Could that be a car door closing outside, the sound carrying in the still night air? Or was the noise coming from inside the house? Maybe Travis was back.

Gently, she took two, three, four steps down the stairs. Her feet, clad in too-small socks belonging to one of the boys, were silent on the steps. She reached for the banister, her hand sliding along its smooth, polished wooden surface.

"I told ya." It was Travis, his voice a yell, the angry grate in the sound setting every nerve Natalya possessed aquiver. "We don't know where she is."

"Shut up, boy." The harsh rasp carried up the stairwell like smoke rising.

Natalya's throat clenched closed. A flash of memory-precognition leapt to her mind: a dour, angry man's face, surrounded by white, eyes closed, and then it was gone, replaced by Kenzi's, pale and drawn, lips blue. Natalya's hands tightened, one on the banister, one on the flashlight, as she brought herself back to the present.

"Where are they?" The raspy voice snarled. A door slammed.

"I dunno. They should be here," Travis shouted back at him.

He was yelling for a reason, Natalya realized. Giving them time to hide. Or at least time to get Kenzi out of sight.

Hands shaking, she hurried back to the mound of children. Tossing the extra clothes aside, she reached for Kenzi's small shoulder first and shook the girl gently until Kenzi's sleepy eyes opened. One of the twins was stirring, too, kicking his feet as he burrowed deeper into the warmth of the others.

"Wake up," Natalya said quietly, forcing her voice to a calmness she didn't feel. "We need to hide you."

Jamie had been sleeping slightly apart from the others, his head pillowed by a folded sweater. He pushed himself up onto his elbows, his eyes blinking awake. "What's happening?" he mumbled.

"Shh," Natalya hushed him. "Someone's here. With Travis. I think..." She let the words trail off. She didn't want to scare them, but the boys were already moving, rolling over, fumbling their way onto their feet. Jamie attempted to pull himself into a fully seated position, before falling back again, groaning in pain, as Kenzi scrambled up.

Kenzi's hands fluttered in fear, her face contorting in a grimace that said more than words.

"It's all right," Natalya said, keeping her voice low. She wanted to comfort the little girl but a drumbeat in her blood was banging out 'danger, danger, danger.' "We're going to hide you. No one needs to know you're here."

She looked at the twins. The restless one was yawning, rubbing his eyes, while the other looked asleep on his feet, his chin dropping onto his chest. Should she let them stay or make them scatter? But a glance at Jamie's bruised face decided her. "Run and hide," she told the boys. "If any of the rooms have locks on the doors, lock yourselves in."

Flashlight in hand, she hurried Kenzi to the breakfast bar separating the kitchen from the larger room. Inwardly, she was cursing herself. Why hadn't she explored the house? Mitchell had said it was big. There might be dozens of better hiding places than these cupboards. But her choices were limited. Travis and his company might already be headed upstairs.

She opened the closest cupboard and peered in, shining the flashlight into the darkness. Empty. No signs of creepy-crawlies or mice. She gestured to Kenzi, who didn't hesitate. The little girl crawled in on hands and knees and wiggled around until she was facing the door.

About to close the cupboard, Natalya hesitated. The darkness would seem so solid behind the closed door. Impulsively, she crouched down and handed Kenzi the flashlight. She met the little girl's eyes with her own. "Keep the light off if you hear voices or movement, okay?" she whispered.

Kenzi nodded, pulling the flashlight close to her huddled knees. Natalya rested a hand on her leg for a moment, hoping to impart warmth and comfort, before straightening and hurrying back to Jamie.

The twins were gone, headed to hiding places she hoped. Her heart raced as she wavered about whether she should try to move Jamie, stay with him, or go downstairs to confront the man she assumed to be Mr. Thompson. She dropped to her knees next to him.

"You should run," Jamie muttered. "He don't know you're here."

She raised an eyebrow. That option was out. She wasn't leaving this child alone to face the man who abused him. "I don't think you're quite ready to do any running." She touched his forehead. Still too hot.

"I'll be okay." Jamie tried to smile, but the expression didn't reach his eyes. "He's not looking for me."

Natalya closed her eyes for a moment and took two deep breaths, trying to focus. Thoughts, emotions—they were just leaves on water, clouds in the sky. Adrenaline was starting to replace the fear. The stiffness from the cold, the exhaustion from the late night, began to fade, replaced by a sparkling energy that made the room seem more vivid, the moonlight brighter.

With a confidence she didn't entirely feel, she said to Jamie, "He's not looking for either of us. So let's let him find us."

"Huh?" Jamie blinked a couple of times, as if he wasn't sure he'd heard her.

She nodded at him and then stood, the corner of her mouth lifting in a faint smile. "Stay there, but follow my lead. If I lie, don't be surprised. Pretend I'm telling the truth."

Moving with sure feet, Natalya went back to the staircase and took a few steps down. "Travis?" she called, trying to infuse her voice with welcome relief instead of the fear still tickling the back of her throat. "Did you bring help?"

Stepping lightly, she ran down to the next floor and around the corner, as if she were eager to greet Travis and his companion. They met her on the stairs, Travis in the lead with a lantern dangling from one hand. The light scattered shadows across the dark staircase as it swung, but there was enough of a glow to see that Travis's lip was fat and bloodied, his face grim with suppressed fury.

After the one quick glance, though, Natalya ignored Travis, putting all her attention on the man behind him. "Mr. Thompson, it's so good to see you again," she said warmly. It was the man from her painting, the angles of his bones and thin lips even more severe in the darkness. As far as she knew, she'd never met him before. But she could have encountered him at one of functions she'd attended for the foster care agency. And the implied familiarity might confuse him, throw off whatever plans he had.

"What?" It was Travis who snapped the word, but both faces were startled.

"Come on up." Natalya turned and led the way back up the stairs. "Travis, I'm so glad you made the smart decision and brought help. I know you were worried about getting in trouble for fighting with your brother, but like I told you before, it's time to own up and take responsibility. Jamie's going to be fine with a little medical attention but we need to get him to a hospital." She was babbling, giving Travis time to recover from his surprise and play along. The feeling of eyes boring into her back made her skin crawl, though. Where was Travis's gun?

"He probably needs antibiotics and some blood work. I know the doctors will want to be sure his electrolytes are balanced. Rehydrating too quickly after being dehydrated can be dangerous. He might need to spend some time on an IV." She reached the top of the stairs and quickly crossed the room to where Jamie lay.

"Did you bring your cell phone, Mr. Thompson?" She turned to face the man, the window at her back. Travis still stood in front of him, his head at the same height as the older man but his frame much smaller. "It would be easier on Jamie if we called an ambulance, I think. The EMTs could start treatment on the way to the hospital."

"Ambulance? No ambulance. Can't afford that." Thompson sounded confused, exactly as Natalya had hoped.

173

Calmly, she suggested, "All right, your car will work. Can you and Travis help Jamie down the stairs? He's gotten weaker since he's been here. We don't want to take any chance of him falling."

"What is this? Where is she?" The words were a growl, the shove that caused Travis to stumble farther into the room correspondingly violent.

The gun in Thompson's hand looked much too familiar.

Natalya ignored it.

She kept her eyes locked on Thompson's face, her calm expression unwavering.

"Mr. Thompson," she said, her voice gentle. "Jamie needs help. Medical attention. I know you want to do what's right for him." Behind her serene façade, however, her thoughts were racing.

Why hadn't she realized the risk in letting Travis go back to wherever Mary and Kenzi had been camping? Jamie had told her he'd revealed the location to Thompson. The man must have been waiting, hoping for one of the children to return there. Travis had walked into a trap, and somehow Thompson had gotten the gun away from him. Had he surprised the boy or had Travis been reluctant to pull the trigger?

"What's right, yes," Mr. Thompson said, as if grasping for the words with relief. "Yes. It's Satan's influence, you understand? It's the mark of evil rising. Not what's right, but what's wrong. But we have to fix it. We can, you know, we can. If we cleanse the world of the marks of sin, we can go back. To how it was. To how it should be."

Natalya's breath stopped in her throat.

Jamie had given her all the information she needed, if only she'd listened. He'd told her life with the Thompsons had been all right. Then came a trauma, the lost job, followed by the long stretches on the couch, the quiet times, ending with yelling and ranting and bursts of energy. A psychiatrist would have made the connections immediately. Thompson's condition presented as classic bipolar 1 disorder, mania followed by depression in a cycle that just kept spiraling down. And it had obviously gotten worse. His words now sounded like a full-blown manic psychosis.

"But I can fix it, I know I can," he continued. "The word of the Lord tells me how."

Oh, how she wished she was in a nice comfortable emergency

room, with a couple of strong assistants standing by with sedatives and a psych consult on speed-dial. She'd realized Thompson could be dangerous, but she'd hoped some sensible self-interest mixed with reason would bring them all to a safer place. Unfortunately, reason and delusions didn't blend well.

She licked her lips, trying to remember from her limited psychiatric experience how to work with a patient displaying psychotic symptoms. All that came to mind was the rule she'd learned on her first ER shift, though: if you think you're in danger, get help. That sounded like a lovely idea to her.

Where the hell was Colin? Shouldn't he be riding to the rescue right about now? He'd always shown up when she needed him before, always.

"Yes, we can fix it," she said, keeping her voice soothing. "You're right. We can make this better." Never argue with a delusion, she remembered that much.

"Yes. Better," Thompson agreed fervently. "Cleanse the world of sin. The Lord made us to suffer here that we might rejoice in heaven, that we might be exalted unto Him."

What else, what else? Orient the patient to reality. Date, time, place, people—remind him of their shared world, break into the inner obsessions. Slowly, too slowly, the bit of experience she'd had was coming back to her.

"I'm a doctor, Mr. Thompson. Natalya Latimer. I don't think you recognize me?" Her chin lifted as she said the words, but her voice was as steady as ever.

"No," he said, sounding apologetic. "No, I don't. We've met?"

"Mmm." Natalya didn't want to invent specific details lest Thompson catch her in the lie, so she kept her confirmation vague, hurrying on to say, "I work with Community Family Services."

"The agency?" Thompson tensed, his shoulders hunching, his hand tightening on the gun. "They can't know. They mustn't know. Annie—she weeps for the sorrow of it all. The wages of sin made manifest. For whosoever causes a child to sin should have a great millstone tied around his neck and be drowned in the sea. Drowned. But that's no child. She is the seed of Satan." With each word he spoke, he grew louder, the fire of his mania heating his tone.

Natalya swallowed, her mouth feeling dry as sandpaper. Oops. Mentioning the foster agency, not a good plan. She wouldn't be doing that again.

As Natalya spoke to Thompson, she'd been aware, out of the corner of her eye, of Travis shuffling to the side, one furtive whisper of motion after another. She thought he might be signaling something to Jamie, but she didn't dare look at him. She didn't want Thompson to turn his attention to the boys.

"Mr. Thompson, I'd like to help you. I think if we can get Jamie to a hospital, the doctors there will be able to help you. To get back to the way it used to be."

"Doctors," Thompson grunted. "Useless. And expensive. Can't afford doctors. No. Cleanse the sin, it's the only way. Mary was a good girl before the evil took her."

"She's still good," Jamie said from behind her. Natalya twitched, startled, and pushed her hand down toward him, fingers spread wide, gesturing him to be quiet. If he saw the gesture, though, he ignored it, continuing, "If she's alive, that is. Did you kill her?"

Natalya winced as Thompson's gun swiveled from her to the boy on the floor. What did Jamie think he was doing?

"Kill her?" Thompson sounded authentically confused. The gun in his hand lowered. "She didn't come home. Just like last time. I went there, where you told me, I went and I waited, but she wasn't there. Thought you mighta lied to me, boy, but her things were there. I took 'em home."

Natalya relaxed slightly. She'd been deliberately trying not to wonder if Thompson had already murdered one person. Not that it mattered—if he'd killed, it was in the grip of a psychotic episode. Either way, he wasn't rationally assessing the risk to himself and his family.

"Where is she then?" Jamie demanded.

"I don't know," Thompson growled back at him. "I know how to find her, though. Kill the Satan spawn. She'll come back then."

"She loves Mac. She'd never forgive you for hurting her."

Natalya wanted to tell Jamie to be quiet, not to antagonize Thompson, but Jamie knew the man better than she did. Maybe this was the right tack.

"She's blinded by evil. It's in the eyes, you know. You can tell by the color." Thompson sounded almost reasonable, as if he were explaining how to change a tire.

"Mac's not evil," Jamie protested. "She healed me. I was really

176

hurt and she helped me get better."

Natalya pressed her lips together, trying not to show her dismay. Would Thompson realize what Jamie had revealed? She looked over her shoulder in time to see Jamie trying to get to his feet and Travis's scowl of frustration as he also recognized what Jamie had done.

"The devil's work," Thompson breathed, before raising his voice and saying in a roar, "Suffering is man's lot in this world. Where is the demon spawn?" He lifted the gun again, pointing it directly at Jamie. "I know she's here. Tell me or face the consequences."

"Mr. Thompson, please." Natalya's legs trembled, but she stepped closer to the angry man, blocking his view of Jamie. "I can see how upset you are. I understand you're a deeply religious man. You want to do the right thing. That's admirable."

Half her attention was on her words and Thompson's face, but the other half was trying desperately to kick her foresight into gear. Surely she'd know if she was about to get shot? It would hurt like hell. She ought to remember it if it was going to happen. Unless she died instantly? But even this close, he'd have to get an incredibly lucky shot, maybe sever a major aorta or her spinal cord, for her to die so quickly she didn't have time to notice.

"Blue eyes," Thompson muttered, staring directly at Natalya.

She kept her gaze steady on his, hoping Jamie was taking his chance to move out of the line of fire. If Travis helped him, maybe she could distract Thompson long enough for both boys to get away.

"The devil's in your eyes, ma'am." Thompson shook his head. "I see it in the blue. You're one of his tools, aren't you? Getting in the way of a man and his duty."

Natalya blinked. He had dark eyes himself and all the boys had brown eyes. But Kenzi's eyes were blue, as were Natalya's own. She suspected the odds of her getting shot had just skyrocketed, but her precognition still wasn't telling her anything at all about the next few minutes.

"Your duty cannot be to hurt a child," she said, voice soft. "No God would ask for that."

"Abraham and Isaac. This is a test, a test the Lord demands of me. I must not fail." Despite the chill in the air, beads of sweat dotted Thompson's forehead. His face was flushed, his hand trembling as he held the gun.

Behind her, Jamie gasped in pain. "I can't, Trav, I can't."

"All right, man, it's okay." Despair filled Travis's voice. Natalya risked a glance. He was helping Jamie back to the ground. Jamie had one arm wrapped around his chest, the other clutching Travis's arm. Kenzi might have healed the internal bleeding, but she hadn't mended his broken ribs.

Travis straightened again, his expression resolute. Natalya tried to caution him with her eyes, widening them in a glare she hoped said, 'run away, run away,' but he stepped up beside her.

"Mac ain't evil," Travis said flatly. "You are."

Natalya bit back her groan. What the hell was wrong with these boys? Did they have to provoke Thompson?

"I don't want to hear no backtalk from you, boy," Thompson warned him, his gaze unwavering, his gun not shifting away from Natalya.

"I'll say anything I like to you, old man. You're a redneck, shithead, motherfucking, son-of-a—".

Natalya's eyes widened as Thompson turned red with fury, but as Thompson turned in his direction, Travis exploded into action, grabbing the arm with the gun and forcing it up and up, over his head. Thompson fired, the crack of the shot ferociously loud in the enclosed space.

"Run," Travis shouted. "Run!"

The surprise had Thompson stilled for a second, but not for long. Travis was hopelessly outmatched as they struggled for the gun. The older man outweighed him by at least a hundred pounds. Even with both of Travis's hands pushing Thompson's right arm up, Thompson was managing to get the gun back down.

Natalya didn't hesitate. She grabbed Thompson's left arm as he swung it around to hit Travis. Digging her thumb into the sinewy muscle directly below the inner elbow and her fingers into the Golgi tendon organ above and outside it, she found the pressure point and squeezed as hard as she could. In automatic reflex, his arm straightened, his chin swiveled, and the fingers on his right hand opened up. The gun fell to the floor with a clatter.

"Grab it," shouted Travis.

Natalya tried to hang on to Thompson's arm, but her sock-clad feet were slipping on the floor, the force of his push sliding her backward toward the window.

"No!" The piercing shriek came from Kenzi, appearing out of the dark kitchen like a mini-avenging fury.

Natalya nearly sobbed in frustration. Why couldn't these children do as they were told? Kenzi could have stayed hidden. She would have been safe in the cupboard.

Thompson roared with satisfaction, but Travis dropped the arm he held and rammed his shoulder into Thompson's midsection, driving the man backward. "Mac, no," he shouted, as she reached the tall man and began hitting him with the flashlight she held. "Run."

Kenzi ignored him, but even with the weight of the flashlight in her hand, her blows didn't hold enough force to slow Thompson down. He swung for her. Natalya leaped on him. Already off-balance from Travis's hard shove, he fell backward, landing hard on the carpeted floor, Natalya on top of him.

"Kenzi, heal Jamie," Natalya ordered. "As much as you can. Hurry!" Thompson was fighting to get up, but Natalya was no lightweight. She might not be strong enough to do damage, but she could hold him down. And then he managed to get in a hard crack on her cheekbone. She grunted with the pain of it as she was knocked to the side, half on, half off him. Travis jumped into the fray, dropping to fall across Thompson.

Seeing stars wasn't just a metaphor, Natalya realized. Flashes of light burst in front of her eyes as an agonizing heat radiated through her face and down her jaw. She shook her head, trying to clear it.

The gun was on the floor next to her. Natalya reached for it, trying not to sob from the pain. Her fingers closed around the metal and she rolled away from the battling Travis and Thompson, sitting up and scrabbling backward toward the windowed wall.

She'd never held a gun before. It was heavier than she would have expected it to be, smoother in her hand, but holding it felt natural, her fingers dropping into place on the grip and trigger automatically. She pointed it at Thompson.

And then she took a deep, shaky breath. Her face hurt. She was terrified for the children. She wanted nothing more than to get all of them safely away from here.

But she was still a doctor.

She flicked a glance at Kenzi and Jamie. Kenzi was swaying, her eyes closing, her skin translucently pale, her lips fading to blue, but Jamie was sitting up, his bruises gone. He touched his side, pressing the skin over his broken ribs, his expression awed.

"Take her and go," Natalya ordered, through lips that already felt swollen.

He looked at Travis and Thompson struggling as he scrambled to his feet. "But…"

"Go," she ordered again, glaring at him. "Get her to a safe place."

Jamie nodded once. He scooped up Kenzi and ran for the stairs. Natalya turned her attention back to the fight. Travis was losing, she could see it.

She could tell him to back off. She had the gun. But a gun was only as useful as the person holding it made it. And Thompson wasn't rational. A threat wouldn't be enough to stop him.

Could she shoot someone? Could she shoot Thompson?

The answer was as clear to her as if it was written in neon across the sky.

No.

A gun in her hands might as well be a hammer.

Turning, she looked at the windows. A bullet hole surrounded by a spider web of cracks marred the wall high above her. She stood, shaky, face throbbing, and hit the glass with the gun. Once, twice, three times, four times, until finally, finally, the glass broke, pieces shattering, falling out the window frame.

"No," Travis shouted. "What are you doing?"

Natalya threw the gun out the window.

A gun was only as useful as the person holding it made it.

∾ CHAPTER SEVENTEEN ⋘

Colin pushed the box of tissues closer to the weeping woman sitting at the table across from him. Her tears were the quiet kind, her eyes simply overflowing in a steady stream dripping down her face, but they seemed endless.

"So the boys went camping," he prompted.

"I told you this already." Her voice shook.

She had, several times. Twice at her home, where her husband had been nowhere to be seen, and now at least three times at the station after Colin requested she join him there. But Colin recognized a lie when he heard one, at least when it was as badly delivered and as implausible as Anne Thompson's lies.

"What sort of gear did they take with them?"

"The usual stuff."

"Sleeping bags, tents?"

"Of course." She sniffled loudly and took a tissue from the box, patting at her face, her head down.

"What about a camping stove?"

"Yes."

"And food?" Colin interlaced his fingers, folding his hands on the table in front of him. He wanted to shake her, to reach out and grab her by the shoulders and demand she tell him what she knew. Instead, he kept his voice gentle and his hands still.

"Yes." She knotted the tissue in her hands, twisting and bunching it up.

"How much food?"

"I—what?" She looked up, her watery brown eyes meeting his.

"You do the grocery shopping for the household, don't you?"

"I... yes, of course."

"How much food did you pack for your husband and the boys?"

She dropped her head again, staring at her lap. She didn't answer the question.

Colin leaned back in the uncomfortable interview room chair. Outside the interrogation room, phones were ringing off the hook, a blitz of volunteers and suspected sightings and reports from teams in the field. People were flowing in and out of the station like cars in a rush hour the likes of which Tassamara had never seen. He wanted to be out there, managing the chaos, not in here.

"Ma'am, if I get a search warrant for your home, how many sleeping bags will I find there?"

The gasping breath she took sounded like the precursor to a child's sobs. Colin bit back the aggravated sigh that wanted to escape and considered what he'd already learned. Mrs. Thompson claimed her husband and foster sons had gone camping several days ago. She didn't know where. She didn't know when to expect them home; it depended on the weather and how the boys were behaving. She didn't know how a picture of her husband could have wound up on Natalya's easel. She'd never met Dr. Latimer and was terribly sorry she was missing, but didn't see how her husband could possibly be connected.

But the tears had started when Colin showed her the flier of Natalya and Kenzi and the long silences had started then, too. She knew more than she was saying.

A knock on the door interrupted his grim thoughts. Standing so quickly he nearly knocked his chair over, Colin excused himself and strode to the door, closing it behind him. Joyce waited outside.

"Anything?" he asked her.

She spread her hands wide. "The roadblocks have picked up three DUIs. People getting started early on their New Year's celebrations, I suppose. A few possibly credible sightings. The likeliest is a woman with dark hair, a child, and a grey-haired man in a blue SUV going through a McDonald's drive-through over in Sweet Springs. The state police are looking into that one. Search-and-Rescue reported in. You were right about the water. The dogs tracked them straight to the lake."

Neither the drinkers nor the dogs surprised Colin, but if the sighting in Sweet Springs was correct, Natalya was definitely under duress. She'd have to be at gunpoint to eat at McDonald's. "All right. What do you need, then?" He tilted his head in the direction of the interview room. "She knows something, I'm sure of it. I'm not ready to give up on getting her to talk yet."

Joyce's expression held the self-satisfaction of a cat in sunlight. "Not what I need, but what I've got."

"What?"

She pointed down the hallway in the direction of her office. "Your search warrant is printing out as we speak. The judge agreed that under the circumstances, Dr. Latimer's drawing constituted probable cause."

"That's great news." An unlabeled drawing wasn't much to build a case on. Colin had done the paperwork to get the warrant, but he hadn't been sure he'd find a judge willing to accept Natalya's art as sufficient evidence to support a search. He'd been afraid he'd need to build more of a case first—at the very least, finding a connection between Thompson and Natalya or Kenzi.

"One problem." Joyce put up a cautionary finger.

"What's that?"

"No one's available to conduct the search. We've got every warm body answering phones or liaising with search teams."

Colin ran his hand through his hair, scowling in frustration. He liked working in a small police department. Four full-time deputies, a couple of part-timers, Joyce to run the office, and a forensics unit consisting of one enthusiastic young tech had always seemed like plenty for Tassamara. But they'd never had to investigate a double kidnapping before. And an inadequate search would be worse than no search. "All right, hang on to the warrant. I'll work on her for a while longer."

He turned to go back into the room, but Joyce put a hand on his arm to stop him.

"Yeah?" he asked.

"One other thing. I don't know if this is relevant to this investigation, but you asked me to look into female deaths in the past ten days in the area. I've checked everywhere. There haven't been any."

Colin blinked in surprise. "None?"

Joyce shrugged. "None that have been recorded. It's possible, of course, that there's a body somewhere out there that hasn't been found yet." Joyce's matter-of-fact tone held undercurrents of bleak pessimism.

Colin rubbed his chin, puzzled. He didn't intend to admit he'd gotten the tip from a ghost, but how could Rose be wrong? And why would she have met a spirit at the hospital if the living person hadn't died there? "No," he said slowly. "The death would have happened at a medical facility."

"Well, no younger women have died in the local area recently. Women under fifty don't die every day, Sheriff." He raised an eyebrow and she added, lips pursed, "Not around here, anyway."

He acknowledged the point with a nod. He'd have to check with Rose, which meant talking to Akira. He glanced at his watch. Under the circumstances, Akira might be waiting with the Latimer family for news, but considering the late hour, her pregnancy, and the long hike they'd had, he suspected she would be sound asleep. Should he wait until morning or call her anyway?

"There is that one woman, though," Joyce continued, acting as if he ought to know who she was talking about.

"What woman?"

"The drug dealer," Joyce answered. "The unidentified woman who got shot in that..." She let the words trail off, obviously searching for the right phrase to use.

"Clusterfuck?" Colin suggested.

She gave him a reproving look. "Language, please."

"Can you think of a better word for it?" Colin lifted an eyebrow.

She snorted. "Not in the least. Fine, clusterfuck, it is. But the Feds still haven't identified the woman who got shot."

"She's not dead, though."

"No," Joyce agreed. "But she's on life support, and apparently there's no brain activity. They're looking for next-of-kin so they can shut down the machines and donate her organs if possible."

So if the spirit Rose had talked to was a drug dealer... Colin wanted to kick himself for missing the connection. He should have thought of that poor unlucky woman the moment they found the plot of marijuana in the forest.

He glanced over his shoulder at the door to the interview room. "When you ran the records check on the Thompsons, did you notice whether they had any kids?"

"One daughter," Joyce replied promptly. "No criminal records for either of them, but they reported their daughter missing, a runaway, about eight years ago. She was only sixteen at the time."

Colin's lips tightened. "Get me the photo of the woman in the hospital, will you?"

He waited silently across the table from Mrs. Thompson until Joyce returned with a printout of the photo the hospital had taken. She'd placed it neatly inside a file folder. As she set it on the table next to him, she murmured, "Coffee?"

"Yes, please," he said gratefully. "Mrs. Thompson, would you like a cup of coffee?"

"I should be getting home," she answered, still twisting the tissue in her hands. Little flecks of white dotted her dark skirt. "It's late. I can't drink coffee this late."

"A few more minutes," he responded, before saying to Joyce, "Maybe some water for Mrs. Thompson."

Joyce met his eyes. He could see the awareness in hers of what they both suspected was about to happen. She didn't say anything but she put a hand on his shoulder for a brief moment before nodding and leaving the room.

"I need to get home," Mrs. Thompson repeated, swallowing visibly.

"Soon, ma'am." Colin put a hand on the file folder without picking it up. "Several years ago, you reported your daughter missing. Can you tell me about her?"

"Mary?" A sob burst out of Mrs. Thompson's throat with the word and her hand flew up to cover her mouth. She held the hand over her lips as if to keep any more words imprisoned inside, but her eyes implored Colin not to say any more.

"Have you seen her since then?" he asked.

She nodded. Her voice muffled by her hand, she said, "She came home. Over a year ago. I was so..." She stopped speaking, her shoulders shaking with silent sobs. The tears were flowing faster. Almost angrily, she grabbed a fresh tissue from the box and blotted her eyes.

Colin waited.

Mrs. Thompson crumpled the tissue and dropped it on the table. Straightening her shoulders, she said huskily, chin high, "But she's gone again now."

"Do you have a picture of her with you?" Colin asked.

"Not a recent one, no." Mrs. Thompson glanced toward her purse, which was sitting on a chair next to her, placed neatly on top of her folded coat. "One from when she was young."

"May I see it?"

Wordlessly, Mrs. Thompson reached for her purse and rummaged through it until she found an old, battered wallet. She opened it, fingers steady. Her tears had stopped, Colin noticed. Carefully, she worked a small photograph loose from the vinyl insert, pausing to look at it for a moment before passing it to Colin.

It was a school photo, a headshot of a girl entering adolescence. She had wavy brown hair, brown eyes, fair skin and the wary smile of a child who already knew the world wasn't a safe place.

Holding the file folder so Mrs. Thompson couldn't see its contents, Colin compared the two photographs, looking for any distinguishing features that would rule out the relationship. But the photo from the hospital was unrevealing. The woman in it was young, pale, but her eyes were closed, her hair pulled back and partially covered by bandages. He couldn't say definitively that the two photos showed the same person but he couldn't say they didn't either. He'd have to ask Mrs. Thompson to look at the picture.

He closed the folder and set it down on the table, pausing as he sought the right words.

She nodded toward it. "Is she dead?" The words were flat, without emotion, as if she'd retreated deep within herself, letting go of her sorrow and fear.

"On life support," he admitted. "But I can't tell if she's your daughter."

She looked at him for permission as she reached for the folder and he nodded, sliding it across the table to her.

He knew before she said a word. She stared down at the photograph, her face suddenly looking ten years older. "Mary. Oh, my baby," she whispered. But her eyes stayed dry as she lifted her face to his. "What do you want to know?"

༺❧

Colin took a gulp of cold coffee and set the cup back in his car's cup holder before picking up his radio transceiver to report in. He'd accompanied Anne Thompson back to her home and seen her into the capable hands of a neighbor who would drive her to the hospital, an hour away.

Once Mrs. Thompson learned about her daughter's condition, she'd been far more forthcoming. But his missing person's case had expanded dramatically. She hadn't seen her foster children in days.

When Mary didn't come home for Christmas, her husband had lost his temper, she'd told him. "His temper... and maybe his mind," she'd said, as her tears started again. "He doesn't make sense anymore. The things he says—I just don't understand what's happened to him."

Colin was interested, but far more focused on where Jack Thompson might be. Unfortunately, Anne had no idea. He'd been searching for the boys and Mary, not sleeping, not eating, barely home.

"He hurt Jamie, bad," she'd confessed. "He's hit them before but never like that. Usually just a smack and then he'd be sorry."

"You didn't call for help?" Colin asked, keeping his voice deliberately neutral.

"I couldn't. I didn't know what to do. They'd take the boys away."

Colin had been tempted to throw her in jail. Even if she hadn't hurt the children herself, foster parents were mandatory reporters: her silence was a third-degree felony, punishable by up to five years in prison. Still, that case would have to wait. His first priority was to find the missing children. And Natalya. Always Natalya.

He looked down at the pictures of the boys Mrs. Thompson had given him. Teenage runaways could be hard to track. If they made it to a city, they could disappear. But the younger boys would be harder to hide. People would notice identical twins. And Natalya had said, specifically, that there was a boy at her door. Maybe it was one of these boys?

Mrs. Thompson had admitted, between sobs, that Kenzi was her granddaughter, the illegitimate product of a union between Mary and the man she'd run away with. According to Mary, he'd died, prompting her return home.

His radio crackled to life. "What's your 10-20, Sheriff?"

Colin frowned at the radio. He didn't recognize the voice on the other end, and the question was unexpected. Then his frown cleared. "Is that you, Rudean?"

"That's a 10-4, Sheriff."

"What are you doing there?" Rudean retired from the sheriff's department long before Colin became a deputy, but Colin remembered him fondly from his childhood visits to the station. The deputy—old even then—always had a candy bar in his desk to spare for his colleagues' kids.

"10-30, Sheriff," Rudean replied, his tone reproving as he suggested Colin was making unnecessary use of the radio.

Colin scratched his nose, his grin wry. Not too many people scolded him these days. "Joyce roped you in to help out, huh?"

"I tried to volunteer for the search, but they said I was too old. Hmph," snorted Rudean. "Too old. What do they know? I know this place like the back of my hand, every square mile of it. But fine, I told Joyce. Fine. You let me sit on that there radio, I said to her. I can manage it."

"I'm sure you can." Colin decided not to mention to Rudean that they no longer used the ten codes. Some departments in Florida still did, but he'd updated Tassamara's protocols per the Department of Homeland Security's SAFECOM procedures. Plain English was a lot more efficient.

"So where are you, boy?" Rudean asked.

"Take a look at the screen on top of the dispatch board," Colin answered.

"10-4," Rudean responded.

"See the number one? Out on Lassiter Road? That's me." The department might be small, but they had the latest GPS technology courtesy of a donation from General Directions.

"10-12, Unit One." The radio fell silent.

Colin waited, wondering why he was standing by. He needed to get back to the station. He'd accompanied Anne Thompson to her home because she needed a ride and he wanted to get photographs of the boys as expeditiously as possible, but he should be at the center of operations back in town.

"All right, you're closest," Rudean finally answered. "10... uh, 10..."

"10-10?" Colin asked, surprised. Although they didn't use the codes anymore, he didn't have any trouble remembering them. He'd spent months reciting them before bed every night back in the early days. "Fight in progress?"

"No." Even over the radio, Colin could hear the snap in Rudean's voice.

"10-9, dispatch," Colin responded, fingers tapping on his steering wheel as he asked for a repeat of the message.

"Ah, hell with it," Rudean muttered, before saying in a stronger voice. "Got a tip. Joyce wants someone to check it out. Some schmo saw lights out at a house on Mud Lake."

Colin frowned. That didn't sound like much of a lead. Mud Lake?

He couldn't even remember which lake that was. "Why me?"

"Joyce said to send the nearest free car. That's you," Rudean answered promptly.

"Did she really intend for you to send the sheriff?" Colin questioned. It didn't sound like Joyce. He was sure she'd want him back at the office, overseeing the action.

"You getting uppity, boy? Too big for your britches?" Rudean admonished him.

Colin rolled his eyes as he turned the key in the ignition and started the car. No wonder Joyce let Rudean take the dispatch duties. She'd probably taken lessons in scolding from him back when Colin was barely out of school.

"All right, Mud Lake it is," Colin said as he pulled out onto the road. "Where is it?"

"Ah, they call it something pretty now. Some developer bought it up."

Colin thought, puzzled for a moment and then his face cleared. "Elsinore Lake, right? Got that gorgeous house by that Danish architect on it?"

"That's the one," Rudean said, sounding relieved. "Lights in the house apparently."

"I thought the developer went bankrupt." Colin felt a trickle of excitement tingle down his spine. "No one lives there."

"That's the place," Rudean said, voice cheerful. "Probably nothing. Fool's seeing swamp gas."

"On my way." Colin slotted the transceiver back into its holder and hit the accelerator. Rudean was right. It was probably nothing. But he'd check it out anyway, as quickly as possible.

Sarah Wynde

Sarah Wynde

Sarah Wynde

190

Sarah Wynde

190

⤙ CHAPTER EIGHTEEN ⤚

Natalya spread her hands wide. The shattered glass behind her back let in a cold breeze, the chill of the bracing night air against her skin not quite enough to distract her from the throbbing pain in her face. "Mr. Thompson," she said, her voice as firm as she could make it with shaky adrenaline pouring through her system, "please calm down now. Let Travis go."

"That don't work," snarled Travis, breathlessly struggling to keep Thompson pinned down.

"Demons," howled Thompson. "The evil must be struck down." With one huge push, he forced Travis off of him and rolled onto his hands and knees. Shaking his head, he paused for a moment before lurching to his feet.

Travis, sprawled on the floor, pushed himself up onto his elbows. "Run," he gasped out. "Run. You can't fix him when he's like this. You just gotta get outta the way."

Natalya ignored him. Stepping forward, she used her most authoritative doctor voice, the one that sent interns scurrying in the emergency room. "Mr. Thompson, we need to get you help. Everything is going to be okay. I need you to trust me. I'm a doctor, and I can help you if you let me."

If Thompson heard her words, he showed no sign of it. He lifted his head to the ceiling, his eyes glazed. "I can't, I can't," he muttered. "I can't." And then, with a groan that sounded like pain, he shook his head as if he were a stunned bull hit by a matador and advanced on Natalya.

She stood her ground, her heart pounding, and said again, voice steady but for a breathless break as he reached her, "Please let me help you."

But there was no getting through to him.

He reached out for her and grabbed, his hands closing on her shoulders only briefly before they slid up and around her throat. Natalya's eyes widened and her hands came up, clutching his wrists, trying to wrench them away, to loosen his fingers. Her nails dug into his skin, feeling the give under them, the dig that said she might be drawing blood, but he didn't relent.

Her head fell back. The pain in her cheek still hurt more than his hands around her throat, but the pressure felt as if it were forcing her larynx back into her vertebrae, a steady weight closing off her air supply. She kicked Thompson, but her bare foot against his shin was a leaf against rock. He didn't react and her toes hurt. Drawing her leg up, she tried to knee him in the groin, but his legs were close together, preventing her from reaching an angle that could do damage.

"No," shouted Travis.

He was hitting Thompson, Natalya realized dimly. But her eyes were already fluttering closed. Her chest burned with the pain of her contained breath and now it hurt, her bruised cheek dimming into insignificance against the fire in her lungs.

"You can't, you can't, you have to drown her!" Travis sounded frantic. "That's what the book says. Drowning. That's what you do, drown evil. Nothing else works!"

The grip on her throat relaxed and Natalya drew in a shuddering breath of air.

"Yes. Drowned in the depth of the sea." Thompson's husky voice sounded dazed, almost flat.

Natalya's eyes opened to the sight of Thompson staring down at her. The moonlight cast terrifying shadows across his face but she could still see the tragic figure behind them.

"The lake," Travis suggested. "You need to take her to the lake."

Natalya swallowed, her throat feeling bruised and sore. What the hell was Travis doing? She supposed she should be grateful he hadn't run away. She could be dead by now if he hadn't intervened. She hadn't expected Thompson to move so quickly, so aggressively. But still—drowning? The lake?

"Yes," Thompson agreed again.

He grabbed Natalya's upper arm and began pulling her toward the stairs, his fingers digging into her so hard she could almost feel the bruises forming underneath them. She stumbled after him, not resisting, confused and unsure. Thompson was too strong. She couldn't fight him, not directly. She needed to get away. They needed to get help. Her mind raced in circles, unable to come up with a coherent plan.

Travis hadn't run. He was right behind them, following so closely that his presence felt threatening. He wasn't going to help Thompson drown her, was he? They hadn't exactly hit it off, but Natalya had stopped thinking he was dangerous the moment he let his little adopted sister wave him off her porch. Was she wrong?

Natalya felt a bubble of hysteria rising. She let out a shaky, gasping breath, searching for the calming, cleansing breath she used to use when a three-car pile-up hit the emergency room on a Friday night, but not succeeding.

As they reached the stairs and Thompson started down, Travis grabbed her free hand and squeezed hard, not letting go. Natalya glanced at him. He jerked his chin down, before slipping by her, against the wall. Three steps down, four, and then Travis kicked the older man—hard—in the back of the knee.

Thompson stumbled, letting out a grunt of surprise, and his grip relaxed, but Travis hadn't waited. He bolted up the stairs, not letting go of Natalya's hand. For a moment, Natalya was caught between them, one arm yanked backward, the other pulled forward, Thompson two steps below her, Travis above. With a grimace and gritted teeth, she raised her foot and kicked Thompson in the kidneys.

It wasn't the hardest kick, but it didn't have to be. Thompson let go and reeled forward, falling down onto the landing a few steps below him. Natalya let Travis pull her away, following him as he ran through the open room to an archway in the wall on the other side, around a corner and through a door.

As soon as she was inside, he slammed the door shut behind them. She could hear him fumbling with the lock.

Natalya bent over, putting her hands on her knees, feeling as if she wanted to throw up. She'd never hit anyone before, much less kicked someone in the back.

Travis leaned against the door, breathing hard. "Shit, lady, you're crazy, you know that?"

Natalya felt a strange urge to laugh. She straightened. "You could have run."

"As if," he muttered.

"Drowning?"

"It was the only thing I could think of. He was gonna kill ya."

"Thanks for saving me." Natalya looked toward the window. This room faced the front of the house, away from the water. The bright moonlight cast only a dim glow, leaving the room shadowed, mysterious.

"Ya ain't saved yet." Travis sounded grim.

"Are we trapped?"

The doorknob rattled. Travis shook his head and pointed toward the corner of the room, as Thompson began pounding on the door. The door shook in its frame, but the lock held.

Natalya followed the direction of Travis's pointing finger but didn't see a door. She took a few steps closer before spotting the metal railing marking a hole in the floor. A spiral staircase led down into blackness.

"We have to get help," she told Travis. "How close is the nearest house?"

He shrugged. "No idea. You and Mac, you should get to the canoe. Paddle outta here."

Natalya wasn't about to leave the boys alone with a man in the midst of a psychotic breakdown. Who knew what delusions would attack him next? She shook her head. "Not likely."

Travis was leaning against the door, pushing back against the wood as it shook with Thompson's battering. "He wants to kill you. You got that, right?"

Thompson banged on the door, rhythmic thuds that sounded like a heartbeat.

"I know." Natalya swallowed. For a brief moment, she reached for knowledge she didn't have. But her foresight stayed stubbornly silent. "But he could also kill any of you. He's having a psychotic break. He's not responsible for what he does."

Travis snorted. "Ain't gonna care too much about that if he murders me." The words sounded full of bravado and in the darkness, Natalya couldn't see his face. But she suspected grief and fear lay under the teenage machismo.

"Come to that, me neither," she said, but her words were drowned out as Thompson roared with frustration, his pounding growing louder, harder. She waved at Travis to indicate they should go down the stairs, but he shook his head.

"Find Mac and get outta here. I'll hold the door for as long as I can."

"I'm not leaving all of you here with him." Natalya took a deep breath and said, in a steadier voice, "We need to get help. And fast.

What's the best way?"

"The canoe," Travis answered promptly. "It's a long way by road, but we go fast across the lake so as not to get spotted by the house on the west shore. There's folks living there."

"Good. Take the canoe and go," Natalya ordered.

"You and Mac should take it," Travis insisted.

"You saw me paddling that canoe," Natalya snapped at him. "We don't have time for that. We need help fast and you're the only one who knows where to go and how to get there."

For a heartbeat, Travis paused in indecision. "Should I look for Mac?"

Natalya pressed her lips together, wishing desperately for better options, then shook her head and said, with an authority she did not feel, "We don't know where she is and every second counts. You don't have time to find her and you'll move faster without her weight. Just go. Quickly."

Travis scowled, before grunting in reluctant acknowledgement. "Yeah, okay. Be careful." Pushing away from the door, he headed for the stairs, passing by her and starting down them without hesitation.

Natalya followed more carefully. It was dark. Seriously, thoroughly dark. Partway down the spiral, hand clenched tight on the metal railing, she paused. She'd heard a sound under Thompson's pounds, a different sound. It took her a second to place it, but when she did, her breath stopped. It was the creak of wood giving way. The door frame must be bending under the force of his weight being thrown against it.

"He's going to break down the door," she warned Travis.

"You gotta find the kids," he answered out of the darkness. "I'll go as fast as I can. Don't let him catch you."

How the hell was she going to manage that?

She could hear Travis moving away. A door opened, creating a patch of lighter shadow against the dark and she saw his silhouette for a moment before he disappeared through it.

She hurried the rest of the way down the stairs, hand sweaty on the railing. At the bottom, she paused. Travis hadn't stumbled or hesitated, so the room must be empty, but she stretched out her hands in front of her as she made her way to the door. As she got closer to the rectangle of light, she realized the walls were lined with shelves. The room must have been meant as a library or office.

Perhaps the room they'd been in upstairs was the master bedroom.

In the hallway, she closed the door behind her. It would take Thompson longer to find his way out without the light. It might give her an extra minute or two.

Where would the children have hidden?

Natalya's cheek ached and her throat felt sore and bruised. The adrenaline had drowned out the pain for a few short minutes, but it was back with a vengeance. And she was cold, bitterly cold, her fingers and toes numb and stiff, despite the fear making her heart race.

The hallway extended to the right, toward the front of the house, and to the left, around a corner. The main staircase ought to be toward the left, she thought, so she started in that direction, moving as quickly as she dared in the dark.

She passed a door and opened it, sticking her head inside. "Kenzi? Jamie?" She kept her voice quiet, not wanting Thompson to follow its sound. No one answered. If she locked the door, would Thompson delay to try to break it down? She felt for the lock, trying to discover if it was the kind she could turn before pulling the door closed or whether she'd have to be inside the room to lock it.

The silence was eerie. All she could hear was the sound of her own harsh breathing. It reminded her of being young, playing hide-and-seek in the dark with her siblings and friends, while their parents enjoyed dinner downstairs. Or Ghost in the Graveyard, outside, after dark, with all the neighborhood kids on spring evenings when the mosquitoes were biting and bats darted across the sky.

Except, she realized abruptly, the silence was because Thompson had stopped battering the upstairs door. He must have finally broken through it.

She was out of time.

She pulled the door closed, unlocked, and ran down the hallway, skidding around the corner, and raced down the next hallway to the main staircase. She passed door after door, knowing the kids might be hidden behind any of them. But she didn't want to call out. If they were safely hidden, maybe she should let them stay hidden.

She had no idea how long it would take Travis to get help. An hour? More? The house was big, but it couldn't possibly be so big they could all stay hidden indefinitely. And with five of them hiding, Thompson only needed to get lucky to catch one of them. This was a game of hide-and-seek they were destined to lose.

But what if they were playing Ghost in the Graveyard instead?

Not literally, not with the children chasing Thompson, but the outside world offered more scope for getting away. He wouldn't be able to corner her, speed would count as much as size, and in the dark night, hiding could even be a matter of standing still in the shadows. Once upon a time, she'd hidden from her brothers for a solid twenty minutes by standing pressed against the house in the corner by their garage.

Unless going outside was horror movie stupidity equivalent to splitting up.

Oh, wait. They had split up.

Natalya wished her brain would shut up as she reached the main staircase and headed down.

She'd get to his car. Smash the window if it was locked, honk the horn as loudly as she could. If she could force Thompson to come outside, maybe she could even lead him away from the house and the children. All she needed to do was distract him until help arrived.

At the bottom of the stairs, she paused, uncertain. She could leave the way they'd entered, but… snakes. And Thompson wanted to drown her. If he caught up with her next to that pool… she didn't want to drown one way or another, but she definitely didn't want to be fighting for her life in that slimy, murky water.

Decision made, she headed in the other direction. She'd find the front door.

Seconds later, she did. It was locked.

Deadbolted, with no key in sight.

She rested her hand against the wood of the door, trying to catch her breath and not to scream with frustration.

It was a big house. It must have a garage, with a door leading to the outside. Teeth gritted, she headed in the direction she thought the garage must be, ignoring the pain in her face and the cold surrounding her.

Despite her fear, she couldn't help noticing the house was beautiful. She'd dismissed it as a McMansion from outside, but the interior was actually stunning. Not the fake glamour of a nouveau riche home, with marble and ostentatious chandeliers, but lovely hardwood floors, plain walls, lots of windows overlooking the lake. She passed through the kitchen and paused.

197

Had she heard something?

"Hello?" she said the word softly.

A door opened. One of the twins stuck his head out. "What's happening?" he hissed.

She pointed at him. "Stay hidden," she ordered. "Travis is getting help. Barricade the door if you can and don't come out until the police come find you."

He nodded and disappeared behind the closing door.

She took a deep breath. Was she making the right choices? She couldn't help worrying as she hurried through the kitchen. Were the boys safer in hiding than they would be if they came outside with her?

She started through a sunroom and paused for a split second. This room would be incredible to paint in. All the windows, light from multiple directions, the view of the lake—and French doors, thank God. They were bolted, too, but with the type of bolt that could be opened without a key.

She crossed to the doors and slid the lock to the side. Opening the doors, she stepped outside. Surprisingly, it felt warmer, as if the exterior air were more temperate than the interior air. The sunroom led onto the patio that held the outside pool, so she stayed as far away from it as she could as she worked her way around to the door that led outside the enclosed space.

The moment she stepped onto the path leading around the house she realized her mistake. She wasn't wearing shoes. The builders must not have finished the landscaping because the path was gravel, not paved and so was the driveway. Swearing under her breath, she winced her way to Thompson's car.

It was an old four-door sedan and he hadn't locked it. She pulled the driver's side door open and leaned on the horn. The sound blared into the night, sounding as loud as a siren. She relaxed her push, then leaned on it again. And again. And again.

When should she run? When she saw him at the door or sooner? But even as she asked herself the question, it was too late. He stepped out of the darkness from the pool side of the house, so close.

Too close.

She yelped and jumped away from the car. Her foot landed hard on sharp gravel and her yelp turned into a cry of pain as the stones dug into her flesh.

Thompson's voice was rich with sorrow as he said, "Satan's minions oppose our heavenly Father's plans. I did not ask for this burden, but I must bear it."

Natalya scowled at him. "That's bullshit."

Thompson paused in his advance.

"God gave you free will and a set of commandments," Natalya continued, her voice rising. "Thou shalt not kill. There's no way around that one. It's not optional. He didn't put any outs in there, no wiggle room. Thou shalt not kill. Period. End of the law. You don't get to say, well, he didn't really mean that, this time it's okay. No, it's not okay."

Thompson rubbed his hand across his face. He sounded confused as he muttered, "The devil quotes scripture."

"Oh, I am not," Natalya snapped. "I couldn't even tell you what book the Ten Commandments are in."

She ought to be afraid. She ought to be running for her life. But the feeling heating her veins was rage. Why hadn't this man gotten help the moment his symptoms started getting out of control? Why hadn't anyone noticed he was spiraling into insanity? Bipolar disorder was a treatable illness. A nice hefty dose of lithium and none of them would be here.

"Get away from her!" Travis's voice was hoarse, ragged with misery.

Natalya looked beyond Thompson. Travis stood by the corner of the garage, both hands gripping the gun, its barrel pointed in their general direction.

"Travis, no," Natalya shouted. And then she froze. Her foresight had kicked into action, exactly the way it used to. She knew everything that would happen in the next five seconds. But she had no way to stop it, no way to avoid it.

Thompson roared with rage as he turned toward the boy.

Travis pulled the trigger.

It felt like slow motion to Natalya. That gun—it was so ridiculously large. Where the hell had Travis found a gun so big?

The bullet tore through Thompson.

Through and through, in and out, the blood already staining his shirt, black in the night. Maybe hit a lung, thought the analytical part of Natalya's brain. Passed right through, tissue only, no deflecting off any hard bones.

But the expression on his face—the wide eyes, the lips parting with shock—how could she have forgotten that? How could she have not remembered that sight? Why hadn't it starred in her nightmares for years?

Her hands fluttered toward her chest. It was going to hurt. Oh, hell, it was going to hurt.

But she was already falling backward as the bullet broke through her skin, penetrated her tissue, lodged deep inside.

It was hot. Shockingly hot. The pain exploded inside her, agony running along her nerve endings. How had she thought her bruised cheek hurt? That was a sparkler compared to a mortar, a gentle rain to a hurricane.

She pressed her hand against her chest.

The blood, so sticky against her fingers. So warm. She could smell it, the metallic earthiness of it. Salt and sewage and death.

She turned her head. The gravel looked huge, gigantic jagged white rocks, like a surreal moonscape.

She let out a breath.

Oh, how it hurt.

Leaves on water.

Clouds in the sky.

But oh, it hurt.

She hurt.

⁂ CHAPTER NINETEEN ⁂

"Got a shot fired on Elsinore Lake," Colin radioed in, keeping his voice calm. He was driving slowly, searching for a driveway. It wasn't marked on his GPS and there were no streetlights showing the turn, but it had to be close.

"10-4, Sheriff. You requesting backup?" Rudean sounded eager to send all units blazing to the rescue.

Colin didn't respond immediately. He'd spotted the entrance, a gap in the trees opening into a long dirt and gravel driveway. Turning in, he coasted along the road, his overhead lights off, his siren silent. He didn't want to alert the shooter to his presence before he had to.

The sound he'd heard might mean nothing. Guns were fired all the time around these parts. Not after midnight, usually, but a local homeowner might be scaring off raccoons messing with the garbage cans. Or the sound could have been a firecracker, set off by someone celebrating the New Year a little too early. While fireworks weren't technically legal in Florida, giant loopholes in the law meant they'd be going off all over the county in about twenty-four hours.

But the scene his headlights revealed had him picking up his transceiver. "Copy, Rudean, I need backup here. And rescue. One down, one injured, and an armed shooter."

His vision had a surreal clarity, as if his car's headlights had become halogen spotlights. In a glance, he took in the license plate of the car in the driveway; the woman who lay next to it, her dark hair spread out in the gravel; the size and shape of the man standing, blood staining his shirt; the African-American boy beyond him with a gun in his hands, shock in his face.

He kept talking, his voice not shaking. "Confirm BOLO on the vehicle, subject is present and injured."

Four missing boys. Could there be another shooter, somewhere out of sight?

His radio exploded with sound as his deputies responded. Colin opened his car door and slid out behind it, staying low, as he unholstered his weapon. He reached into the car and flipped the switch to turn on his rarely-used speaker. "Drop the gun," he ordered, his enhanced voice echoing into the night.

The boy looked down at the gun in his hands as if he'd never seen it before. Colin didn't wait. "Face down on the ground. Now," he ordered.

His radio crackled. "Where the hell are you, Sheriff?" Rudean demanded. "This damn machine has you out in space somewhere."

Colin didn't answer. A dark pool of shadow was spreading along the ground off Nat's left side. It held his eyes as if they were magnetized. "Drop your gun," he shouted again.

Wait for backup. Secure the scene. Maintain control of the situation. He knew the procedures.

But that was Nat bleeding out twenty feet away from him.

This shouldn't be happening.

Couldn't be happening.

But it was.

The man, Thompson, dropped to his knees. He swayed. Colin could see his lips moving, could tell he was muttering something, but the words were indistinct. The boy hadn't moved.

"Drop your gun," Colin shouted again, not bothering with the speaker. He had his weapon free. He could step out from the car and shoot as many times as it took to take the kid down. But he'd never fired his weapon out of fear before.

And that was a kid.

The boy bent and set the gun down on the gravel road in front of him. Colin inhaled, a gigantic gulp of air that felt like the first he'd taken in since he'd seen the blood seeping into the ground.

"Step away from the gun," he shouted. "On the ground, face down."

The boy didn't listen. He turned and ran, disappearing around the side of the house in the seconds it took Colin to step out from behind his car and lift his weapon.

"Where the hell are you, Sheriff?" The radio crackled again. "This thing don't make no sense."

Colin grabbed the radio transceiver. "All units," he barked. He fell into so-familiar official language as he gave his location and demanded two ambulances and backup, but with every word he was aware of the heartbeats that were passing, that were pumping blood into the dirt.

The moment he was through, he ran for her.

He fell to his knees next to the car, ignoring the sharp gravel digging into his skin, the pain that told him this was no dream.

Fuck, fuck, fuck.

Her eyes were open, alive. One hand covered the hole in her chest, but without pressure. Immediately, Colin dropped his against it, firmly pushing the fingers into the soft tissue.

"Nat." The nickname said everything.

Her eyelashes fluttered. She pulled them open again as if it were a great effort. "Not Travis's fault," she breathed. "Thompson wanted to kill me."

"Nat," he said again, his voice broken.

Her lips curved into the tiniest of smiles. "Not how it was supposed to be. Huh." Her eyes closed.

"Natalya Latimer," he snapped. "Don't you dare. Don't you dare." He hadn't cried in so long, in so many years, that he didn't even recognize the feeling inside his eyes.

She opened her eyes again. "Gotta stop the bleeding," she whispered, tongue tracing her lips. "I'm so cold. So cold. Not a good sign."

"The ambulance is on its way," he promised her.

Behind him, he heard a scuffling noise. Was the boy back? He could be picking up the gun, aiming at Colin's back, but Colin didn't even look. He didn't care. Not while Nat still bled.

It was a breath, not a chuckle, but somehow Nat conveyed amusement through it. "Tassamara," she said. "Love the place but..." She paused and gasped, pain crossing her face. "Middle of nowhere's not where you want to get shot."

"What can I do?" Colin demanded.

She grimaced. "Pressure. No arteries or I'd be dead already. But..." She fell silent.

"Tell me what to do."

Her head fell to the side. "Not Travis's fault," she whispered again. Her eyelids closed. He could barely hear the words as she breathed, "So cold."

"This isn't right. This isn't how it was supposed to be." He choked out the words, fighting to get them past the knot in his throat.

Her eyes didn't open.

"You should have moved on," he told her, not shifting his hands.

"Gone to art school. Gotten married. Had kids. Lived the life you deserved to live. This is wrong."

A tiny flutter of her eyelashes said maybe she heard him, but she didn't respond.

Colin didn't move. He just pushed harder, his fingers pressing into hers, into the blood still seeping out of her.

And he waited.

The air was still, quiet. Colin strained to hear the sound of sirens. Was that them in the distance? But a scraping noise on the driveway behind him drowned out the faint wail. Without moving his hands, he risked a glance over his shoulder.

Thompson had somehow pulled himself to his feet and gotten to the gun. It dangled from one hand while he made his way toward Colin, one laborious step after another.

Colin's position didn't change. He turned his gaze back to Nat.

He'd just failed Police Basics 101, secure the scene. Under other circumstances, he would have been cursing himself up, down, and sideways. But Nat was dying under his hands and he couldn't bring himself to care what Thompson was doing.

Colin didn't want to die. Life had tasted so sweet these past few hopeful days. But he should have been dead already. If Thompson shot him and he died here next to Nat, well, it was way too Romeo and Juliet for his taste, but at least he'd be with her. Maybe they'd turn into ghosts like Rose and haunt this abandoned mansion together.

It wouldn't be the worst fate.

Thompson reached his shoulder. Colin looked up at him. Thompson's shirt was stained with blood, his face grey and beaded with sweat. He was struggling to breathe, his chest heaving, but as he gasped for air, he said, "Blood washes away sin. Faith. I have faith in the Lord."

Bending at the waist, he set the gun on the ground next to Colin, but as he tried to stand again, he overbalanced, toppling forward. He caught himself with one hand, breaking his fall, and landed hard in the gravel. He moaned, a hoarse, guttural sound, and gave a wheezing cough.

The sound brought Natayla's eyes open again. Her lips moved as if she were forming words. Colin leaned closer, but he couldn't hear what she was saying.

"Don't try to talk," he told her automatically. "The ambulance is on its way. It'll be here soon."

He could read disgust in the faint wrinkle of her nose, the flutter of her eyelashes. Yeah, maybe it was a stupid thing to say. She had to know even better than he did how dire her situation was. Her eyes fell closed again but with what looked like enormous effort, she shaped her lips into words. "Find Kenzi."

Oh, God, it was just like Nat to still be worrying about the little girl for whom she felt responsible.

"I will," Colin promised her. "I'll take care of her. You don't have to worry."

"Not... not..." She fell silent again, her face relaxing. She was slipping away, he knew. Leaving him behind. But what did she mean? Not? Not what?

Sarah Wynde

✂ CHAPTER TWENTY ✄

In her fifty-plus years of afterlife, Rose had never been so darn annoyed.

She'd been trying to pour her own energy into Natalya, to use her own life force to keep the woman's heart beating.

It wasn't working.

Oh, maybe Natalya felt something. A sense of peace, perhaps? Some relief from the pain? Having a bullet in her chest didn't seem as agonizing as Rose would have expected it to be. But Rose's energy couldn't heal the wound or even slow the bleeding.

She needed Kenzi.

The first time Kenzi had healed Jamie, Rose hadn't tried to help. She'd been too unsure of what might happen if she did. But the second time—when the very bad man was fighting with Natalya and the boy—Rose had poured her energy into Kenzi like a broken drain pipe gushing water. And it had worked. Jamie wasn't just better, he was healthy.

Kenzi's gift needed energy. Rose had energy. It was a perfect match. Like Bogart and Bacall. Hepburn and Tracy. Dean and Castiel.

But Kenzi wasn't here and Rose had no way to summon her.

"Oh, drat." Rose sighed.

Natalya was sitting up, looking around in confusion. She passed straight through Colin's hands. He was leaned over her, his hands still pressed to her chest, talking to her in a desperate voice. "What's happening?" Natalya asked.

Rose clenched her fingers into fists, not wanting to explain. Sure, death was a natural part of existence. Everyone moved on eventually. But not today, not Natalya. "Do you see a passageway?

"A what?"

"A door," Rose said, crouching down next to her. Colin had seen his right away. If Natalya couldn't see hers, then she wasn't supposed to die. If she did, she'd linger as a ghost, trapped at this house indefinitely. Rose wouldn't mind having another ghostly friend, but most ghosts didn't enjoy their afterlife as much as Rose liked hers.

"Over your shoulder, maybe."

"I don't—" Understanding started to smooth Natalya's expression. She looked around her, down at her body, at Colin, and back at Rose. In a bleak voice, she said, "No, I don't. Should I? Are you—do I know you?"

"You're not supposed to be here. You need to keep fighting." Rose put her hands over Colin's where they were pressed against Natalya's chest, ignoring her question. She closed her eyes and concentrated, trying to push energy into Natalya's body. A bizarre sizzle of power tingled against her fingers, unlike anything she'd ever felt before. It wasn't unpleasant, but it was strange. She ignored it.

Colin was talking, words, low and frantic, spilling out of his mouth. He was reminding Nat of the time she'd broken her collarbone, when he'd walked her home and he'd wanted to carry her, but he couldn't because it hurt her too much, so he'd held her hand. He told her how brave she'd been, how strong, how she had to be strong again now.

"Listen to him," Rose added, making her voice gentler. "Hear what he's saying to you."

Natalya looked at Colin and her face softened. She reached up a hand, touched his cheek, and disappeared.

A minute or two, that was all they'd gained. Natalya was back in her body, and fighting to hold on, fighting to stay with her physical being, but without help, she couldn't last.

Maybe it would be enough. Rose hadn't noticed the sirens getting louder, but flashing lights were harder to ignore. Police, ambulances, unmarked cars, a fire truck—a veritable flotilla of assistance was pouring into the driveway.

As the paramedics spilled out of their vehicles and rushed to their patients, Rose stopped leaning over Natalya and stood. Clasping her hands together in front of her mouth as if saying her childhood bedtime prayers, she waited.

"Move out of the way now, sir," a paramedic instructed Colin. "I've got her."

Colin let his bloody hands drop. He backed away, standing up. Looking around at the chaos, he seemed dazed, before shaking himself into awareness of the situation.

"We've still got five missing kids and the potential one or more of them could be armed and dangerous," he said to a man in a uniform similar to his own.

"Are we in an active shooter scenario, sir?" The deputy asked, eyes bright, voice eager.

Colin looked at him. "You hear any shooting going on?"

"Uh, no." The deputy looked sheepish.

"We can take our time," Colin said wearily. "We need to establish a perimeter around the house and assess the situation. Better to go in slowly than take any chances."

"No!" Rose protested. "That's a terrible idea." She stamped her foot on the ground, wishing it would make a sound. "You need to find Kenzi. Quickly. Right away."

A woman jogged up and handed Colin an absorbent towel. He took it but instead of wiping the blood off his hands, he stared up at the house as if strategizing a plan of approach.

Rose paused.

Blood.

Akira had once mentioned that blood made ghosts stronger. Could that have been the sizzle Rose felt when pushing energy into Natalya? The idea disgusted her, but she suppressed a shudder of revulsion and stepped into Colin, putting her hands over his. She could sense the blood now, crackling with life under her fingers, although it was dimmer, less powerful than when it flowed directly from Natalya.

Rose concentrated, thinking ferocious thoughts about how stupid Colin was being and how angry she was he couldn't hear her and how desperate she felt about Natalya's condition. Did he have any idea how close he was coming to losing her? He needed to think. To remember. To realize. To connect.

Colin shivered convulsively as the temperature dropped.

"Sheriff?" The woman who'd handed him the towel drew back in surprise. "You—are you okay?"

"Yeah," he said with surprise. His breath condensed in the air in front of him, turning into a puff of vapor. His eyes widened. "What the hell?"

The woman stepped back, farther away. "That's... that's so weird. It's really cold around you. You're freezing."

Colin looked down at his hands. Rose concentrated even harder, trying to make her thoughts vicious. Angry, vengeful ghosts created the coldest energy, she knew, but it didn't come naturally to her. Still, she'd told him if anything bad happened to Kenzi, she'd be haunting him and this felt like it counted.

"Change of plans," Colin said. With two abrupt swipes of the towel, he wiped most of the blood off his hands, then dropped the towel on the ground and took off, running for the house. "Gotta find the kids," he yelled back over his shoulder.

Rose raced after him, exultant. She'd tried and tried to tell Natalya she was present earlier, but the woman had never figured it out, even when her hands were almost blue with cold. But Colin had put the pieces together. Even better, she was sure he'd deciphered her message—not only that she was with him, but that she wanted him to find Kenzi.

Colin ran for the front door. He tried the handle. It didn't turn. He slammed into the door with his shoulder. It didn't move. With a growl of frustration, he stepped back.

"This way," Rose called, heading toward the right, to the side of the house with the open pool door.

Colin ignored her, charging toward the left, toward the garage.

Rose shrieked with exasperation and followed him.

"What are you doing?" called out one of the deputies.

A side door led into the garage. Colin tried it, but it was also locked. Turning, he sprinted toward the large garage doors.

"Sir, what's going on?" shouted another deputy.

Colin pointed toward the front door. "Use the Halligan bar," he barked. "Don't go inside."

"But sir!" protested another deputy. "That's not procedure."

The sheriff waved her off. "I'm not risking another fuck-up like we had last week. Get that door open but stay out here. Wait for my return."

"What are you doing?" Rose protested. "That's not how it works on television. You're supposed to break the door down and then you all rush inside with lots of yelling."

But Colin was moving again, grabbing the large garage doors by the handles at their bases and yanking at them. They didn't budge. "Hell," he swore. "Kids had to have gotten in somehow. Caller said there were lights inside the house."

"Use the pool door, you dummy." Rose jumped up and down, bouncing on her toes with impatience. Oh, why wasn't Akira here? Rose knew where Kenzi had hidden but how could she tell Colin?

And why wasn't he letting everyone in to search? It would go faster with more people.

He ran, charging around the side of the house, Rose chasing after him. Ghosts didn't get tired, but she hadn't gained magical speed and he ran faster than she did, so he reached the open French doors before her. But he paused there, putting a hand over his holstered weapon. He was breathing faster than usual as he said, voice low, "You're here, aren't you, Rose? Do you know if there are any more guns in there?"

Rose stopped next to him. That's why he was being so careful. He didn't want to risk his deputies getting shot. Or shooting back. But drat it, he needed to hurry.

A corner of his mouth pulled into a wry smile. "Damn, if I'd been thinking ahead, we could have made up a code while we were hiking." He closed his eyes and rubbed a hand over his face, looking desperately tired. A streak of blood from his not-entirely-clean hands remained on his cheek as he tilted his chin up and asked, in a stronger voice, "If you believe anyone inside this house is armed and dangerous, make the air freezing again." Belatedly, he added, "please."

"Oh, dear." Rose paused, uncertain. She didn't know the answer. She hadn't seen any other guns and the boys didn't seem dangerous to her, but then she hadn't expected Travis to start shooting people, either.

"All right, I'm going to take that as a no."

Rose yelped in protest. She hadn't even decided yet, much less had time to make the temperature drop. But it was too late, as Colin entered the house without taking his gun out. A few steps into the sunroom, he stopped, unhooking a flashlight from his duty belt. Turning it on, he let the light flicker across the empty space.

"Kenzi?" he called out. "It's Sheriff Rafferty. Where are you, honey?" He stopped moving and listened.

"She's upstairs in the movie theater room," Rose said quickly. "Hurry. The stairs are this way." She headed toward the stairs by the garage, but Colin didn't follow. He stayed by the light from the wide windows overlooking the lake, heading into the dining room, a living room, and back into the kitchen. He moved with steady assurance, not lingering, but sticking close to the walls and pausing at every doorway.

Rose wanted to scream with frustration. "You don't have time for this," she wailed, returning to where he stood.

"Kenzi?" He tried again. "It's the sheriff."

"She's upstairs, darn it."

But a muffled thump had Colin swiveling, one hand dropping, as if by reflex, to his gun. Rose turned, too. Could Kenzi have come downstairs? She hurried forward, passing straight through the wall of the kitchen and into a small shelved space behind it. The pantry, of course.

"Shut up," hissed a twin, shoving his brother.

"The sheriff. That's like police, isn't it?" The second twin ignored the push, leaning up against the door and pressing his ear to it.

"She said wait for the police. Nothing 'bout a sheriff," whispered the first twin.

"We heard the sirens."

"Until they come find us. That's what she said. You wanna get shot? I bet it hurts."

"He's out there, though, ain't he? That's finding us."

"We don't know who he is. Maybe he's a bad guy. We gotta wait."

Rose popped back through the door. The sheriff leaned against the wall next to it, his head tipped as if he were listening to the conversation. "Boys." Colin knocked on the door. "I'm here to help you. Come on out."

A squeak came from behind the door, followed by a smack and a protesting, "Ow."

"Dumbass," one of them grunted.

"Don't hit your brother," Colin said, voice firm. "And open the door. Is Kenzi there with you?"

The door inched open. Colin tilted his flashlight at the crack as a brown eye peeked out. "Are you the police?"

"Yes," Colin answered, quickly aiming his flashlight back at the ground. "And I'm in a hurry. I need to find Kenzi. The little girl, the blonde one. Is she with you?"

The door opened all the way. Both boys stood in the darkness. Colin let the light play over them, steering clear of their faces.

"She was upstairs before," one of them volunteered. "But she's probably hiding now. She's a good hider."

"We heard a sound. Really loud. Like a crack. Was that a gun going off?" asked the other.

Colin ignored the question. "Where upstairs?"

"All the way up, the big room," said the helpful twin.

Noise drew their attention, all heads turning toward the left. A metallic clang, followed by another, a third, and then the sound of breaking wood.

"That's the front door. They're getting it open. Come on," Colin ordered. He turned and hurried toward the foyer. The boys exchanged glances.

"Don't be stupid," Rose said. "Go with him."

One twin hugged himself, crossing his arms over his chest and looking worried, but the other twin shrugged and charged after Colin. After a moment's hesitation, the second followed more slowly.

"Stay here," Colin ordered when the boys reached the foyer. He called out, loudly enough to be heard through the wood, "You've got two boys here. Take good care of them."

Before the deputies had finished getting the door open, he'd moved on, heading farther into the house. "Kenzi!" Colin shouted. "Where are you?"

Rose was too impatient to wait for him. She hurried up the main stairs to the second floor and around the corner into the movie room. Unlike the rest of the house, this room was furnished. Three rows of cushy chairs, four seats each, sloped down and faced a wall where Rose was sure a movie screen had once stood. Now Travis and Jamie stood there, Kenzi between them, arguing.

"Man, they'll lock you up. You won't even get to juvie. They'll put ya in a padded cell and drug ya until you're like some zombie kid." Jamie blocked Travis's path up the low steps.

"I got no choice." Travis looked ready to drag Kenzi out of the room, but she was tugging, resisting his pull.

"They'll lock her up, too," Jamie protested. "Experiment on her like a lab rat."

"You watch too many movies," Travis snapped.

Jamie waved his arm at the wall. "We heard the sirens. There's police out there, ambulances, everything. The doc's gonna be okay. But if you tell them about Mac, you won't be."

"You don't get it."

"I do, man, I do," Jamie tried to reassure Travis. "You didn't mean to do it."

As the boys talked, Rose pushed back through the door to the outside of the room. Maybe if she created a cold patch right by the door, Colin would notice. And it wouldn't be too hard to find some strong negative emotions to build up her temper. In their own way, the children and Colin were all hoping to keep one another safe. But while their fears held them back, Natalya was dying.

"Kenzi?" Colin called from the bottom of the stairs.

Rose listened, hoping he'd be able to hear the boys arguing. But the theater room must have been sound-proofed, because all she could hear was something that sounded like a garbage disposal, a rhythmic beat, beat, beat.

"Aw, hell," Colin muttered. He leaped up the stairs, taking them two, then three, at a time.

The garbage disposal was a helicopter, Rose realized. The blades weren't grinding food, but churning air. That meant they were almost out of time. If Kenzi was to have any chance to help Natalya, it had to be soon, before the helicopter evacuated her to the distant hospital.

"Kenzi!" Colin yelled again. "Where are you?"

"Over here," Rose called from the door, as he ran past the second floor and up to the third. "Over here," she tried again, with a sigh for the futility of her efforts.

Maybe she should give up and go outside? She could welcome Natalya to the afterlife, help her get used to the idea of being a ghost. But the door behind her opened. Travis stuck his head out, looked from side to side, and listened.

"Come on." He gestured behind him. "We gotta take the back stairs, get out that way. Can't let them catch us."

Kenzi followed him out the door, Jamie trailing after her and they headed down the hallway, away from the nearby stairs.

"This is a bad idea, Trav." Jamie was still arguing, his voice low. "You don't know what you're doing."

Kenzi's lips quivered as she looked back at Jamie. Rose hurried to catch up to her, resting her arm on Kenzi's shoulder and letting warm thoughts of love and encouragement send powerful energy into the little girl. Kenzi felt it, because her face cleared and her shoulders relaxed.

Colin stepped out of the darkness in front of them. "No more running, guys."

The boys froze. Kenzi started to move forward, but Travis

stopped her, scooping her up into his arms.

"You don't understand," he said, his voice breaking with stress. "I gotta get out there. I gotta get to the lady doctor."

"It won't work," Jamie muttered from behind him. "They got ambulances. They'll fix her."

"She's hurt bad," Travis was keeping his voice steady. "You saw that. Mac can... Mac can help her if you'll let us."

"He ain't gonna believe you," Jamie said, like some Greek chorus of disapproval. "Nobody does."

"She did," Travis replied. "The lady doctor did. Right away she did. She didn't even ask any questions." He clasped Mac tighter and she put an anxious hand on his cheek, looking into his eyes.

Colin strode forward, relief lightening his expression. "I do, too," he said simply. He held out his arms. "Give her to me. Let me get her to Nat."

Travis pulled back, his head turning in disbelief, as Jamie stepped forward, eyes wide.

"Yay!" Rose cheered, jumping up and down. "But hurry," she added, stopping abruptly. "You're running out of time."

"She already saved my life," Colin added. "I know what she can do."

"This—this is the weirdest place ever." Travis shook his head as Kenzi leaned out of his arms, eagerly turning to Colin. "You're the police. They never believe anything."

Colin ignored him. Taking Kenzi, he said, "Hang on tight," to her and "Meet us downstairs," to the boys and rushed away.

"Yay, yay, yay!" Rose cheered again, before chasing after him.

They burst out of the house into a scene more orderly than it looked. A crowd of people gathered down the driveway—volunteers and rescue workers, waiting for news. A technician was putting bright yellow police tape up around a wide area of the house and car, while Mitchell and Michael stood on the side porch, talking brightly to two listening deputies. The helicopter had settled down on what should have been a lawn, if the developer had finished landscaping. Paramedics and EMTs were clustered around it, loading stretchers into the open doors.

Colin raced straight for the helicopter, Kenzi bouncing in his arms. The paramedics were talking, hushed voices, words and numbers with no meaning for Rose. Colin ignored them, dropping

Kenzi at the edge of the door.

"Go on in, honey," he said to her. She crawled forward.

"No," one paramedic protested, as he hooked an IV bag onto the wall. "What are you doing? We can't take her."

The other ignored all of them. "Blood pressure's dropping," she reported, voice tense. "We need to get moving." She turned to the pilot who was in his seat already, head tilted up, watching them, and nodded.

Rose clambered aboard, eagerly following Kenzi as the little girl slipped forward to take Natalya's hand. She tuned out the noise as the helicopter revved up and the paramedic argued with Colin and the pilot radioed in, focusing all her attention on pouring energy into Kenzi.

Natalya's eyelids flickered slightly in her pale face. She was still in there, Rose realized, still fighting, still holding on. "Heal, heal, heal," Rose chanted. "Stay here, be strong, you can do it." She didn't think the words helped, but they couldn't hurt. The helicopter shifted, starting to lift, but Rose kept all her attention on Natalya's face. Was a little pink appearing in her cheeks? Was the bleeding stopping?

Her focus was so intense that when Natalya started to move, her body drifting slowly up and up and up, Rose blinked in confusion. As the helicopter passed straight through Rose, leaving her to float gently back to the ground, she realized she'd forgotten to concentrate on the vehicle's movement.

And they'd left without her.

❧ CHAPTER TWENTY-ONE ❧

A sun lodged in her chest, burning her from the inside out.

Natalya whimpered.

"Hang on." A worried male voice. She ought to recognize it. But, oh, she hurt. Connecting the sound to a face was much too challenging.

A tingling warmth started in her arm and ran up through her body and down, down, down. In its wake, the sun shrank and faded.

She floated.

She faded.

Was she having a conversation?

She thought she might be talking. But the words didn't make sense. Flowers? Of course she liked roses. Who didn't?

She slept again.

Natalya opened her eyes.

She licked her lips. They felt dry and cracked and her mouth tasted disgusting, as if she'd been eating blue cheese before falling asleep. And her chest—oh, it hurt, an ache as deep as an ocean running through the core of her.

She turned her head. Her father sat in a chair next to her, his head tilted back, his eyes closed.

"Dad," she whispered.

His eyes popped open. He leaned forward, fumbling for her hand. "Nat. You're back."

"Didn't go anywhere." She blinked, trying to clear her eyes. He looked older, the lines around his mouth and forehead deeper than she remembered.

"No. No, you didn't," he agreed. He pressed his lips together. The glimmer in his eyes might have been tears. He nodded toward an IV. "Do you need another dose of painkiller? There's a button I can push."

Natalya's free hand fluttered toward her chest. "Not... not yet." She closed her eyes and breathed. Leaves on water. It hurt, but she could bear it. "What happened?"

"What do you remember?"

She thought. Her brain felt sluggish, slow, as if her thoughts were underwater.

He didn't wait for her to respond. He started to tell her about her condition, the blood loss, the surgery to remove the bullet, the doctor's surprise at the way her heart had closed around it... but she wasn't listening.

Her gift was back.

And it felt like a gift. She remembered everything her father was telling her and so much more besides.

"Dad," she interrupted him.

"Painkiller?" He reached for the pump.

"No." Her head rolled weakly from one side of her pillow to another.

"Water? A wet washcloth? Do you need me to call the nurse?" Max stood, clearly torn between fear she needed medical attention and a desire to fuss over her.

Natalya's lips curved up. "Nothing," she said, before correcting herself. "No, water. Water would be good."

He fussed. The nurse was summoned. Water procured. Natalya helped to a sitting position. Her sheets smoothed. Her teeth brushed, with help from the nurse and a cup to spit in. The room temperature adjusted. The television turned on and off again.

Finally, Natalya stopped him. "I need you to do me a favor."

"Anything, of course. What is it?" Max dropped back into the chair next to her bed.

"My foresight is back."

"Wonderful," Max said with relief. "You're not going to get shot again, are you? Because if so, I'm building you a tower, like Rapunzel, no way in, no way out. I'll send your food up by dumbwaiter."

Natalya's chuckle turned into a groan as the pain shot through her chest like jagged darts.

"Sorry, sorry," Max apologized, reaching for the morphine pump again.

"Don't do that." She waved him away from it, leaning back against her pillows and trying to catch her breath.

"You sure?"

"Positive. Got too much to do." She closed her eyes. The pain was ebbing again, easing off its tight grip on her.

"Honey, you're in the hospital. You've been shot, had major

surgery, and nearly died. You're not doing anything today." Max's tone was firm, no-nonsense, her father laying down the law.

Natalya restrained her chuckle, but her lips curled into a smile, before she opened her eyes. "So this is what you get to do then." She took a moment to organize the thoughts, and then started talking, loving the way her words triggered her foresight, memory after memory of the future piling up in her mind.

Partway through her list, Max pulled out his phone and started taking notes.

"All right," he said when she was done, looking down at his phone dubiously. "I think I have it all."

"You can let the last couple wait until I get home," Natalya offered. "It won't be too long."

"The doctor said weeks." Max raised his eyebrows.

"The doctor was wrong," Natalya answered, taking a shallow breath. God, it hurt. She was glad she knew how quickly it would stop. "Will be wrong," she corrected herself.

A knock on the door forestalled Max's next question. He stood as Colin poked his head around the door. The rush of warmth and euphoria that hit Natalya was so strong she glanced at Max to make sure he hadn't pushed the pain relief button. His hands were nowhere near it.

"Okay if we come in?" Colin asked.

Natalya nodded and the door opened to reveal Kenzi, her small hand held tight in Colin's. Her other hand held the doll Grace had given her, tucked close against her side. She was wearing an outfit Natalya had never seen before, purple leggings with a blue and purple cotton dress, and her hair was neatly brushed and braided in two short braids. Her face looked solemn and wide-eyed.

"I'll go get started on my chores, then," Max said. As he left, he clapped Colin cheerfully on the arm and touched Kenzi's head with gentle affection, but he didn't say anything further.

"Hope you don't mind," Colin said, unsmiling, his eyes intent. "Kenzi wanted to see you."

"Not at all." Natalya turned her palm up, holding her hand out to the little girl. She came forward, tugging Colin along with her. "How are you, Kenzi? I mean Mac."

"I like Kenzi," the little girl said, voice soft. She set her doll down on the bed next to Natalya's hip, propping her up carefully, not looking at Natalya. "I want to be Kenzi."

"Yes," Natalya said in quiet agreement, feeling a warm contentment entirely at odds with the pain and misery messages her body was sending her. She already knew that, of course, but Kenzi deserved the chance to say it.

"Kenzi's talking now," Colin pointed out needlessly.

Natalya smiled at him. She knew enough about the future that she would have liked to laugh, but it would hurt far too much.

"My mama said it was okay," Kenzi replied. Natalya saw Colin flinch, his hand tightening on Kenzi's. The little girl looked up at him. "She did," she insisted.

"I know." Colin forced a smile. "It's all right."

"The nurse says I'm wrong." Kenzi's lower lip slid out. "My mama is gone now. The nurse says I didn't talk to her, but I did. She said I could talk now and not to hide any more and she told me good-bye. And she said she was sorry and she loved me and she'd see me again soon, but not too soon." Kenzi paused for a response, but when it wasn't forthcoming, she added insistently, "She said. She did."

"Yes," Natalya said, keeping her voice soothing. "She did."

"You believe me?" The lower lip slid in and Kenzi's eyes narrowed. For the first time she looked straight at Natalya. "He said it was a dream." She tilted her head toward Colin.

"Mmm," Natalya murmured noncommittally. The hospital wasn't in Tassamara, and Colin was used to pretending, for the outside world, that reality was what outsiders expected it to be. She suspected he knew it was no dream.

"Do you know what a Wookie is?" Kenzi went on. "Because I didn't but my brothers did. And it's like a bear. A really big bear. I'm not a bear. But maybe I'll be really big someday. I don't want brown fur, though. Maybe white fur."

Natalya's lips twitched. "That would be nice." She was fading in and out, just a little bit, her memories and reality and the pain, the pain, all mixing together. "Feathers would be good, too. Maybe blue ones? Or purple ones?"

"Or pink ones," Kenzi agreed. "I like pink. But not all pink, sometimes I like orange, too. And yellow, but not with crayons, yellow crayons don't work right. They don't have the right shine. But I liked the yellow with your funny chalks."

"That's a good yellow, isn't it?" Natalya agreed.

Kenzi rubbed one foot along the back of her other leg. Her eyelashes dropped and she stared at the bed. "Will I get to use your chalks again?"

"Yes," Natalya answered without hesitation. She moved to push herself up on the bed but stopped, grimacing with the pain radiating through her. She leaned back again much more carefully. "Yes, you will."

Kenzi shot her a sideways glance. "I was really sick, but I'm all better now. I'm supposed to go home soon."

"I'm sorry you were sick." Sudden tears pricked at Natalya's eyes. Kenzi hadn't been sick. She'd poured so much of her energy into keeping Natalya alive her own systems began to shut down. They were going to have to be very careful with her gift in the future. Little injuries—skinned knees, minor burns, sprained ankles—those were okay. But she needed to learn to protect herself. And then Natalya realized she was answering the wrong question. "Max is taking care of it."

Kenzi's forehead furrowed with puzzlement, but it was Colin who asked, "Taking care of what?"

Natalya flicked her fingers dismissively. "Whatever needs to be done." She closed her eyes and concentrated on breathing for a moment. Her last dose of morphine must be wearing off. The pain was gnawing at her chest, digging into her bones.

She opened her eyes again. Kenzi and Colin wore identically worried looks.

"Sorry," Natalya exhaled the word, not wanting to take the deep inhalations that would force her chest to expand. She tried to smile at Kenzi as she said, pausing between sentences to take shallow breaths, "My dad will work with Carla. Remember her? Until I get out of the hospital, you'll go stay with him and Grace."

Kenzi dropped Colin's hand. Her smile lit up her face. Oh, Natalya thought blearily, she was going to be a gorgeous teenager. And that first boyfriend—that asshole would break her heart. She'd have to make sure Colin didn't learn about it until much later or that kid would wind up with more traffic tickets than was strictly fair.

Kenzi took her hand. Natalya felt the small fingers gripping hers. And then the energy, the soothing warmth, like sunlight reaching into her, stroking up her arm, gently cushioning the pain. For a second, or maybe ten, Natalya didn't resist, but then she pulled her hand away.

She felt—not great, not good, but too much better. "None of that," she said firmly, softening the words with a smile. "No need to rush. You'll like staying with Max and Grace." But the pain was better, enough so that she lifted herself up, leaning away from the pillows to pick up the doll and stroke its hair.

"I think Colin wants to talk to me now," she said, handing the doll to Kenzi. "Is Grace out in the hallway?"

"Uh-huh," Kenzi answered eagerly. "Lots of people are. Grace, and the lady who's going to have a baby and gets confused a lot and talks to invisible people, and the daddy, and some other people, too. They're all waiting to see you, but the nurse says only one person at a time. Except me and him, we got to come in together, because I was supposed to go somewhere, but they didn't know where. And the confused lady, she has to have a rose hold her hand, except she doesn't have any flowers and it doesn't make sense."

Natalya met Colin's eyes and she could see her own amusement reflected in his. Kenzi was making up for lost time.

"You go wait with them," he told Kenzi. He waited until she was out of the room and sat down in the chair next to Natalya's bed. It was a recliner, the type of big, ugly plastic chair hundreds of worried relatives had probably slept in over the years, but he perched on its edge, leaning forward and looking uncomfortable.

"Nat," he started.

"Police business first," she told him. "You've got Travis in jail, right?"

"Isolated, because of his age," Colin agreed. "Thompson's alive, but not talking. Or not saying anything coherent, anyway."

"No surprise." She stretched her shoulders back. She should have stopped Kenzi sooner. She felt so much better. She still hurt, but it was more like an intensely painful bruise than the cracked sternum she was sure she had. "How soon can you get him out?"

"Uh, that's not gonna be so easy," Colin answered. "Best we can tell, he shot two people."

"With one bullet?" Natalya let sarcasm creep into her tone. "It was self-defense. Or rather, my defense. Thompson was trying to kill me, to strangle me, while suffering a psychotic episode caused by severe bipolar 1 disorder. Travis shot to save my life. He couldn't have known the bullet would go straight through Thompson and into me."

"Still..." Colin protested.

Natalya tilted her head to one side and smiled at him sweetly. It wasn't that she didn't respect his position, but she wanted to get through this discussion and on to the next, far more entertaining conversation they were going to have. "Get him out. Or I'm going to sic my dad's lawyers on you."

Colin groaned. "Not Bill Piero."

"Who else?" Natalya spread her hands. "Where are the other boys?"

"All in the group home over by Sweet Springs."

Natalya nodded. They might not be happy there, but she'd take care of that as soon as she could.

"I need to get a statement from you. Can you answer a few questions?"

She shook her head. "Our police business is done," she said, head still tilted, voice still amused. "Try again."

"Nat." Her name was a guttural moan. Colin closed his eyes. "You..."

"Don't start there," she interrupted him. He opened his eyes and looked at her. She gazed into them and the pain of her chest meant nothing. "You were wrong," she told him.

He buried his face in his hands, and maybe he was laughing and maybe he was crying, but his voice was muffled as he agreed, "I was so wrong."

"I was right," she said.

"You were right," he agreed, lifting his head.

"Can I say it?" she asked wickedly.

"Say it."

"I told you so!"

He laughed, and then his expression darkened. "Nat," he said again, and this time she waited. "I wanted you to move on. I wanted you to have the life you should have had. I wanted you to get married and have kids and be an artist and live... happily ever after. And I knew you couldn't do that with me, because I was going to die. But I didn't know..."

"That I couldn't do it without you, either?" she prompted him, her voice so gentle.

"You were dying," he said, his expression bleak. "You were..."

"Bleeding out," she told him briskly. "Gunshot penetrating the right ventricular cavity, chance of survival, uh, about nil. Maybe ten percent if the hospital is close enough, but it wasn't."

Colin rubbed a hand over his face. "That makes me feel better," he admitted.

"Because of Kenzi?" she asked him.

"If I realized what could happen, I would never have put her into that helicopter. You're the love of my life, Nat—the only one for me, now or ever—but Kenzi nearly died trying to save you. When I found out they had to resuscitate her and you were in surgery, in critical condition, and they weren't sure you were going to make it, I thought I'd killed her for nothing." He took her hand, his strong fingers folding around hers.

"If you could have seen the future, you would have done exactly what you did," Natalya reassured him.

"Does that mean . . ." He shot her a quizzical look.

"My precognition is back." She tried to look serious, but she couldn't stop the smile playing around her lips.

His own smile started slow. "And?" he asked. "Are you going to tell me?"

"My future—our future—looks great."

"Does that mean you forgive me?"

Natalya raised her free hand and touched the bandages over her heart and the tubes coming out of her chest. "I shouldn't have survived this. That I did—it's a gift. I'm not going to waste it."

"Oh, Nat." Colin stood. Moving carefully around her IV and wires, he sat on the bed next to her and slid his hand along her cheek and around to the back of her neck. Leaning forward, he gently kissed her, his lips soft against hers.

She kissed him back, harder, fiercer, leaning into him, wanting to press against him, to feel his warmth against her, until a jolt of pain reminded her of where they were and why.

He caught the wince and pulled away. "I don't want to hurt you."

"Life hurts sometimes," she said simply, but she settled back against her pillows again. She could wait. They had time. "Are you going to ask?"

He blinked in momentary surprise, and then took her hand again. With solemn eyes and a serious face, he started, "Natalya Latimer, will you—"

"Not that," she interrupted him, pulling her hand away and putting it up in laughing protest. "I'm not wearing a hospital gown when I get proposed to."

He looked puzzled for a moment and then his expression cleared. "Oh, that. I already know."

She kept her face straight. "Oh, really? So which are we having first, a boy or a girl?"

"Girl, of course," he said promptly, grinning at her.

She shook her head at him, eyes innocent.

"No? But—" His head turned toward the door and the little girl waiting outside it.

"The twins are already available for adoption," she told him. "Their paperwork goes through much faster than hers."

His mouth opened and closed and opened again, before he finally closed it firmly, swallowed hard, and said, "Okay."

Laughing would have hurt too much, so she opened her arms to him and beckoned him close for a gentle kiss. She'd let him find out the rest in time, the way most people did.

But she knew already that they would fill the house on Lake Elsinore with children, pets, love and laughter.

ॐ EPILOGUE ॐ

"I'm sorry I couldn't do more."

Mary's smile didn't change, and her gaze didn't waver from Kenzi, who was leaning on Grace's knees, the two of them with heads together, talking intently about something Rose couldn't hear. "It's all right."

"Not really," Rose said sadly. "If I'd realized you were still alive, I could have brought Kenzi here days ago. You wouldn't have died."

"I might have died anyway." Mary shrugged. "And she might be dead with me. It's better this way."

Rose pressed her lips together to stop the words from escaping, but she wanted to respond with heated protests. It was not better. It was not right. Kenzi needed her mother.

Mary must have felt her reaction, because her head turned and she looked at Rose. They were sitting, side by side, in a crowded waiting room. Rose sat next to Akira, so she could whisper in her ear about who not to talk to. Akira sometimes didn't notice ghosts weren't living. It made life awkward for her.

"You helped me so much," Mary said. "You saved my daughter. I'm so grateful. There are no words."

"But you could have lived, too," Rose insisted.

Mary turned her hands up. "I got to say goodbye to my mother when she came to the hospital. I got to see my father and know he's getting help, whether he likes it or not. I know the boys are safer, even if they won't be together the way they wanted. I don't have any regrets."

"They took you off life support just before we got here," Rose tried. "If we'd been a little faster..."

Mary looked calm, serene, as different from the anguished ghost Rose had encountered a week ago as night and day. "I'm ready to go." She tilted her head toward her shoulder. "My door's been waiting for me for a week."

Rose shook her head. "I don't get it."

Smiling shyly, her cheeks pink, Mary said, "Well, my father would tell you about heaven. No sickness, no death, no tears, an eternal perfection. But I'm hoping Dumbledore got it right."

"Dumbledore?" Rose asked.

Akira, who had been pretending to ignore them, turned her head, raising her eyebrows.

"From Harry Potter?" Mary responded.

Rose shook her head. "I don't know it."

Mary's eyes widened. "Oh. Ah. Well… Dumbledore says death is the next great adventure."

Rose turned to Akira. "Do you know him?"

Akira tilted her chin in a nod so small most people wouldn't have noticed it.

"Hmph." Rose snorted, feeling vaguely disgruntled, although she couldn't have said why.

"It's not important," Mary said peacefully. "I'm glad my baby will be safe, but I'm okay leaving her for a time."

Max had been on his telephone, alternately rolling his eyes at whatever he was hearing and scribbling notes on a paper napkin Grace had found for him.

"Wait, emergency hearing?" he said, his words loud in the quiet room. "With what judge?" He listened, beginning to nod. "Lovely, lovely. I know Judge Sheridan well." He paused again. "Oh, you know. Golf buddies. Metaphorically speaking. I don't golf. Nothing against it, good way to get exercise, but not my thing. But Katie Sheridan and my wife worked together on a couple of non-profit boards. I'll give her a call, explain the situation. I'm sure she'll be willing to help out."

"Are you sure you don't want to come with me?" Mary asked.

Rose turned her attention back to Mary, frowning. Of course she didn't. But then she paused. She glanced at Akira who watched her steadily, bottom lip tucked under her teeth. Rose had visited the other side once already. But maybe she hadn't given it a fair chance. She hadn't felt ready. She'd mostly been annoyed to be there. Oh, sure, the love was wonderful. Being washed in joy and peace, surrounded by cushions of affection, it wasn't as if it were unpleasant. She'd just felt—not ready. As if she weren't done with what she wanted or needed from this dimension.

Max closed his phone with a satisfied sigh. "Kenzi, dear," he said.

The little girl turned away from Grace toward him. "Natalya wanted me to arrange for all your brothers to come live with you, too. Is that something you want?"

The little girl nodded eagerly.

"What?" Grace spluttered. "What?"

"Oh, wonderful," Mary sighed. "Then the boys are taken care of, too. I think that's my cue." With a last smile toward Rose, she stood and disappeared.

"All of them?" Grace asked.

Max tipped his head, lifting his shoulders in a small shrug. "It seemed... well, I did wonder whether it was the drugs talking. She gave me a lengthy list of instructions."

"What else?" Grace asked suspiciously.

"She plans to marry Colin in June," Max replied promptly, without looking at his phone. "She asked me to book Maggie to cater and that local bluegrass band for the music."

Akira put her hand over her mouth, stifling a squeak; Zane grinned; and Grace shrugged. Rose clapped twice and clasped her hands together, delighted. Weddings were so much fun. She hadn't been to one in decades.

"Not a surprise," Grace said. "They should have done it a long time ago."

"She did say I could wait on those details, though. But they're going to adopt all the children." Grace raised her eyebrows and Max continued. "And she asked for the house on Lake Elsinore for a wedding present."

"The one where she nearly died?" Grace protested.

Max shrugged. "She liked it. With five kids, they'll need a big place. And apparently there's a movie theater in it?"

"Nat wants a movie theater?" Grace laughed. "She barely watches television. That doesn't make sense."

Max looked down at his phone again and rubbed his chin. "I don't know," he said. "Maybe this was the drugs talking."

Akira leaned forward and asked, "What did she say about the movie theater?"

Max chuckled. "She was very clear, actually, even if it was the drugs. She wants the highest-end home theater system available with an extensive library of classic movies, including the entire Mystery Science Theater 3000 collection. She said she owes a debt."

229

Rose gasped. The entire MST3 collection?

"Huh, the house, all right, but the theater sounds like drugs to me." Grace said. "Let's hold off on that one."

Rose, eyes pleading, turned to Akira.

Akira, smiling, leaned back in her chair and said, "Let's go ahead with the movie theater. And include all the Harry Potter movies in the library, please."

Rose clapped her hands again and jumped up, out of her chair, twirling around the room and ignoring a passing nurse who walked through her. Maybe someday she'd be ready to move on. But first she needed to find out who Dumbledore was.

❧TO MY READERS❧

If you're an active reviewer and want a free review copy of either the next book in the series or the next book I release, please send an email to reviews@sarahwynde.com with a link to a review you've written about one of my books, and let me know which title you'd like to receive and in what format (epub, mobi, or pdf).

The review can be on any site, including a retailer, Goodreads, LibraryThing, Shelfari, your personal blog or a group blog, and it definitely doesn't have to be nice. Be as critical as you like, but please write at least a few sentences—two-word reviews don't count!

If you'd like to know when I'm releasing a new book or get an occasional free short story or missing scene in your inbox, sign up for my mailing list at sarahwynde.com/find-me/.

You can also email me at sarah@sarahwynde.com or find me on Facebook as Sarah Wynde or on Twitter as Wyndes. Or you can find me on one of my blogs. Wynded Words at sarahwynde.com is my home site, and The Write Push at writepush.wordpress.com is a group blog where I and a couple of other authors post about our progress and our thoughts on what we're learning. On tumblr, I'm at wyndes.tumblr.com.

Best wishes and thanks for reading!
Sarah

❧OTHER WORKS❧

A Gift of Ghosts
Akira has secrets. But so does the town of Tassamara.

Akira Malone believes in the scientific method, evolution, and Einstein's theory of relativity. And ghosts.

All the logic and reason in the world can't protect her from the truth—she can see and communicate with spirits. But Akira is sure that her ability is just a genetic quirk and the ghosts she encounters simply leftover electromagnetic energy. Dangerous electromagnetic energy.

Zane Latimer believes in telepathy, precognition, auras, and that playing Halo with your employees is an excellent management technique. He also thinks that maybe, just maybe, Akira Malone can help his family get in touch with their lost loved ones.

But will Akira ever be able to face her fears and accept her gift? Or will Zane's relatives be trapped between life and death forever?

A Gift of Thought
Sylvie swore she'd never go back to Tassamara. She was wrong.

At seventeen, Sylvie Blair left her infant son with his grandparents while she went shopping. She never returned. Twenty years later, she's devastated to learn of his early, untimely death. But although Dillon's body is long since buried, his spirit lingers on.

And he's not real happy.

He doesn't like his mom's job—too dangerous. He doesn't like her apartment—too boring. And he definitely doesn't like her love life—non-existent.

But when Dillon decides that his parents should be living happily ever after, he sets them on a path that leads deeper and deeper into danger.

Can Sylvie let go of the past and embrace the future?

And can Dillon survive the deadly energy he unwittingly unleashes?

The Spirits of Christmas (A Tassamara Short Story)

Akira's plans are simple: write wedding invitations, bake Christmas cookies, and eat red meat. (The last surprises her, too.) But when Rose, the ghost who haunts her house, asks for a favor, Akira can't say no. Although she's faced danger before, even death, a toddler who doesn't like peanut-butter-and-jelly might be her worst nightmare.

☐

A Lonely Magic (Coming June 2014)

Fen, a street-smart, 21-year-old orphan with anxiety issues, thinks she has her life under control until a gorgeous stranger tries to kill her and a mysterious boy comes to her rescue. Now she's caught up in the adventure of a lifetime, one that will take her from the cold streets of Chicago to the glorious blue waters of the Caribbean, and into a world she never imagined existed.

☐

Made in the USA
Middletown, DE
03 March 2017